LAY BABY

First published in 2020
by Black Spring Press Group
Suite 333, 19-21 Crawford Street
London, WIH IPJ
United Kingdom

Graphic design by Edwin Smet
Author photograph by Neil Reid
Cover image by Neil Reid
Printed in England by TJ Books Limited, Padstow, Cornwall

Set in Bembo 13 / 17 pt
ISBN 978-1-911335-72-6

WWW.EYEWEARPUBLISHING.COM

LAY BABY

V.A. SOLA SMITH

A NOVEL

THE **BLACK SPRING**
PRESS GROUP

DRAMATIS PERSONAE

LAYLA / LAY BABY – the narrator
MUM / MS DINSDALE – Layla's and Cal's mother and Dom's step-mother
TERRY – Layla's mum's boyfriend
DOMINIC / DOM – Layla's elder brother (estranged)
CALEB / CAL – Layla's eldest brother and LA Sarah's partner
JIM / JIMMY – Layla's ex and Bull's younger brother (deceased)
BULL – Jim's elder brother, Laura K's ex and one of Caleb's closest friends
LAURA K – Bull's partner and La's best friend (deceased)
LA SARAH / LA – Cal's partner and Clit's and Maggie's housemate
CLIT – Maggie's partner and LA Sarah's housemate
MAGGIE / MAG – Clit's partner and LA Sarah's housemate
MISS – Layla's closest friend, fellow student at Wayside School, Dave's daughter and Jasper's twin sister
JASPER / JAZZ – Miss's twin brother, Dave's son and member of the Gallows Hill 353
DAVE – Miss's and Jasper's mother and Pru's partner
PRU – Dave's partner
SANAA – toddler daughter of Dave's and Pru's next door neighbours
LYNN GREEN – leader of the Lancashire Education Medical Service
ANDREW – Layla's classmate and fellow Student at Wayside School
RYAN – Layla's classmate and fellow Student at Wayside School
HAZEL – Layla's classmate and fellow Student at Wayside School
DANNY – Layla's classmate and fellow Student at Wayside School
NICOLE – Layla's classmate and fellow Student at Wayside School
LEA – teacher at Wayside School
CAROL –teacher at Wayside School
CHRIS – teacher at Wayside School
MR RAMSEY – substitute teacher at Wayside School
BRENDA – teaching assistant at Wayside School
MRS MCQUAIDE – head teacher at Wayside School
PETER – Layla's social worker
CRUSTY DON – owner of The Hammer and Sink Nightclub
ANNETTE / NETTY – barmaid at The Hammer and Nightclub
BRIAN - drives the free minibus to The Hammer and Sink Nightclub
FLOWER – Polly's partner and later Biddy's partner
POLLY – Flower's partner and Sam's closest friend and classmate
SAM / SAMMY DOLL – Polly's closest friend and classmate
BIDDY – Kyle's ex and DM's mother
DM – Kyle and Biddy's toddler son
ABERDENIE JEANIE / AJ – Biddy's closest friend
TRIX – friend of Layla's and fellow 'dreg'
RICH / RICHIE – friend of Trix, Richie's parents once fostered Trix
STEVIE – Layla's childhood friend and classmate, now a drug dealer and a leader of the Aldgate 212
BOY – former Range Estate 608 member turned drug dealer and contact of Stevie's
MONICA / MON – Layla's Mum's closest friend and neighbour and mother of Alastair and Benny
ALASTAIR – Mon's son, Benny's older brother and a founding member of the Dacrelands 414
BENNY – Mon's son and Alastair's younger brother
JOSEPHINE / THE MAD WOMAN AT NUMBER NINETEEN – Layla's Mum's neighbour
MARY / THE WHITE KEYRING QUEEN – neighbour of Layla's father (deceased)
DEANO – childhood friend of Layla's and Dom's and shotter for Mary, the white keyring queen
KIM LOVEDAY – head of A levels at Lancaster College

I used to be able to feel Jim's stare. That vibe, like when someone is watching you? I still get that feeling sometimes. I'll be really into a book or toking with the guys or whatever, then I'll just feel it. Like folk who have limbs amputated get phantom pains. You see it at Pok, where's there's plenty of crusties and smackheads with stumps where their arms, fingers, toes, a leg or two, have gotten gangrenous and had to be lopped off. An amputee will go to scratch an itch only to remember, or rediscover, they ain't got no leg for it to have an itch. Some are so fucked off their nut they just carry on scratching.

I don't. I never scratch the itch. As long as the itch is there, I can go on feeling it. Feeling like Jim's there, grinning back at me like a fucking smartarse.

It were a book of Philip Larkin's poems, the first book I asked to cadge from him. And the first time Jim floored me with that fucking grin. The next day, at the Steps, Jim snuck up behind me, placed his hands over my eyes so tight I couldn't prise them off my face or break out of his arms and wheeled me around, whispering right in my ear as I struggled and failed to free myself.

– I'm gonna take you to the best fucking place in the whole wide world. Better than a come up. Better than sex. Better than Christmas morning. Better than that first smoke of the day. Better even than Etihad Stadium. I'm gonna change your life, Lay Baby.

I remember Jim letting me go so I could finally see what I was facing, and my shoulders dropping.

– Lancaster Library?

Jim loved libraries. The idea of there being a place in every city where you could go and sit, be warm and dry, and pull books from shelves like levers in to secret worlds. Somewhere you didn't need money or status or ID or even to become a member to enter.

I already had a library card. My mum got my brothers, Cal and Dom, and me our own library cards and used to walk us there every Sunday. Cal got too old to want to tag along pretty quick, and Dom were only really interested in terrorising the library hamsters, Enid and Blyton, but I took out eight books – maximum on a child library card – every week, until the divorce.

Mum never read to us that I can remember, but she'd wait for hours, literally, while I picked books and then while the librarian let me stamp each book out. Then she would carry them all home for me. She had a cotton tote bag she kept rolled up in her handbag just for when we went to the library. She bought it at a carboot sale and nailed a hook in to my old bedroom door to hang it from like a stocking always full of books.

Sometimes, at night, Cal would creep in to my bedroom with his hand over Dom's mouth to stop him from calling my name in the dark and waking our parents. They'd squeeze into my single bed and Cal would read us book after book from the bag till me and Dom fell asleep. Cal used to change the names of characters to mine and his and Dom's; us having adventures or solving crimes or casting spells. Dad never featured, maybe 'cause he weren't Caleb's dad. Cal only ever snuck our mum into the story if the book had a witch in it. We'd all laugh, our faces pushed into the duvet so Mum didn't hear us and know we were still awake.

I didn't even remember any of that till I were telling Jim about it and that if he ever wrecked my library card, I'd wreck his face. He'd tried to snap my library card in two. Jim said you couldn't trust a person to return library books on time, and you can't trust any person who does returns library books on time. But he never tried to snap my library card again. I've still got the card, though I never use it no more, except to rack lines.

Jim would distract the staff so I could sneak out books we could've checked out for free just so we weren't on no time limit to return them. We also snuck out cassettes, which made sense; you've to pay to borrow music.

We'd head back to Jim's brother, Bull's place or to Pok and rifle through our loot. Jim would read aloud poems or passages from the books. I'd play him my poets – Lou Reed, Jim Carroll, Iggy Pop, Nick Cave on Cal's old cassette Walkman. When we'd bored of them or moved on to sommet new, we'd sneak the books and cassettes back on to the shelves.

I used to be mad on the library, but I'd never thought about the idea of what a library is, what a library really is, until Jim made me face it.

The way they see it, all I've got to do is 'be good' for nine months, until I turn sixteen, until I'm free from school and guardians and binned into the council-housing-raffle-barrel. The way I see it, well, I don't see it. And that, they tell me, is the problem.

★

My mum threw me out again on Friday. As she pushed me over the front step, I tried to grab a key from the rack on the hallway wall. The door slammed straight on my hand.

The doctor tells me I've fractured the scaphoid, this little nub of bone located in the anatomical snuffbox. The way he tells it, four hours after waiting around in A&E, it suddenly becomes urgent to minimise the risk of avascular necrosis somewhere between the proximal and distal borders.

Translated: I buggered my right hand up and now the whole thing is in plaster for a fortnight.

★

Always the same routine. Sam's mum pretends not to be listening in the hallway. Pretending I don't know Sam's mum is listening in the hallway, I punch in my mum's number on the cordless in the living room, and push 'dial'. My mum picks up the phone, recognises my voice and hangs up. I give the line a moment to clear. At the sound of the dial tone, I say:

– Yeah, Mum, no worries. I'm at Sam's place... Yeah, y'know, Sam. Do you want me to put her mum on? ...OK. Thanks... Yeah, I won't be any trouble... Bye, then...

I replace the handset and make for the stairs. Meanwhile, Sam's mum makes for the lounge to check the last number dialled, in case I faked the call.

Sam's room is in the attic. After climbing this little ladder you have to scramble through a tunnel in the rafters, which eventually opens up into a loft decked wall-to-wall with plastic dolls. Bedding down between all that synthetic hair and those tiny polyester-dresses, I'm always waiting for a house fire. Knowing that the last thing I'd see would be the bubbling faces of synthetic cherubs.

Sam don't even look up from the bed when I crawl in. She's just pierced her navel with the bent tine of a sausage skewer and is busy cupping the blood in the crease of her stomach to try keep it from staining her faded *Sleeping Beauty* bedsheets.

I drop my bag onto the bed, roll a one-skin joint and crack the skylight.

Sam slips a ring into the new piercing and then tosses aside a few tops from an open drawer, before finding a black vest and pulling it on. She takes one last look at her handiwork in a full-length mirror, before rolling her top down and inspecting her face in the glass.

— I want to go to the Steps.

Sam lisps. Her bottom lip clamped with BBQ tongs, she unflinchingly drives a hole through the skin beneath her lip with one of her mum's pearl stud earrings.

— It's boring here.

★

There's about twenty kids in baggies, and a handful of crusties too, smoking single-skin joints and dozing against the stone pillars that line the museum steps. Apart from to accept whatever is being offered round in paper cups like nuthouse meds, nobody looks up much, not even when Sam and me approach; most folk are too preoccupied trying to stave off Sunday comedowns. All except this new guy, who starts chatting like he's dropped a whole roll of pills to anyone who gives him eye contact. He's talking about the knees-up at Willibob Park last night, like we weren't all there. Tan skin, a pink Mohawk that's suspiciously bright and neatly styled, and wearing baggies with pristine hems, this new guy looks like an office intern got up as a punk for a fancy dress party. In comparison, even Aberdeenie Jeanie in her neon goth togs looks washed out, or just washed up.

— He looks hot.

Sam whispers in my ear as we drop our bags down to sit on.

—He looks like a pig.

—'Flower' ain't a cop name, Lay. And anyway, he's with Polly.

Sam has a point. Undercover cops don't fuck underage lasses, least – if they do – not on the job if they know what's good for them; small time drug busts tend to pale in comparison to paedophile cop scandals in the eyes of the law, and the newspapers, after all. And, at fifteen, Polly's legally underage and not the sort of lass who calls a guy she ain't yet fucked 'hers', so anyone who has reservations about this latest newbie gives him room and divvies up their shit, all the same.

The nickname 'Flower', Polly smirkingly tells me, was Bull's doing. Nicknames always get doled out by the older lot. And Bull's nicknames mostly always come from fantasy novels, or Monty Python skits. In Terry Pratchett's DiscWorld Series, Twoflower is the name given to a character said to be the world's first tourist. Round here, 'tourist' is the name folk call anyone who dabbles now and then, but who couldn't get a dealer to give them so much as directions to a pub without us dregs lending a hand.

Bull slumps down beside Flower and passes him a takeout cup, which Flower don't take a sip from, but holds politely until Polly takes it from him. Polly sniffs at the open cup, flinches, takes a swig and passes it on to me. I take a pull and hand it over my shoulder to

Aberdeenie Jeanie, who gags when she smells it, but still takes a gobful.

— Yeah. Lancaster's alright. The great thing about a little city is all the secret places: the gazebos at Willibob Park, The Place of Kings, The Forgotten Rest Rooms, Smokers' Alley...

Bull counts off the names of local haunts to Flower as if casting an enchantment. I take Bull's tobacco tin and help myself to a fair whack of his grass while Flower asks more about The Place of Kings. Somehow, along the way of things, Bull has taken on the gig of explaining all the basic shit needed to best avoid a kicking if you hang about the museum steps, probably on account of how long he's been a dreg. I think only La, and maybe Clit and Scraggy Mag have been hanging around the Steps as long as Bull and Cal. Them and Laura K. But Laura K ODed last year, so I guess she don't count no more.

I've only ever known the Steps as always having been littered with dregs. People always appearing, and disappearing. The only thing that's changed is the steps. The first wave of what locals came to call 'the dregs' were a loose tangle of art students that'd wash up at Dalton Square during their lunch breaks or after college; that's how Bull and Cal first met — at art college. That's how the Steps began. After 'the accident', nobody wanted to sit at the steps beneath the pouting statue of Queen Vic in Dalon Square though. Nobody wanted to face the road where it happened. To face what'd happened. Instead, everyone just shifted arse to the Museum Steps in the City Centre.

— The Place of Kings? Pok, it's just an old factory behind the theatre up toward Gallows Hill. S'nowt special; just where you go if you need anything bigger than a few grams of owt. Only place no one fights. Course, don't mean any old fucker can just roll up there, mind. No-man's land in more ways than one, Pok is. But that's a point right there; there's plenty of places to avoid too.

Bull gabs on. The town centre before me looks plod-free, so I spark the joint. Beside me, Sam is twitching so bad to join in with the storytelling that if our shins were kindling we'd be ablaze. Flower glances at the blood-encrusted pearl earring protruding from Sam's lip, and, noticing, she grins at him, forcing the earring to jut out, and breaking the scab that's formed around it.

— Yeah, like, Trix went down the Quay last week and got thrown in the river by The Aldgate 212. He could have died, like, but then he got out, but then they saw and threw him back in. He caught sommet from all the shit in there too and ain't been right since. He must have gulped down some of the river. Like, he got rabies, or it might've been typhoid, you know, like, from all the shit he swallowed?

Sam pauses only to suck her lip and stem the blood, her eyes widening.

— Like, *literal* shit.

— Speaking of shit, Sammy Doll, you don't half chat some. Trix ain't never had everything up there dancing right.

Bull taps his head.

— Ain't no amount of river water what done that, just five years of group homes and foster rents. But Sam's only half wrong: Trix did get himself tossed in the river. Silly cunt what he is, thought he'd just shortcut into town via Aldgate subway. Daft twat oughta be called Billy Goat.

He clears his throat, hocking whatever was in there onto the cobbles.

— See, Flower, it's like this: there are five main gangs round here. Mainly, there's the Aldgate 212 this side of the river and the Range Estate 608 south of the Lune. Avoid them both, mate, and anywhere with those numbers sprayed on the walls. It's all territory, you follow? S'all bullshit too like, but bullshit hurts all same when it's served with a claw hammer, course. Ta, La.

Bull accepts the paper cup from La, swills what's left and downs it.

— Apart from them, there's the 353 run by The Wyatts up Gallows Hill way, a scuttle crew. They're nowt too crazy, but getting there quick enough. Then there's just the Dacrelands 414 on the Dacrelands Estate where Lancaster borders Morecambe, oh, and The Old Pier crew. They run Morecambe, district next to this one. You been to Morecambe yet? Pubs are cheaper than here and the beach ain't half bad when the weather holds up. They import sand from Spain.

Bull nods proudly, as if Flower's wide-eyed goggle is caused by disbelief at having found himself so close to such a scenic coastline.

– Fucking gorgeous it is, the Bay. Got a bore tide like a fucking slotty shelf. They call it the 'killer tide' 'cause of all the illegals it drowns what're here cockling for the Old Pier lot and that. Clears the poor fuckers out like prizes, the bay does. Shame that. But s'fucking immense to clock, like – the bore tide, I mean. Not the bodies, course.

I smoke some more of Bull's grass, watching shoppers skit about the flags while Bull and Sam shit up Flower some more with stories about how everyone who comes here seems to die, or at least get their head kicked in some time or other.

As the people milling about town gradually trickle out like hourglass sand, the crowd at the Steps thickens like a shadow behind me.

Flower's asking if Trix called the police on the guys who did him over. A few of the guys laugh, glancing Flower's way, as if to see if he's larking. Bull frowns, dribbling cider from a three-litre bottle and spitting onto the cobbles.

– Call the filth? For what? Last time the plod involved themselves there were riots what made the

nine o'clock news. National an' all, not just regional.
You had little'uns pelting rocks at riot cops. Nah, in the
mid-nineties the police learned not to stick *their* nab in.
'Nough molehills round here as is, no need to be making
no fucking mountains of 'em.

Sam edges in closer.

– Yeah, there was this huge rivalry back then
between the Aldgate 212 and Range 608. No one
remembers about how it got started, but –

Bull cuts Sam off with a growl.

– Every fucker remembers how it ended. Ain't worth
mentioning. The 212 and 608 tolerate each other well
enough. For now. Problem is, Flower, lad, the 212 pretty
much runs Lancaster and since The Dacrelands kids hit
puberty they've been trying to make out they're rock
hard and all that, you know?

Flower don't look like he knows much too much of
nothing.

– Aye, Lancaster's darker than it looks, mate. Don't
let a handful of tearooms and hanging baskets fool you
otherwise.

Flower's eyes glance off Sam's weeping lip piercing
to the DIY tattoos circling Bull's eyes.

– So what about you guys?

– Us? Ha. Us are just 'the dregs', ain't we?

Bull barks, gesturing air quotes.

– Mostly dragged up on the estates, like, but we're
the fallout. The scum on the surface. That's why we got

known as 'dregs'. We don't want to fuck no one up over who can walk where or who sells what. Like I say, s'all bullshit, Flower. Pure bullshit, man. Better to sit out in full view –

– And get hassled by the cops...

Sam says, rolling her eyes, like she's ever had hassle off a cop. Bull grunts.

– Least there's a complaints procedure when the pigs give you a kicking.

Behind me, I hear Scraggy Mag muster a dry, cystic-fibrotic laugh. Turning my back on the last of the anorak-clad militia and their offspring in time to catch Mag shake her head, I pass Flower what is left of the joint.

The big clock on the museum tower is chiming. Distantly, the cathedral bells holler back.

Gradually, the black wave of hoodies and baggies scattered along the museum steps become upright like some occult gathering, readying themselves to sacrifice the museum steps to the drunks soon spilling out the pubs and clubs. Sam and Bull are still discussing Lancaster like it's some ghetto in The Bronx as we climb the hill. Flower slows, gazing up at the castle as we pass beneath its ancient oak trees and Narnia lampposts, to descend onto the flattened grave slabs at the rear of Lancaster Priory. He says something about how grand it looks against the sunset, like a postcard picture, and how it'd be amazing to get inside. Sam laughs, causing her pierced lip to start up bleeding, again.

— It's easy enough to get in.

Wiping the blood from her chin with her sleeve, Sam drops her voice and hangs back, gesturing ahead to Bull.

— He just did four months in the Castle wing. That's how come we all partied at Willibob Park last night; Bull didn't want to spend his birthday here, even on this side of the walls.

She gestures theatrically.

— Welcome to Her Majesty's Prison Stonerow Head!

— Shit. Isn't it dangerous, you guys all coming here to get high at the back of a prison?

Passing by us on his skateboard, Trix makes to slap Flower upside the head. Sam pulls Flower from Trix's path in time, and grins.

— Don't worry, s'not like they let the murderers out to roam about. Except when they release them, course. Anyway, Bull weren't in for smoking weed, were he?

— What was he in for?

Flower glances toward Bull who's lumbering along just ahead of us. Sam shrugs.

— Grievous bodily harm. But ain't like the guy didn't have it coming. Ask Lay Baby. Jim — Bull's baby brother — he were her boyfriend.

It were an accident, I tell Flower, and remind Sam.

— Jim's still dead, and that guy's still driving around the car what killed him. Someone had to do sommet.

Like I need reminding that Jim is dead. And like it's

worth reminding Sam, Jim weren't my boyfriend.

Talking about 'love' when you're a teenager is like trying to sell fool's gold; nobody's buying it. Anyway, sex weren't what me and Jim shared; at least, sex weren't all we shared. Jim and me, we fucked and we hung out with a bunch of people besides each other in the two years we knew each other. We just liked stuff that set us apart and got us laughed at, or plain put people on edge, even at the Steps. Stuff like poetry.

When Jim died it was like getting my throat ripped out, not my heart.

★

You can only get so fucked up, until you're just plain fucked, and when there's no place left to end up you end up here.

Wayside, they call it. Special school, everyone else calls it. I've been here for three months, since I took to street sleeping after Jim kicked it. When Jim kicked life, I mean, not the gear. Jim didn't disappear to get clean; Jim just disappeared.

When the police laid hands on me, The Social and Welfare Services stuck me here. My mum and me, we both signed the agreement: she'd house me, until I turn sixteen. And I'd stay in her house, except to go to special school and engage in socially acceptable and age-appropriate recreational activities. Like anyone I know wouldn't just reckon I'd face planted a bag of speed if I invited them on a bike ride or suggested a game of five-a-side.

So, it's official. But official is all it is: I ain't kipped at my mum's for more than a couple of nights at a time since, but I turn up at Wayside, most of the time, and my mum's stopped reporting me to Social Services when the teachers call to tell her I ain't turned up. Neither of us fancy getting banged up. It's about the only thing my mum and me do agree on.

I got straight As at mainstream school – before I got permanently excluded, I mean. Mostly on account of Jim's giving me a kick up the arse, though, not the school teachers. Fact is, the best teacher I ever had weren't to be found in school, but after school in the city library, where he almost always were. School, of any kind, it just began to feel like playing chess when your aim ain't to win but to lose in the end, and because losing gets to feel like the only way to win sometimes.

Jim taught me to play chess. He nicked a portable set from a bric-à-brac stall in Morecambe market, and set it up at Pok, while around us crackheads piped and junkies rummaged for veins and dealers clocked in and out. Some watched, offering advice or whooping and cheering when one of us took the other's piece.

I hated chess, instantly. Suicide ain't an option on a chessboard. Trying to lose a game of chess takes as much effort as trying to win; every time you are placed in check the only move open to you is to try save yourself. Being at school ain't unlike playing chess, in that regard. I can play the game. I know the rules. I just can't whoop or get all crazy about winning. Whoever they had chatting or teaching us weren't ever chatting or teaching about any life I could even imagine. How can you want sommet you can't even imagine?

Grades weren't a problem, or *the* problem, I were.

They say, I had to leave that school because I assaulted a teacher. Way I see it, I left school because it were getting in the way of my education, just like that teacher got in the way of the desk I kicked. Their chat and efforts weren't aimed at me, just like that desk weren't aimed at her. We just got in each other's way.

That's why I ended up here. That's why any kid ends up here; we're damaged goods and we know it. Everyone knows it.

Thing is, even here, even at Wayside, even at Special School, everyone is waiting for *us* to sort ourselves out, but things in special schools don't sort themselves; they can't. I mean, that's the whole reason shit ends up in places like this.

Special school is the last stop: it's the limbo between normal society and prison, or the crazy house, or the morgue, or whatever place us kids ain't ticked enough boxes or blown enough candles out yet to end up. Kids in special school either get sorted or eventually they just get tossed, like mail in sorting offices. For now, we just wait to be returned-to-sender each noon, to some address where no one's waiting for us, not no more – if ever anyone were waiting. Nothing to wait for except the enforced routine of being returned here every morning to wait for noon. Over and over, going nowhere fast. And that's how it is for us – how it gets to feeling.

You see it in the new ones, when they first arrive: expectation, hope, even. The social workers and welfare officers tell them here's a safe place. What no one tells them, tells us, is that here's only safe because by the time you get here it's because there's little left to fear. After a while of waiting you just get lost in the dull rhythm of this whole bureaucratic apparatus. So when there ain't been a new kid for a while, everything starts getting real quiet; just two rooms containing six or so slouching kids, waiting for whatever happens after this. Not because owt does happen, just because there's nowt else to do, but wait.

It could almost look like a scene in a normal school, if the scene didn't play out in two basement rooms of a Quaker Meeting House and according to a three-pupils-to-one-teacher ratio. But then they send another kid, or a kid disappears and it sort of jerks everyone out of their fugue.

This morning, my only mate in this place, Miss, is sitting between me and the new kid, Danny, pretending to be asleep. The radio competes with the crap being gabbed by Danny.

I close my eyes and press my forehead against the passenger window. When Bald Fella's taxi don't arrive and instead Sweating Pits pulls up or Heavy Breather crawls along the curb side on Monday, Danny will soon realise the futility of conversation and fizzle out. Everybody does, in the end.

★

At the hospital, a technician uses a power tool with a circular blade to cut the plaster and then prises the cast open like a razor clam. My hand's all shrivelled where the cast's been rained on or got wet when I've been in the shower, so my skin's peeling off along my palm. The whole thing looks more gruesome than when the cast was slapped on, like sommet from a low-budget 1970s horror film.

The doctor inspects my wrist, and then carries on about x-rays, more casts, physiotherapy. Realising the doctor reckons my hand ain't fully healed, I ask if I can cadge something for the pain. He hands over a box of Paracetamol. I say it hurts *bad*. The doctor adds to the Paracetamol a strip of Ibuprofen and takes a long, hard look at the size of my pupils, holding and lifting my chin like I'm some inanimate ornament he's inspecting and shining a torch at me like a miniature spotlight.

He tells me to wait a moment, and disappears

through the curtain divide. Before he returns, with
more questions, and likely with someone employed by
Social Services, I duck out through the curtain wall and
make for Pok to cadge some grass to punt and kill some
time till Sam finishes school, and to score some actual
pain relief.

★

A cigarette hanging from her lips, Polly is poised at
Sam's vanity desk, watching Sam sleep via the mirror
affixed to the desktop. She has a tube of red lipstick in
one hand and a wad of twenties in the other. She makes
it look offhand, but she's been sat like that for half an
hour, chain-smoking and waiting for Sam to wake. So,
when Sam does wake, instead of being hit by the sight
of Polly cross-legged in a mini skirt brandishing a roll of
money, Sam is just hit by a room thick with smoke and
waves her hand about, swearing and coughing.

– Fuck school. We're going shopping.

Polly delivers the line, undeterred by Sam, who
looks more choked than impressed by the scene she
wakes to. I tell them I've shit to sort up at Pok, as I
search Sam's underwear drawer for sommet to wear,
sommet that don't have some cutesy logo, and Sam
tosses this look at me like I've just pissed on Christmas.

– But you can go up to Pok anytime. Polly, tell her,
will you?

Polly slips a twenty from the roll and drops it into Sam's underwear drawer.

– Go get your shit sorted. Then we can go. But we are going.

Polly blows me a kiss and winks at me. In reply, I toss the crumpled notes out the drawer and on to the bed, where Polly has sprawled. Polly retrieves them, climbing over the dirty washing I've been sleeping amongst. She starts catapulting Sam's knickers out the skylight window, before forcing the notes into the pocket of my jeans and squeezing my arse with her hand still in my jeans pocket so Sam don't see.

– I'll even buy you some knickers of your very own. No frills, Lay Baby, I promise.

★

Catching back up with Sam and Polly at the Steps after swinging by Pok to cash Polly's twenty, we head straight up the ginnels, through Bashful Alley and over the hill past Lancaster Castle to the railway station.

Bunking table seats on the last carriage of the airport train, I leave my sleeve rolled back and rest my arm on the table. There's still the ghost of a bruise haunting my wrist and thumb where my mum slammed the door on it, and my whole arm, knuckles to elbow still smells faintly like wet dog from where the cast had been.

When I tense my fist, the freshly-healed scars where

the door's edge cut into my hand turn from purple to white like secret ink. Polly grimaces and sprays it with deodorant till I can feel it burn my raw skin, like my hand is some upturned bug we're watching keel.

By ten-thirty we're sitting beside the tropical fish tank in the Manchester Piccadilly Station bar, Polly passing us condensated highball glasses of coconut rum and iced milk. I duck out to the loos. When I return, Sam is leaning forward over the table, chewing the straw in her drink and asking Polly where she got the money from.

– Pipe down, shit for brains. Do you want us to get IDed?

Polly glares at Sam until she blushes, and then tells Sam she laid these blokes when she were at her auntie's in Scotland.

– What, and they paid you? Sam gapes.

Polly shoots me a grin before she turns back on Sam.

– That what you think of me, Sammy Doll? You think I'm a whore?

Sam falls for Polly's bullshit every time. Polly tosses another grin my way, which I deflect with a raised eyebrow.

– I'm a kid. Where d'you think I got the money, you fucking div?

Sam frowns, more at being called a fucking div, I reckon, than at how Polly might've happened upon what looks to be about half a ton.

— My mum don't give me hundreds of quid. Lay's Mum don't give her owt.

— What, you gonna accuse me of being some scummy drug dealer now too? Lay Baby's mum's on welfare. She ain't got no fucking money. And your mum's so uptight it's a wonder you exist at all.

I don't say as much, I don't say nothing, but my mum's not on benefits. She just has a shit job, and no husband. She'd get more money on welfare, but then she'd not be able to level with anyone who questions how me and my brother, Caleb, have turned out. Not that I *am* a drug dealer. I ain't. I just shot for folk sometimes, is all.

I finally cave and ask where Polly did get the money, more to kill her fun than to kill any curiosity.

Polly considers me for a moment, crushing an ice cube in her teeth. She sucks the shards smooth before spitting the pieces back into her empty glass.

— My 'rents made me go stay with my great aunt for the week, except when I got there this time the old biddy was dead.

Sam literally spits a hail of milk onto the glass table between us. Polly ignores her.

— My 'rents thought she was, like, sitting on a fucking goldmine or some shit, but the house barely covered her fucking bingo debts. If they'd have ever fucking gone see her they'd have seen that too. Cunts. She left me four hundred quid. S'all she had.

– What and you actually like found her, like, *the body*?

Polly rounds on Sam like she's actually thinking of lamping her, and Sam quickly changes tack; she tries to reach over to hug Polly, but Polly slaps Sam's arm away.

– What, you trying to hire me now? Fuck *off*, you fat fucking dyke.

I don't ask myself, let alone Polly, if her aunty really died or, if she did die, whether Polly found her body. Sure, Polly is a total bullshitter; it's in her nature, like it's in a cat's nature to torture its prey, but if it ain't true yet about her aunty, so what? It will be, someday.

Peeling back the notes for the seventh time in the twelfth shop and still in Piccadilly Gardens, all the toing and froing between shops and temperatures has me feeling mazy. I barely make it out of some knock-off make up shop and to the gutter before throwing up. Sam and Polly looking at me like *I'm* something been hocked up.

– Maybe you've got an allergy to the deodorant stuff Polly sprayed on your arm.

– Maybe it's cotton fever.

Polly tries to sound innocent. Polly only ever tries sound innocent when she's being sly. Even Sam don't buy Polly's 'concerned mate' BS.

– I don't think a person can be allergic to cotton.

As Sam frowns at the curdled rum and milk I've upchucked into the gutter, Polly eyeballs me. She knows

I ain't got cotton fever — she knows that I don't even use needles, so I don't chance getting sick off dirty cotton filters. Polly's concern ain't for my wellbeing, it's for her reputation, which don't allow room for giving a shit about elderly relatives. Like I need Polly threatening to let slip to Sam what I were doing when I disappeared into the train station toilets earlier, or what I spent that twenty quid on that she shoved into my jeans pocket, to stop me from taking the piss with the guys at the Steps about someone dying. Like anyone, besides Polly, would even find that funny.

Catching the way I clock her, and warnings having been flashed both ways, Polly drops the digs towards me and I relax my fists. She suggests I'd feel better in Afflecks, already leading the way over the tram tracks and towards the Tib Street Horn, this urban-gothic structure fifty feet high which marks out Affleck's Palace and the gateway to Manc's Northern Quarter.

On the subject of needles though, if you have ever seen them posters they put up at needle exchanges of magnified photographs showing how after each use a pin barbs, that's kind of how all the shards of wheel trim and general junk welded to the sides of the Tib Street Horn looks; sinister more than inviting, like it's a dirty needle permanently poking at the bruisy-looking clouds that seem to hang over Manchester, whatever the season.

Afflecks is essentially an indoor market, an emporium in a gutted red-brick former factory. Now, independent traders and designers punt vintage clothes, costume jewellery and oddball homemade art here. I've seen framed inkblots and gas masks and bags of 'used' pinballs from arcade game machines with price tags in Afflecks.

The place is full of ripped-out bus seats, old tin fire buckets full of cigarette and joint butts and life-sized papier-mâché Daleks draped in plastic leis. The buckled corridors are jammed with old untuned pianos, retro arcade games and funhouse mirrors. Some stalls are lit up by black lights and UV plastics or sprayed with graffiti, like the record store on the ground floor. We pass a tiny Japanese woman who sits on a three-legged milking stool like an automaton, hemming silk-lined kimonos beneath strings of coloured bonbori lanterns on the second-floor landing. Outside Top Café on the third floor is a shop that sells clocks made of old bean cans, and rip-off Andy Warhol Pop Art prints. The only security guard in the whole place is literally a joke, in the form of a tarantula called Boris, kept in a tank in the first-floor jewellers' place.

When I was a kid, my brother Cal used to bring me to Afflecks with his girlfriend La. That were back when La first appeared and everyone still called her 'LA Sarah' on account of her California drawl. While Cal and La shopped for neon hair wool and black lipstick, they'd dump me in a vintage denim shop: The Queen of the Blues. I used to crawl beneath the heavy racks of

old leather jackets, gazing up at yellowed portraits of
Ella Fitzgerald and Billie Holiday, Carmen McRae and
Mildred Bailey, tacked with nails and peeling tape onto
the chipped plaster walls. Surrounded by the smell of
old leather, the sweat of the shoes and strange musk of
the fabrics, I'd close my eyes, my fingers feeling the deep
grain of the old, uneven floorboards while Chet Baker's
trumpet or Sarah Vaughan's 'Black Coffee' warbled out
the old bar-room blues jukey.

I first heard Dinah Washington's version of 'This
Bitter Earth' play here whilst hiding beneath a rack of
1950's Sunday dresses. That voice, sad sway of violins,
ache of cello and scent of those fabrics brushing about
me like ghosts in some old-time jazz lounge winded me
like a sucker-punch straight to the gut. The Queen of
the Blues – the shop, I mean – is long gone now, too. It
was one of the first things gone when the chains started
sneaking in.

While Polly checks everything Sam tries on, offering
to buy her anything long as it makes Sam look even
tubbier than she is, I browse the newest stalls, the stalls
that weren't here the last time I was.

More and more high-street names are nudging their
way in, killing off the last of the original designers
and fumigating the whole place with health and safety
bullshit.

Eventually, they'll just gut this place and turn it
into a wine bar for the city trendies or another luxury

apartment block. Or even student digs for the uni kids. It ain't even so much that it'll happen, more that it happens so slow. The brands have been breaking out like an ugly rash for a while now; it's like watching someone you know get eaten alive from the inside out.

These days, I walk the rickety funhouse corridors and exit the lopsided stairwells bracing myself for the smell of joss sticks and grass to be overpowered by ground coffee and chlorine bleach. Meanwhile, everyone just pretends it ain't happening, just how people always do when that's all they can do.

Polly asks if I want anything. I shrug, parting a rack of black mesh vests in what were once The Queen of the Blues. It now sells coffins and any merch to do with tacky vampire movies. The sort of place where they spell vampire with a 'y'. They didn't even bother to take the portraits down, just painted them over. You can still make out the shape of faces like ghosts beneath the thin veil of black emulsion. The musty smell of broken-in leather has been almost entirely choked up by the smell of dry ice from a machine in the corner where the jukey used to sit. It lingers, the dry ice, like a fog so you can't tell where you're standing and occasionally crunch down on lost friendship beads like skulls. Some of which probably are skulls. Glass skulls and plastic hearts.

I try to find the spot where I first heard 'This Bitter Earth', moving nearer to where the counter now stands, and the guy behind it, who's wearing fang veneers and white facepaint, runs his tongue over his pointed teeth and winks at me.

Polly sneers at the guy. Snatching an acid-washed vest from me, she steers us back out into the corridor. As though the dry ice really were some mad intoxicating fog, my mind instantly begins to clear. Polly lets go of my arm before I can prise her fingers from my skin, but is still cursing the cheek of the guy in fang veneers.

Sam wants to check out the sex shops to browse the pick'n'mix condoms and cocktail flavoured lubricants, but Polly has other ideas. And seen as Polly has money, we follow her, taking the warehouse lift with its Halloween muzak, looped warnings crackling out whenever the lift shifts between floors.

Reaching the top floor, Polly drags me to the piercing and tattoo studio, Prince Albert's, which is tucked away in the far corner. The corridor leading to Prince Albert's is sandwiched between two clothing stalls, so you've to sort of push your way through tie-dye, hemp, hippy-shit togs to find the place as if passing through some psychedelic acid trip wardrobe on your way to Narnia.

The guy behind the counter straightens up as we enter and Polly's acrylic nails dig in my arm. He's tall and skinny, covered in tattoos, with anti-eyebrow piercings like tears of mercury dotted along his cheekbones. He looks about the same age as the guy Polly accused of being a paedophile.

— That's the beauty of being underage, Lay Baby.

Polly whispers in my ear, like I ain't fifteen and don't already know as well as she does that all blokes who hit on you are paedophiles when you're underage, except the ones you actually *want* to fuck, of course.

Polly leans her tits onto the counter, to try to create the illusion of cleavage, and slips the guy a note from the dwindling roll of twenties. Sam, having put on a sulk over missing the dildos and seemingly unimpressed with the real thing, slopes off to check out the rubber genitalia advertising barbells in locked glass cabinets while I fill out the form. No, I'm not an intravenous drug user. No, I haven't consumed alcohol, used drugs or had any other form of body modification in the last twenty-four hours. Yes, I am over eighteen. After I sign some phoney name, the guy shakes my hand and tells me to call him George.

From a small, sterile side room I watch people on the open market below pointing up at the window. I'm topless with George standing between my legs. George has my right nipple clamped between metal teeth and is brushing my breast with iodine. Some guy on a fruit stall with bigger tits than me is cupping his chest and gesturing over to some blokes in a burger van.

George glances out the window between fiddling with my tit, like we're on a date at the zoo watching the chimps toss their shit at us.

— Most excitement they get, poor sods.

As the needle reaches through my nipple a mound appears on the left side. I watch the skin rear, tear and slide reluctantly along the shaft. It's like hot barbed wire dragging beneath my flesh.

George slips the needle back out, leaving the straw in my nipple and trimming it so he can remove the clamp. I lean into the open window, where the air is cool and George puts his hands around my waist and turns me back to face him. He pulls at the straw, feeding the bar through the tunnel in my nipple before pinching the end to screw on a small titanium ball.

When the blood begins, George reaches for an empty coffee mug.

– Your blood's thin. You ain't taken owt, been drinking or owt?

– Thin blood. Anaemia and all that.

– So, how many have you had? Piercings, I mean?

He holds the coffee mug beneath my breast, making conversation like we're office colleagues at a water dispenser.

– I've never counted.

Jim used to tell me I look like a derelict house that a pisshead with a nail gun has been renovating. I glance down at myself.

– Not much you can't see.

And seen as I'm topless, that's mostly true.

– You a masochist?

– Are you?

George smiles for the first time, wipes my breast clean, and then laughs. He bins the blooded wipes and throws me my vest. Catching it, my mind automatically begins reeling through morning-after protocol. I pull my top back on and try to push the thought of chemists, paperwork, and morning-after pills from my mind, along with the feeling of having my freshly pierced nipple chafing against the vest, which suddenly feels two sizes smaller and does nothing to hide the evidence of what's just taken place.

Outside the cubicle Polly and Sam are smoking by a large, open sash window. A fat woman with green hair, large, gold hoop earrings and a septum ring is behind the counter. She looks like one of those dummies in the fortune-teller machines along Blackpool promenade, only half-melted, like someone tried torching her at some point.

George walks around the counter and hands me an aftercare sheet and a smaller bar to wear once the swelling subsides. The fat woman with green hair smiles up at me. I half-expect her to hand me a sticker or stick of sugar-free gum and tell me how brave I've been, but she just says to take care and then turns on Polly and Sam.

– Make sure she eats and has a sugary drink. And no alcohol –

– Or anything else.

George interrupts as he's eyeing the marijuana

leaf badge pinned to Sam's rucksack and her beaded homemade earrings, which feature the molecular structure of MDMA.

I turn down Sam's offer to go upstairs to the café, where plastic flowerpots are glued to the green-carpeted ceiling so everything looks upside down, and La used to buy me banana milkshakes in sundae glasses the size of vases. Instead, Polly leads the way to a pool hall, just off Portland Street where you can't identify the things hanging from the ceiling and the only flowers are apologies wilting on stools beside guys who know they'll need them in about six hours time. The kind of pub with permanently blacked-out windows where I half-search and half-avoid meeting eyes with the patrons, just in case I happen to find my dad amongst them.

I ain't seen him or my brother, Dominic, since I were ten, and since I woke up to find the flat emptied of everything and everyone but me, and a shit ton of maybes. I don't even know if he's still in the country. Maybe he took my brother, Dom and went back to Spain, after all. Maybe he took Dom and jumped in the ocean. Maybe they got beamed up by aliens, along with all the liquor emptied out the drinks cabinet.

All I know is, the compulsion to clock every face of every drunk in every pub I set foot in, I can't kick it, even now. The thought, not so much of seeing my dad again, but of seeing someone who might know where

Dominic is, someone who might know *how* he is, it's forever lurking in the back of my mind, like a hangover you just cannot shake. Sometimes you think it's gone. That's when it sucker-punches you, when you least expect it. Sometimes, people just disappear.

– Oi, bitch tits, Sam's about to feed twenty quid's worth of whiskey to the carpet. Fancy lending a hand at all?

I turn back to the bar to see Sam trying to overload a tray with shots, and take it from her. Polly loads what's left of the drinks on to a second tray and we make for a corner booth. All the time, Sam keeps asking if George and I did owt.

I finish the first double shot of whiskey in a swig. Following suit, Polly slides a shot across the table to me. I wipe my mouth with my hoodie sleeve and reach for what smells like tequila.

– Come on, you didn't make a move?

Polly rolls her eyes, leaning forward to pick up her own shot, and handing me a lemon wedge.

– Make a move? Sam, he had a needle through her tit, you fucking virgin.

★

A few miles south of Lancaster is a town called Galgate. Galgate used to have its nose in the air on account of every council house family dreaming of living there.

Then in 2002, some lass who lived in Galgate became the youngest kid in Britain to die after doing ecstasy there. She were ten years old and the newspapers said she downed forty times the lethal dosage, whatever that is.

Anyhow, Galgate's still got its big thatched cottages, three-acre gardens and yacht-littered marina, sure, but it's true when you're taking the Blackpool bus through Galgate you don't overhear parents complaining how *if they didn't have kids they could have moved up here* so much, anymore.

Out the window, the grey concrete melts away like snow to reveal plush green fields, patchwork drystone walls and kissing gates as we near the village, and the house. Eventually, even the human traffic seems to be replaced by broods of sheep and swathes of heather which gives the far-off hills the impression of having turned necrotic, like neglected track sores.

Polly's grandparents make a stop-off at the village shop before we reach the house. Polly picks up some horror flick DVD, crisps, chocolate and Coca-Cola while I wait in the car. I have a bottle of bourbon in my jacket I cadged from Sam's place. I left a twenty in place of the whiskey and only took it 'cause Polly wouldn't let up. Even knowing I've got the bottle, Polly keeps whining that I should've taken the bottle of single malt instead, seen as Sam's mum is going to be pissed at me anyhow. But I don't know what the fuck difference whiskey being single malt makes when it's mixed in a glass of warm Coke and downed by stoned fifteen-year olds.

Pulling up and seeing the house, I start wondering if it's true that Polly's parents really do send her to all their well-to-do relatives that are likely to kick it within the decade, to try to get mentioned in their wills. This garage alone is bigger than any place I've ever lived. Their back garden opens onto the canal, where they've a barge, Polly says. Polly says they never use it, like anyone else has an old fridge-freezer or broken-down sofa out back, or plastic patio furniture and hanging baskets when they're trying to front to the neighbours, like my mum does.

We enter the house through the garage to avoid the rain and Polly's grandfather directs me up a central staircase, telling me to take the second door on the left. Inside, the bedroom is made up of four walls of built-in wardrobes and storage compartments, all with this like filigree, lustre, gold stuff on them. Set into the centre of the wall to the right of the door is a dressing table, mirror and stool, all upholstered in matching gold and sort-of-lilac material. Even the television and DVD player are fixed into the walls, like the room is purpose-built so nothing can be nicked.

Dropping the DVD and munch onto the floor, I swig some of the bourbon and roll a cigarette. I also take the opportunity to chase a couple of lines in the en-suite. I've never been inside a hotel, but I bet this is what they look like, the posh ones in cities like Manchester and London. Or at least, I bet this is what they looked like back in the 70's or whatever heyday decade Polly's grandparents are stuck in, like old folk always are.

I pick up an ornament. Surprising how little it weighs, and to find little fuzzy-felt stoppers applied to its base to prevent its rough edges from scratching the lacquer off the sideboard. In the middle of its base, hallooed by a coarse ceramic lip, is the stamped logo of a department store.

I trace the letters, and think of my mum. All the Sundays of my kidhood that I spent being zipped into thick layers of second-hand highly-flammable polyester coats that smelt like other people and came from 50p clothing rails at car boots and were stood in front of bowing trestle tables of perilously arranged pottery and glassware. I'd be made to hold some clumsily-stamped, mass-produced, hollow owl ornament while my mum literally counted out pennies to the sum of anything up to a quid, and I'd try to figure out, what is there to love about this? It's like my mum filled the house with all her ticky, tacky knick-knacks just for some reason to cry when my brothers and I, or my dad returning drunk, shattered them.

I replace the ornament on the sideboard. The whole place seems unreal, a movie set I'm about to have wheeled away from all around me.

Catching my reflection in the full-length mirror, I

try imagining who I might be if this were a movie, if the set designers and wardrobe department had made me like this not just fifteen years of council estates, car boots, underage drinking and climbing things that are fixed with signs that warn *Danger! Do not climb!* beside little images of faceless stickmen being electrified to death.

It's like a detective story, one of the battered Raymond Chandlers Jim used to leave lying about and jokingly paraphrase parts from when he'd wake to find me half gouged out and half naked, sprawled like a murder victim up at Pok.

I am a New York teen from the wrong side of the tracks brought as a hooker to some aristocrat's hotel room. I've accidentally stumbled over some mafia secret. Now I'm being buttered up, coaxed into being conned back onto the streets. Wandering around the room, I actually start to imagine what the secret might be, while Polly's grandparents downstairs are no doubt asking their granddaughter what the fuck she's doing inviting something like me into a place like this, a places like theirs. Anything to avoid thinking about that, or about my mum and all her garish ornaments that crowd her house like hollow, heart-shaped booby traps.

– I had to sit at the table and eat tea with them. I said I weren't hungry, but they made me. I could see them eyeballing me, like I'm some anorexic.

Laughing, Polly, pushes the door closed and hands

me two glasses.

I take my hand from the glazed porcelain hind of some breed of dog I recognise as that type you see posh folk use to hunt with on TV, whenever the issue of whether to ban hunting crops up on the News. My fingers leave smudges where my hand had begun to sweat with the effort of not just picking the ornament up and slamming it into the wall, or Polly's face. At the vanity desk, I pour whiskey and cokes, the now duck-arsed cigarette I rolled ten minutes earlier still hanging unlit from my mouth.

– You can smoke. They never come in here, only the cleaner does. It just tobacco?

I nod, lighting up the cigarette and Polly sets about putting the movie on.

– They're going to Preston tomorrow. They asked if you want to come. They usually buy Sam stuff. I'll get them to buy you sommet, but don't take the piss.

We sit on the bed staring at the TV for a while. I'm knocking back shots of whiskey from the bottle cap, waiting for Polly to decide the movie is shit and turn her attention to me, like usual, when I notice this plastic button the size of my fist, fixed on the skirting board. I think like maybe it's some panic button for old people, like if they fall out of bed and can't get up or something.

– Push it.

Polly dares me, crushing crisps in the bag and knocking back the crumbs. Swinging one leg off the bed, I kick the button. I mean, I figure the worst that can happen is nothing. And when there's no alarm or noise, no lights, no feds busting through the French doors from the balcony, the silence gives me a moment to think nothing *will* happen.

Then the door swings open, sending light jutting into our smutty darkness. I hadn't even noticed it'd gotten dark. Back lit by the landing light, Polly's Grandma stands in the doorway donning an open, pale yellow, quilted dressing gown. It's the same lemon-yellow the Queen always wears for televised celebrations. Her cobwebby hair is full of pink plastic curlers as all five feet of her demands someone put their hands up. I don't put my hands up. Instinct keeps me from moving at all, at least while she's focusing what looks like a handgun on me, her hands shaking. Blinking through half-light, she recognises it's me, lowers it, and looks around for Polly.

– Paulina, did you push the button?

Her voice is as unsteady as her hands, not with anger so much as terror by the look of her. Like she's the one staring down the mouth of a gun barrel.

Polly slides the ashtray beneath the duvet and washes down the chewed clump of crisps with a swig of whiskey and Coca-Cola before answering.

– Lay Baby did. Was an accident, is all, Gran.

Trapped between Polly, who has actually turned back to gaping at the bloodshed on the screen, and her

Gran, who is frowning at the carpet, firearm trembling in her arthritic hands, there I am. Like being dropped into a kaleidoscope of mad, posh shit and held there by a plush rockery of scatter cushions all been meticulously arranged to look disarranged, suddenly I've to suppress the urge to laugh. Is this seriously how the middle class live, packing heat out of fear of kids like me might be pocketing firearms and dreams of raiding OAPs' ornament collections?

– Right. Well. As long as everything's OK...

I can't even figure if that's sarcasm in Polly's Gran's voice or just some coded SOS message.

– Night then, both of you.

She starts to leave, and then hesitates.

– Be up before seven if you're wanting a cooked breakfast. We'll be heading out soon as the traffic's thinned.

Polly grunts in reply, crushing up a mouthful of multi-coloured, sugar-coated chocolate balls without turning from the TV. Just as my jaw has begun to unclench and my mind started cleaning the room of the chaos, her grandma and the gun reappear, as if to prove I had just been in the literal firing line of some old woman in a lemon-yellow house robe and carpet slippers.

– Paulina, pet, you haven't. Um. Been smoking in here?

Polly shakes her head, still without moving her eyes from the TV. Her Gran dithers slightly as if Polly might mind her enough to at least offer some bullshit excuse for the haze of roll-up smoke lingering in the room. But only when she's finally turning to leave, does Polly turn from the TV and call to her.

Her Gran hesitates again, clocking me and her gaze loaded even if the gun ain't. Like I'm going to shoot some common sense into the situation. Maybe she just figures I've more experience of situations involving guns. Maybe that's what scares her.

— You do trust me, Gran?

— Well. Um. Yes, well, of course I trust *you*, but...

I expect Polly's Gran to toss me another glance. Instead, she is looking down at the gun, turning it slightly in her hand as though able to twist the gun so far into the sleeve of her robe it'll disappear completely.

—Thanks, Gran.

Polly leaps up and takes the gun like she's doing her Gran a favour, before shuffling the reluctant old woman from the room. I resist the urge to leave with her.

— Your name's Paulina?

— Says 'Layla Garcia Casares'.

— My dad were Spanish. *Is* Spanish.

I shrug, unsure which tense applies.

— And my family are middle class.

Polly shrugs back.

— And pack heat. Your Grandad just lets your Nan run around like that?

— You going to argue with someone who's got a gun?

Polly grins, weighing the gun in both her hands.

I move across the room to refill my glass, aware that the gun is tracking me. If I thought Polly could shoot straight and wanted to kill me then, fuck it, you know? It's not like I'd have to deal with the consequences, or aftermath, after all. As is, I'm more concerned Polly will accidently shoot one of my kneecaps out trying to act clever. The thought of hospitals, of pissing into a bed pan while Disney characters' faces leer off the paediatric ward walls around me, of trying to convince underpaid, overweight nurses to give me real painkillers, of being surrounded by kids dying of cancer or all battered up and stuff. And then the police coming to visit instead of my mum or dad, asking questions about guns and wanting to have little chats in gentle, patronising voices. Informal little chats that lead to big, formal, realities... I swig some whiskey neat, before diluting the rest with pop.

– So, are you really suicidal, Lay Baby; do you *really* want to die?

I look up at Polly. She's posing in the silk slip she's got on as a dress like a kid dolled up for some amateur-dramatics production of *Lolita*. I don't know what's the bigger mindfuck, the gun or the fact that Polly is recreating an image I've had seared in to my mind ever since I discovered *Lolita* being guffawed over by some old guy in Lancaster Library, like he actually had his hands on Lolita rather than just the book. I picked up the dog-eared paperback after to find out what he were getting such a kick out of, and unlike that guy, I couldn't put it down again.

Holding the gun with both hands, she tilts her head to one side, bites her lip and pouts. Usually, I say nothing. Usually, I just let Polly's bullshit slide. Usually, I don't have a gun pointing at me.

Thing is though, what can I say? Like, how the fuck does a half-drunk council estate kid explain to her sociopathic fifteen-year-old fuck-buddy that her thinking is so fucking abductive? Or that that's *why* I'm pissed at having been created?

I try to imagine what Jim might've said, what Jim might've done, faced with a gun. All I see is a vague grin, floating in my mind like smoke rising teasingly from silver foil.

– Think all people who want to be rich want to be bank robbers?

As I ask her, I return my attention to the half-poured drinks. She still has the gun hovering level with my head. I keep my eye on it in the reflection of the dresser mirror.

– You said you wished you'd never existed.

I turn from the mirror and watch the gun slow its fall until it stops as if a spotlight over my heart like I'm part of some interrogation. I walk over, like I'm being reeled into the barrel until it kisses my skin open-mouthed and cold, and point blank against my flesh. And I offer Polly the drink with the gun pressing against my chest hard enough to leave a mark.

— If you really think an inanimate hunk of metal can reverse a person's existence...

I push my chest harder against the mouth of the gun so Polly has to push back or else take a step back.

— *Do it.*

I know this ain't the fun Polly had no doubt hoped for, but I'm not Sam.

When I don't break eye contact or waver, Polly extends her arm until the whole thing hangs above us both. Then, and without taking her eyes off me, Polly's fingers outstretch, like a game of This Little Piggy, slowly extending one by one until the gun seems to hang in the air unsupported. We're still fixed on each other, locked in some Wild West style stare down, so when the gun does fall it passes through my peripheral vision like a shadow or flash like the shit you see during the onset of a migraine. Or during speed psychosis.

The gun hits the floor between us with a heavy inanimate thud, like a body. No shot, no rogue bullet, no drama follows; there is nothing, nothing, but the guttural screaming coming from the TV, which ebbs to a foamy death rattle as the scene fades out, I guess to save the audience from having to witness what comes next, or just because no amount of special effects can compare or compete with the reality of what the human imagination can conjure up.

★

The bedcover has been pulled back and the French doors are wide open. I squint at the light and figure it's around midday based on how bad I want a smoke. And a smoke. Bad enough my skin's crawling with goose bumps, but I lie for a moment soaking up the luxury of an empty bed.

Polly's grandparents must have left without us. I wonder if her Grandma came to check on us this morning, to see if we were going shopping, or just to see if we had blown each other's brains out.

The open doors, the pulled-back sheets, Polly's bullshit fills the room like one big magic-eye picture. The sort they put at the back of kids' magazines. You know, those acid-trip style patterns you can look at forever without seeing what is actually there; but once you do see it for what it is, you can never unsee it? Like, even when you look away, the image remains burned into your retinas, like when you stare into the sun too long.

A trail of peeled-off clothing leads to the open doorway of the ensuite, like a dare. Beyond, Polly's body appears pixelated through the frosted glass of the shower door as if censored.

I take the joint Polly has left for me to find in the cleaned-out ashtray and reach beneath the bed. I'm feeling for my jeans and the lighter I know is in the back pocket, when my knuckles hit upon something cold, and heavy.

I hook the gun with a finger and pull it out by the trigger guard. The heft of the whole thing in my palm, I turn it to face me so my sight narrows to the entrance of the barrel. I don't even know if it's real. Or how real a gun needs to be to kill at point blank. Looking straight down the barrel, it's like a mouth locked in a 'o'. It's like staring into that Edvard Munch painting.

Back when my brother Cal were at art college, pissing his life away, as our mum put it, he'd stacks of books full of famous paintings, all smattered and marred with Indian ink and acrylic and charcoal fingerprints. Some of the books opened naturally where the spine had been bent on his favourites. I used to sit cross-legged at his feet while he painted and open the books on random pages. Caleb would say the name of each image before I'd time to read the text. I've probably forgotten a hundred or more paintings Cal showed me in those books, but I can't shake 'The Scream'.

I face it till I've stared so long the running water starts sounding like a broken metronome tick-tocking unevenly, as though time itself is stretching and dripping. And I get mesmerised by the chaotic rhythm, stuck in this face-off with that black hole, until the metal has warmed against my flesh and I can no longer appreciate its weight, its reality. The 'o' seems then a comic mask and I imagine when I squeeze the trigger the gun will melt or burst or fall apart, not me; the whole world will shatter around me like some surreal prank.

I rest the gun against my temple and curl my finger. The trigger curves up for what feels like forever. I'm beginning to think the gun's a dummy, when the sound hits. After what feels like so long, it's so sudden, not like a firework or an explosion though. It sounds as if Death itself just tutted in my ear. I feel the shock reverberate throughout my body. For a moment, that is all I can feel. All I know.

And then, realising I can, I run my fingers over the solid curve of my skull, and stare down at the gun I have no recollection of dropping. I am trying to feel anything; the sudden lack of anything, of everything. But there's nothing *to* feel, except the realisation: of course some old woman ain't going to hand a loaded gun to a kid. And I'm the reason why, not Polly.

★

Morning rush hour. What an oxymoron that is.

I rub my temple where I'd rested the gun, as if I can erase the moment from my mind. A faded bumper sticker clings to the fender of the car in front. From the back seat of the taxi, I watch it blur in and out of focus as the gap between us widens and closes. And in that way, moving in the only direction we can, we enter the one-way-system.

The traffic slows to a crawl over Greyhound Bridge. There is nothing either side of me but a fifty-foot drop into the Lune, which is almost perfectly black like Indian ink. As if laughing at me, the words continue to blur in and out of focus: *Don't follow me; I'm lost too!*

I slip out of the taxi in a dream. Hazel is already rushing over. She slips me two-twenty for a ten deck. On account of having facial piercings, I'm the only one who can get served by the old bloke at the newsagent's across the road.

Returning from the offie, I smoke my ten per cent on the lawn overlooking Lancaster Railway Station, before heading in. Winter sun is shooting off the tracks. Laid to take people who live here away, and fetch in the ones who don't. I take slow long pulls on the smoke, wondering why folk don't just live where they're needed. Same logic, I guess, has those commuters paying their taxes to be spent on taxis to make sure us runaways, junkies and thieves turn up for school each morning, only to then go and put the school next to a train station, across the road from an off-licence, and two minutes from the town centre.

It's hard to know when you're a kid what's most screwed up: the idea adults know what the fuck they're doing and do it anyway, or the idea that they have no fucking idea themselves and ain't even got what it takes to admit it. Or just the idea of becoming one of them. Not just employed and that, but someone who will likely never actually see the consequences of the actions and the decisions they get paid to make day in and day out for what'll be the majority of their lives. Or the fact that they consider themselves the 'successful' ones.

Reluctantly, I turn my back on the railway station and face Wayside House, its fresh-cut lawn still dewy, the huge front-facing windows streaked with rain, as if the glass is scarred. They occasionally let us out onto that lawn for break. We huddle awkwardly, watching our breath form in front of our faces and dream of cigarettes as the cold seeps into our broken soles. All the while, the women attending good parenting groups bounce babies on their knees and peer at us from the front hall through massive church-looking windows. The teachers call it a treat.

When I first got here I'd light up and blow smoke at the windows or press my face against the panes. Once, I plain screamed into the glass till it were so misted the people inside became like some abstract figurative painting, like I were erasing all their horrified expressions. Then Brenda and McQuaide dog-piled me on the grass and literally carried me off.

Now, between nine and noon they keep me hidden from the general public, providing I turn up at all to let them, that is. That's the bit I figure is craziest of all: not me, but how it's like I'm a part-time crazy. When the plastic shatterproof wall clock hits noon, they just release me. It's like, whatever kind of fucked-up they think I am when I walk through the doors each morning is done for the day – and not just getting started.

Inside, I slide into a seat beside Miss, passing Hazel the cigarettes under the table. I'd put the cigarettes on the table like a normal person; but I'm not a normal person; I'm a fifteen-year-old at a special school.

Like usual, our trays get placed in front of us along with our lesson slips. This slip tells me that in the next room Carol is waiting to teach me all about probability. It's only McQuaide who insists on being called by her surname. All the other teachers introduce themselves by their Christian names and wear casual clothing, like they want us to think they're our friends or something.

I stand up, like I'm actually going to try to follow the instruction on the slip, but I know before I do, before I can, the scene that's about to play out. McQuaide, seeing I've gotten up, takes her cue. Like this whole scenario is scripted, she starts demanding I hand over the cigarettes. Nicole, who knows I've been on a smoke-run, hums Beethoven's 5th, grinning as she passes me with her own tray. Only Andrew disappears into the next room, on account of God having given Andrew Asperger's instead of social skills, leaving Hazel, Miss, Ryan, Danny and, of course, Nicole still watching.

– Let's not play games. Just hand them over, Layla. One of the taxi drivers saw you smoking, and don't think I didn't notice you were late in. You must think I'm stupid.

When I don't reply, McQuaide buries a hand in the place where twenty years ago her hip might've been.

– The cigarettes? Now, Layla.

She points where she wants me to place the smokes on the table, tapping an acrylic nail against the veneered plastic surface and scanning everyone else for guilt.

And then she waits. And I wait. And Hazel waits. And Miss waits. And Danny waits. And Ryan waits. And Nicole waits. And, no doubt, sat in the next room to be taught this morning's lesson, Andrew waits too.

But trying to outwait the likes of a kid fucked up through having spent their first years alive crying never to be answered and the next ten hiding from the only answers ever come to them is, well, that really is like trying to outwait a junkie. We are experts at this shit. I mean; that is why we're at Wayside. Yet, somehow the teachers still try their hand occasionally, usually when there's a new kid and protocol has to be observed.

Fortunately, observing protocol at Wayside lasts about as long as the kids do here. When McQuaide catches Miss stifling a genuine yawn and Hazel leaning against the doorframe, she snaps.

– Fine. OK, Layla. Have it your way. Just remember, your review meeting is on Monday, that's all I will say.

I say nothing. There is nothing I can say, after all. If I had it my way, I would put the cigarettes on the table every morning like a reasonable person. And Hazel would buy her own smokes like any reasonable person.

But like they keep on reminding me; I don't make the rules.

★

Like usual, Miss and I arrive at Dalton Square late. Everybody's gone already, having caught the first free bus, which is actually a transit van with seats welded into it that Crusty Don puts on to get folk to his club.

Waiting for the free bus to circle back, we sterilise our tongues with the bourbon her mum gave us, burning up our thoughts until the words fizz and sting in our throats like stuck pills.

I'm thinking of how life is like waiting for a train at a bus stop. Beside me, Miss is sighing. For the umpteenth time, she flips her mobile open, checking the time on the lit-up screen against the huge old clock beyond the statue of Queen Vic on top of the Town Hall like she don't trust it.

– The bus is late, Lay.

– You say that every week.

– It's late every week. What if it ain't coming back?

– You say that every week.

– You say *that* every week.

And like every week, I say nothing after that; just swig more whiskey like I can somehow disinfect my mind with alcohol, or at the very least sterilise my tongue.

Sure enough, the bus circles back, and as Lancaster melts into the pocked West End of Morecambe my daydreams of Brian, the bus driver, crashing the minivan dissolve into the usual dreams; I am anybody but me, anywhere but here.

I'm a Ryu Murakami rockstar like out of the novel, *Coin Locker Babies*. One of the English teachers at Wayside told me to check out Murakami. She meant Haruki Murakami. I didn't realise there were two famous Japanese writers called Murakami. Neither did the teacher, till I went in raving about Ryu. The worlds Ryu Murakami describes are electric. They stick in the mind like those garish neon signs glow with faux-glamour in the dark outside of 24/7 off licences and dodgy Manc sex shops when everywhere else has closed its doors; when I close my eyes, it's Ryu's world that I end up lost in, at least it is whenever I'm on speed and I can feel my blood rushing through my veins like boy racers in their souped-up scoobies do alongside the River Lune most nights.

Tonight, I've spiked hair and solid black eyes. I have sharp cheekbones and tattoos like punctuation. I'm being delivered via tour bus to some smoke-and-cocaine-fuelled psychosis of a bar to be reunited with a guitar shaped like a gash and the tabbied colour of a scab. I'll plug it into an amp set on permanent distortion and thrash at power chords while thinking about the harem of neon ladyboys waiting backstage to offer me

Class As and blow jobs.

I reluctantly open my eyes and trip out of the van
onto the promenade, to see the manmade structures that
scar The Lake District glittering like smashed glass in
the moonlight, littered across the countryside around
Morecambe Bay.

Bypassing the queue, we head for the heavily
graffitied double doors beneath a hanging sign with an
illustration of an emaciated human staring into a mirror.
The genderless figure has been painted with a hammer
in their right hand and their face obscured by long
matted black hair, above the words: *The Hammer and
Sink*. Beneath the sign, the bouncers step aside for us.

I've never been turned away from a nightclub, round
here. Or queued to get in one. Or paid to enter one. Or
been IDed at the door. I'm Caleb's baby sister, after all.

Apparently being 'Layla' ain't enough and being
'Layla, Caleb's baby sister' is too much of a mouthful.
So, I'm Lay Baby. A bite-sized abbreviation. A
shorthand explanation. A golden ticket, for some.
Whatever. I'll take a Get Out of Jail Free where and
when it's offered. Hell knows, I usually have use for one,
sooner or later. And there are worse shadows to live in.

Inside, up a flight of wide stairs, The Hammer
and Sink houses two bars: the imaginatively-named
'The Hammer Bar' and 'The Sink Bar', in two separate
rooms split by a removable dividing wall. The wall
gets wheeled away during the day so the huge hall-like

space can be used for bare-knuckle fights, or fundraisers whenever another batch of cocklers wash up or the Lune overfills and divvies out its surplus into the city's social housing.

A mezzanine level surrounds an upper floor of The Sink Bar, as if the centre has been removed like a flesh plug to expose the dancefloor below. A café operates on the mezzanine level throughout the night where the fucked-up throw chips and ketchup over the balustrades into the mosh pit like poorly supervised kids at aquariums who flick sweets into shark tanks, then cry when some monster comes up on them to rip their arm off. But that always happens later in the night.

For now, at The Hammer Bar, where it's quiet enough to talk, Netty pours out four tequila slammers and two tall whiskey and Coca-Colas, without asking what we're drinking. Miss taps out salt with a level of care anyone else would reserve for racking lines of speed or coke, and arranges glasses. When we've cleared the round, Miss takes a swig of whiskey and hands me a CD she's been banging on at me to get my brother to play. I drain a second glass of whiskey and I make my way into The Sink.

Beneath the DJ booth in The Sink, which juts out from the stage-side over the dance floor like a theatre balcony, is a lass whose fingers are gripping at the partition like a survivor on the outside of a lifeboat. She's trying to attract my brother Caleb's attention from the mosh pit, and failing.

I climb into the booth from the stage side to hand Caleb the CD. The DJ booth, wherever the party, has always been and is the place me and Cal get along best. I guess because there ain't room to fight here. All the BS beyond stays beyond, along with everyone else vying in the mosh pit below.

Clocking me as I push through the curtain, Cal lassoes my neck with his arm, pulling me in to kiss me between song changes, smearing his red lipstick across my forehead in the process like some voodoo priest blessing a sacrifice. His pupils are huge as saucers, framed by a panel of thick electric blue eyeliner. A white halo circles his left nostril and is glowing in the UV light. Coke, I figure, glancing up at him and feeling his heart racing against my chest as he manoeuvres about me, pressing lit up buttons and flicking switches.

Some 80's synth pop tune gives way to something German and industrial sounding and Caleb starts *sieg heil* saluting the mosh pit and goose-stepping on the spot. A few randoms expose themselves by returning Cal's salute, which regulars know is the cue for the pit to dive them. After all, nobody who's just performed a Nazi salute is about to bitch about getting jumped. And anyone who returns a Nazi salute of course deserves to get jumped.

Slipping back onto the dance floor, while Cal is distracted, the girl clinging to the partition eyes my

torn jeans and braless chest, on full view through one
of Miss's XL mesh shirts as I pass her. I meet her gaze,
and hold it till it's clear she ain't going to approach me
though. And knowing that when Caleb is done with
her, she'll be the one crying to her friends, wishing she'd
never used that fake ID and gone to that nasty club, and
left with that bastard DJ, I don't approach her either.

A whole bunch of empty shot glasses are strewn
across The Hammer Bar where Miss is still sat, where
I knew Miss would still be sat. Trix, on a stool beside
Miss, asks Netty for a fork.

– Ta muchly, Netty, love.

Trix bows to her. He then proceeds to push the
entire handle up his nose until only the tines stick out
and runs towards the door to the entrance to The Sink,
screaming. Some nameless bouncer instantly chases him,
like afraid Trix has actually suffered some fork-related
accident or something. I drop a bomb of whatever the
powder is that Cal slipped me while Miss is preoccupied
watching Trix and the bouncer, like an acid trip Charlie
Chaplin chase scene.

The ladies' toilets are always jammed full of
underagers and anyone who still get a kick out of
sneaking joints in the toilets. I'm watching some of
them when Miss's head appears round the door.

– Layla, have you taken owt?

Miss always thinks I must've done coke when she
hears someone wants to kick my head in. So, I always

figure someone must want to kick my head in when Miss asks if I've been doing owt. 'Owt' means nowt but coke when Miss says it.

Polly and Sam are re-applying dayglo lipstick at the sinks. Blotting her lips on the back of her hand so it leaves a smear like that stuff cops us to expose blood or cum at a crime scene, Sam says she's also heard some lass is looking for me.

Some real mean looking Old Pier Crew type girl, Sam qualifies, rubbing lipstick from her hand onto her laddered stripy tights.

I take Polly's grass and roll a joint while the three witches try working out who could want to knock seven bells out of me. Teasing, Polly asks me whose fella I've been shagging. Sam jumps on the idea I've been scamming on some other lass's guy.

– Sam, she don't even know this girl, do you, Lay?

Miss levels with me, rolling her eyes exactly like her mum, Dave, does, only without a hint of sarcasm in her voice, or face.

– That don't mean she don't know the lass's fella though, right Lay Baby?

Sam elbows me in the side. She's trying to wink. She's trying to be Polly, but just looks like she's tweaking out off a bad batch of speed.

– She ain't been shagging other lass's blokes, Sam. I know 'cause Trix were the last person you had, right, Lay?

Miss looks at me. I actually think Jasper, Miss's twin brother, were the last guy I fucked, but I guess Miss don't know that, or don't want to; she wants me to tell her she's right. So, I do. If people want to treat sex like trump cards, collect each experience, rate each fuck, organise it, that's their deal. Even if it is my fucks they're collecting. It's not like I've any use for them.

Miss sighs, eyeing me like there's only one thing she don't know about me, and this is it. Whatever this is.

– You must have done sommet.

Polly smirks, I guess assuming she's the last 'thing I've done', but I don't know if girls even count.

Outside the toilets, Aberdeenie Jeanie is leant in the corridor, her face lit up by the fluorescent light of her mobile. When she sees me, she drops her mobile into her bag and pounces, pushing a bottle of amyl nitrate up my nose until my head hits against the corridor wall. I try and steady myself, but before I can she has her tongue in my mouth and a bare leg between mine. I grasp it with my thighs, if only to avoid hitting the carpet.

– Did you feel it, Lay Baby, could you feel it?

She flashes her titanium-studded tongue at me and winks. I hadn't noticed the addition of a third bar when it'd been in my mouth; I was too preoccupied trying to feel anything that weren't the poppers rushing through me. AJ offers Miss some. Miss declines. Miss is weird about anything that ain't alcohol or weed; she's only been hanging at the Steps a few months, since we met each other at Wayside. She watches as Aberdeenie Jeanie recaps the little bottle and goes chasing some girl who has iridescent tubing in her hair and is wearing a pink gas mask.

— Is AJ actually gay or what, what is her deal?

I don't answer. I don't have an answer for what Aberdeenie Jeanie is.

Still trying to shake off the amyl nitrate, I sneak a pint off a nearby table while the couple it belongs to are busy snogging, in an attempt to try and flush the stuff out of my head before a migraine kicks in. I figure drugged-up and dazy is how old people feel all the time, wandering about half-blind and confused, having to grab onto stuff and hoping whatever that might be is more solid than themselves. If amyl nitrate didn't have other uses, I'd wonder why the fuck anyone bothered with the stuff.

— She's always kissing you, touching you...

— You kiss me an' touch me. Everyone does.

— I've never whipped you with a bamboo cane or branded my initials into your arse cheek, though...

I swig the last of the pint, placing it on the bar and raising my hand to call the bar man over.

— You've never been to one of Scraggy Mag's parties.

— I just figured, maybe you and AJ actually like each other...

Some new barman at the bar in The Sink refills our glasses and I have to convince him to chalk the drinks up as Cal's expenses.

– Burn your initials in my arse if it'll make you happy.

I slide a glass over to her, without looking at what I'm sending her way; AJ is in the mosh pit, swinging her handbag full of amyl nitrite, and most likely cocaine. I cut through the pit, making a point of roping Miss in between us when AJ dumps her glass and bag onto the stage. Spitting what is left of her cigarette over our heads, she begins really dancing, screwing herself into me and Miss like she is trying to fuse us all together. But before the song is a minute in, some force spins me off like a bottle cap and stops me with a hand slamming down on my shoulder so I'm left staring into the face of 'the girl who wants to kick my head in'. I don't even recognise her but then clock the girl who'd been groping at the DJ booth trying to get Cal's attention, standing about three feet behind her, and looking more like someone in a queue at confessional than someone on the peripherals of a mosh pit.

Miss detaches herself from AJ, who latches onto some other lass totally oblivious to anything beyond an unexplored pair of tits. We are all being pushed and shoved as the dance floor fills up.

– Oi, you, what you been saying about my mate? 'Cause I dare you to say it to *my* face, you lanky bitch.

– Have some confidence. Your face ain't that bad. Like, I've seen worse –

I'm shouting back as the girl's mate carries on screaming at me, getting pushed into her by some bloke diving off the stage into the pit. I stay pressed against her, speaking into her ear so only she can hear.

– You and your mate? You're a fucking circus act. You dress up, paint your faces, put on shows like this... Still, irony is a small mercy for you; you don't even know what you are, do you?

I don't even know what I'm shouting, it's just the first load of bullshit my mind offers up, and I'm laughing as I say it. The girl is now uneasily trying to peel herself off me. She glances Miss's way, bewildered, as if Miss is supposed to be my carer or hired translator or something. Still pressed against the girl, I shout right into her mush:

– Your face is the least of your problems.

Miss tries to wade in to stop the girl's punch. The girl from the DJ booth is just standing there being shoved by the mosh pit. Her friend's fist, knocked by some mosher, glances off my forehead. Miss is trying to hold the girl back, but failing, and waves a slap at her. I catch the girl's nose just as she turns to avoid Miss's palm; Miss jumps back, letting go, as the girl's nose plain bursts. The girl stumbles. I catch a handful of her hair, pulling her head forward, face first through the chaos of hips and thighs, jarring my knee into the mess of blood that is her make-up. I can't even feel if it's her eye or nose or chin I'm pounding with my knee. Whatever it is, I feel it break.

Like sharks drawn to blood, other people begin jumping in. A bouncer tries to restrain the bleeding girl, or rescue her, it's hard to tell. She rears up from the floor and grabs for the fishnet vest I'm wearing, ripping it until the strap clean breaks. My new nipple bar must've caught on the fishnet, 'cause something that looks like black drips of ink under UV lights is spreading over my chest and stomach beneath the mesh.

Limbs are coming from everywhere, like the dance floor is one giant squid. I reach for the girl from the partition who's doing all she can to stay upright as the mosh pit gets more wild. She makes a pointless attempt to get back to her friend, who has two bouncers trying to carry her away, forcing their way against the tide of the crowd. Another bouncer tries to pull me out, too, but all fifteen stone of Miss, who's actually audibly sobbing now, lands on his back, clinging round his throat so he lets go of me and starts gagging. People are still joining in. I glimpse Caleb scanning the scene from his booth, no doubt looking for me to see if he can blame me for this later. I pull the girl from the DJ booth away and into the Sink Bar, out of view of the mosh pit before Caleb clocks me.

All the while, this girl's saying she's got to go find her mate.

— I've got to get to my mate. I've got to —

— Like, I've got to tear your face off for setting your mate on me?

I hand the lass, who tells me she's called Sasha between sobs, a double vodka and coke and cross my legs to veil the blood and snot crisping up on my jeans. Only then, I notice my whole right breast is covered only by blood. I grab a handful of bar napkins to wipe what blood ain't already been soaked up by the waist band of my jeans and pull what is left of the fishnet vest up. The nipple bar is still there, though it looks a bit lopsided. I shout over the bar for a plaster from the first aid box, rolling up the vest to tape the piercing straight again.

Sasha has stopped crying, mostly, and is eyeing me now. She looks like a half-drunk child in a hooker's workwear. Looks like she's realising for the first time the reality of where she is. Looks like. In reality, she is probably older than me. Legal, even. Maybe.

I tell her not to fret, and promise to introduce her to Caleb. Then, I order another round and wait. Sasha mentions that she drinks alcopops. I order tequilas and fix her a bomb out of the crumbs of powder left in the wrap.

The bouncer who'd been reaching for me in the pit eventually finds us, towing Miss along by the arm. Netty runs out from behind the Sink bar. She pulls the bouncer's arm off Miss and shushes him, asking Miss and me what the fuck happened.

When Miss has finished explaining, her eyes still filling every few seconds, Netty brings over a tray

of whiskeys by way of an apology and tells the new
bouncer to fuck the eff off and stop bothering regulars
if he values being gainfully employed. Sasha is too
drunk already on the free booze to notice the looks Miss
is tossing me. I'd envy her, if I didn't remember being
her.

The Hammer and Sink gradually clears for the
night; then, Miss, Caleb, Sasha and I share a few beers
and some smoke with Crusty Don, the owner of The
Hammer and Sink, before catching a staff taxi into
Lancaster.

Caleb tells the driver to take us to Meeting House
Lane, Clit and Scraggy Mag's place, where I get on with
introducing Sasha to new glamorous narcotics and new,
albeit not so glamorous, people. When she's too wasted
to trail me anymore, I introduce her to Caleb seen as
Cal's girlfriend La ain't there like Cal were hoping, and
leave them to it.

I'm in search of a pick-me-up-bump when Miss sees
I'm alone and drags me outside, slamming the door
behind us.

– Why do you do it, Lay?

Sitting on the curb, I roll a cigarette. I figure we'll
be out here a while and look up for an indicator of the
time, but all the heavens tell me is that the moonless
night is fast becoming a sunless morning.

– Why did you have to say that to that girl? Why did
you have to start a fight?

— I didn't *have to* say or do owt. Speaking of doing 'owt' though, you got owt on you?

I know Miss won't be holding anything, but I also know one day she will be, so I ask anyhow. After all, someday, one day *will* be today.

— Exactly. So why do it?

Miss asks again.

I pass Miss a cigarette rather than reply. She stares at it, like there's any chance she won't take it, before she sits down beside me and sparks up, staring into the dried blood on my jeans and eyeing her ruined sweater.

— Will you talk to me, please? I really want to know, Lay: why the fuck —

— Do you ever feel like you're waiting for a train at a bus stop?

Miss gapes at me like I've just said something unreasonable.

— I feel like you're avoiding the fucking subject. That's how I feel. Why'd you invite that Sasha girl here?

— I invited you here, introduced you to these people —

— Yeah, and you're my best mate, but —

— But what? What makes all this OK for you, for me, but not for her? Who made you judge?

— Who made *you* judge?

— Who's judging? She wanted to meet Caleb. I could make that happen.

I shrug.

— She wants to fuck Caleb, and she prolly is doing

right now. He has a girlfriend, Lay.

– And he has a choice. So did Sasha.

I run my hands over the stain on my trousers and Miss looks away like it's her blood.

– You're an arse when you do coke, you know that? You didn't have to lie to Netty, or that bouncer or –

– And you had a choice too. And now, here we are.

I put my arm around her shoulders, pulling Miss into me. She hesitates before resting her head against my cheek.

– And I love you, Lay, you know that, but –

– But what?

Behind me, the noise has lulled to a murmur and about me the night has burned out.

Cross-legged on the curb, Miss and I linger in the brief expanse of not-ness. I guess this is what Larkin meant by 'soundless dark'. We sit for a spun out moment in silence before Miss sighs, wiping her eyes dry and getting up.

– Nowt, mate.

I listen for the door latch to click shut before slipping my knife out of my back pocket. Flipping it open, I run a finger along my thigh ahead of the blade. As if summoned, the sun wells at last. It swells pinkish in the thick air before slicing through the clouds. Light runs along the blade.

★

Peter-the-Social-Worker and my Mum are already at Wayside when I arrive. Miss gets ushered into the other room, leaving me with bits of the weekend still stuck in my hair, spilt on my vest and scabbed beneath my jeans.

Lynn Green, leader of the Lancashire Education Medical Service, is sat at the head of a rectangular table. I sit down, where I'm told to. McQuaide sits at the opposite end of the table, beside Lynn Green, separated from me by three chairs, four decades and what might as well be an ice age.

Brenda shuffles in, placing mugs of instant coffee between each person. When she reaches me, the tray is empty. She squeezes my shoulder as she passes. Meanwhile, I'm watching my Mum pulling her scarf off and accidently dipping it into her mug. Her handbag strap slips, dragging her coat away from her shoulder. The coat is the same shabby, ankle-length black one she always wears. I've no memory of her going shopping for it. Like most of her wardrobe, it's just always been her coat, and her only coat. She looks shattered: I wonder if she were up late last night, watching TV with Terry, her boyfriend, or on the phone to her mate, Mon; or waiting for Caleb to get in; or if it's just from having spent the last however many years of her life, and all of mine, as a supermarket cleaner mopping up other people's messes.

I think back on the copper colour her hair used to be and how it used to appear all different colours in the sunlight, like the freshly dropped conkers she used to take me and Cal and Dom to forage for in Willibob Park when we all still lived together. It still amazes me, the rare times I see her now outside of her house, how grey her hair has turned, how dull, how old. I swallow back on the sick and whatever other nasty shit is rising in my throat.

— I thought, as this is her first review, it might be an idea to give a general overview of Layla's attainment so far. Mrs McQuaide?

This is the first time I've seen Lynn Green and her cool grey skirt suit since she exposed the YMCA reality of my Mum's place on a 'home visit' to assess my suitability to attend Wayside. That was four months ago, and were actually her second home visit to my mum's place. I was still officially 'missing' when she first visited to discuss the possibility of me securing a place at Wayside. My mum hadn't thrown me out, though, not that time. She hadn't had to. That were just after Jim had died.

I think back on meeting Bull at Lancaster train station, ready to take the train down to Salford. Bull had said it were OK if I wanted to go to the funeral. He hadn't told me until I met him on the station platform who'd be there though.

As Bull had begun to list names I didn't know or recognise and explain that his and Jim's stepdad had paid for the funeral, it hit me. Faced with the reality, I couldn't board that train.

I remember Bull saying he had to go. The train were pulling in alongside us, though maybe he meant he had to go because his mum was waiting for him at the other end.

All I know is that the thought of watching that box get lowered and knowing what was inside were enough of a mind fuck. The idea of watching Jim and Bull's stepdad toss dirt on Jim's name while their mother cried beside him, fuck that.

The light from the window makes my eyes burn until I swear I can actually feel my pupils constricting. I yawn. McQuaide clocks me and tuts.

Must be nice, to get through fifty years thinking yawning is something people do – people only do – when or because they're so bored they can't be arsed to breathe no more. Never having to yawn – or have your body scream out for air – for any other reason.

I don't remember Bull getting on that train. I don't remember 'running away'. I just remember waking up at the back of that supermarket at the arse end of Morecambe Promenade and everything being dark, like when you wake from a nod and know a grain more on the foil or in the spoon and you'd have gone over; there'd have been no coming back.

– Of course. I've samples of Layla's grades here. Just to clarify, Layla came here to study English Language, Double Science and Maths, but Layla showed an interest

in Art, and an aptitude for it. Consequently, I told Layla
she could study Art as long as her behaviour and grades
in her core subjects didn't suffer. I hoped this would
serve as an incentive, but unfortunately Layla's erratic —

— If you could just give us an idea of Layla's academic
progress please.

Lynn Green sets her watch down on the table
before her, and I can almost feel McQuaide sag slightly,
hoiking up her smile like it is actually heavy, before she
continues speaking.

— Layla should be aiming for all As in her core
subjects, but has been removed from sitting her Art
GCSE due to unacceptable behaviour. She is currently
expecting to scrape Cs in all four subjects, though these
averages are based on very erratic grades.

Lynn Green then asks McQuaide about my
behaviour, using some word I don't catch.

— Layla's mood fluctuates dramatically, and her
attitude and language remain unacceptable. Layla was
caught smoking after entering class late on Friday, was
late today, and is still dressing very inappropriately, as
you can all see.

I can feel everyone's eyes briefly fix on me and I
turn to face them. I bare my teeth and watch as their
eyes scatter like cats from a growling dog. All except
McQuaide, whose eyes never leave the papers in front of
her. And my mum, whose eyes never leave McQuaide.

— On top of that, Layla has a lot of unexplained

absences, which was part of her problem in her previous school. This all indicates that Layla hasn't been taking her medication –

– Um, if I could just say a few words?

I'd almost forgotten Peter-the-Social-Worker existed, or were here. Seems everyone did, as I feel the room prickle.

– Layla was offered certain. Um. Medications, but chose not to. Um. Accept them. We do need to, well, respect Layla's decision.

In another life, I'd be grateful for Peter's attempts to speak up for me. As is, I keep my eyes out the window, trying to ignore the sound of McQuaide chewing on the little, earnest attempt Peter makes to level the playing field.

– Peter is it? Or would you prefer Mr. Granville? OK, well, Peter, I'm in charge of Layla, and all the children here, and the problem with that is that Layla needs to accept some form of treatment, if she's to remain at Wayside. This is a school for youths *who want to change*. The children here need to *want to recover*.

I feel myself frown, for the second time. Recover from what?

– We are all here for Layla, but there are only a few months until the GCSE examinations –

– If you're trying to say Layla needs to be medicated then I'll get her in with the doctor soon as I leave here.

My mum's sudden interruption shatters the veneer of

civilisation in an instant. I finally blink, my eyes burning like crazy, so I can't see what face my mum's pulling for the afterglow.

McQuaide takes a deep breath and turns to my mum.

— What I am trying to explain, *Ms* Dinsdale, as someone who has spent a *significant* amount of time with Layla over the last few months, is that *Layla needs to change*. Layla has continued to be disruptive and difficult. You, yourself have involved Social Services on several —

— My daughter will go to the doctor tomorrow. I'll make bloody sure of it; I'll make the appointment myself. That everything? 'Cause this is my only day off and I'll be beggared if am wasting any more of it here.

Outside, my mum shakes hands with Lynn Green, McQuaide and Peter-The-Social-Worker. I walk with her down the drive, sparking a cigarette as we walk.

— Oh, put it out. You don't have to take the fucking meds, do you. I'll make an appointment tomorrow morning. Just turn up.

My mum gives me the once-over before turning away.

— And take a shower, Layla; you're a state. And, for fuck's sake, wear a bra; y'not a child anymore.

*

The pointless sound of How Are You repeats and reverbs in my head till I realise the doctor is now telling

me he knows how hard life can seem when you're
fifteen. I sit there mute, zoning back in occasionally,
just to hear the doctor say things like, it is normal to feel
insecure about my appearance, or to get nervous about
school.

— You're taking your GCSEs this year, am I right?

I could just walk out, but somehow I don't; I just sit
there, counting off the time until the doctor brings up
hormones, or drugs.

— Layla...

He inhales the sigh rather than letting it go, and
forces a smile because that's his job.

— If you are willing to accept it, help is available.

What would help me right now is if this guy tells
me 'help' ain't just semantic bullshit for meds and meds
ain't just semantic bullshit for drugs what don't get you
high. I'm bored of the meds speech. Bored of drugs that
only compound the reality. And, I'm bored of being
told everybody understands: apparently, everybody
understands me, except me. And I'm bored of doctors
who give the same speech all the time like it's printed
word for word in some medical text and you can't
graduate medical school until you can recite it like the
Miranda Rights.

I get language, sure, but when you're pointing at
people and regurgitating words like doctors and social
workers and adults do, like *that's* the reason people are
a certain way, and not that people are a certain way

because people and the mind ain't simple and can't be reduced down to the consequence of some mutated gene or that time their parents forget to pick them up from school, well, being 'crazy' starts seemingly like the only logical fucking option. Might as well diagnose the whole of humanity with a terminal case of tough fucking luck.

But there's no point saying any of that, not when you're fifteen. Not when you're already at special school. Not when you're diagnosed crazy already. Not when you're anybody who's ever sat this side of that big fat desk.

– Hormones can play a part at your age, of course, but it's all about recognising teenage mood swings and more serious episodes of feeling, which become even more difficult and far more serious if a person is using illegal drugs...

The doctor goes on. I stare determinedly into the black expanse of desk between this me and this middle-aged man in a suit. If I could make you understand, I wouldn't have to. If crazy people could just explain it, they wouldn't be crazy. And if the people who off themselves without leaving suicide notes – the vast majority – could write one, I don't figure they'd need to actually *do it*, you know?

– But that's us, Layla, at least for today. Think about what we've discussed. OK?

The doctor stands up, glancing to a black and white

clock suspended on the wall above us, its red hands like those on a pressure gauge.

★

The door is unlocked when I get there. When the door is locked I've often to hammer to get let in – if I do get let in. But when the door is unlocked, I've always to force myself to enter.

My mum locks everyone out, but only ever locks herself and Cal in. I figure her boyfriend, Terry, must be in there. Following the sound of voices to the lounge, I halt in the doorway as I clock my mum in her armchair. The chair, her chair, faces the TV. My mum is sat with her legs folded under her. She's twisted herself to face the sofa, and she's nursing a baby.

For a moment, I think I've walked into the wrong house, trespassed on some family dynamic – I don't even recognise my mum, initially. Her face, her expression, it's like looking at someone who's just had Valium slipped into their tea, her arms crossed around something besides herself, locked around something beyond her own chest, and so gently. It's like tripping into some TV family drama – then I recognise Louise, the mother-of-four from number five, sitting on the sofa – this must be her fifth. It's weird, how a baby can shatter the image of a person you think you had the measure of as much as a haircut or a new wardrobe. It makes me think back on the story of my own babyhood. It ain't really a story about me at all though. It's a story about my mum.

Before the story begins, you have to know my family – my mum and dad, my two brothers (Caleb, who were my mum's kid and Dominic, who were my dad's kid by some other woman) and my grandma all lived in a one-bedder on the Aldgate Estate, 212 territory, when I were born. The flat had a small lounge, no carpets, and parents had to chain up their kids' prams to the stairwell on the ground floor on account of the lifts never working. I didn't have a crib. They kept me in a fruit crate that my mum or whoever would push with a foot from room to room. They were still together then, my mum and dad, but they didn't share the bedroom. On account of the cancer, my grandma had the bedroom, and the only bed.

When I were little my mum used to shout the story at my dad during rows. Since my dad upped and left, she's taken to shouting it at me: *you any idea what that's like, eh, for me? Have you? Well, have you? Sitting up every fecking night praying the babby don't wake and y'own mother does!*

For years I thought my mum spent every night praying to God for a refund on me, like she could somehow sacrifice me in exchange for her own mum. Of course, I didn't understand. How could I? Until now, the only thing I've ever seen my mum nurse is a hangover.

I stand in the doorway to the living room and try not to stare.

When I don't say nothing, Louise, who, along with all her brood of now-five kids, lives off of benefits, and who my mum calls a sponge when the windows are shut, smiles and asks me if I'd like to hold the kid. Glancing at my mum, who's still holding the little baby, it feels like being dared to try take a puppy from a bitch.

★

I try make the most of not sharing a bed, but the bedroom that's supposed to be mine is directly above the kitchen, has no carpet and the floorboards ain't sealed. I can hear everything that happens in this house, like it or not. And the noise at my mum's place ain't noise like sirens or death metal or people fucking; the noise in this house refuses to be ignored, or reasoned with. It's noise without rhythm. It's the sound of my mum existing in the only way she knows how.

— Don't dry your hands on that. You blind? That's a *tea towel*, Caleb; use the cloth.

The cloth is a rag, but you ain't to call it that. Unlike with the towels, Mum only washes the cloths three or four times: in bleach. Then, they begin to get thin and get used for the floors. Tea towels are for drying clean crockery, not hands. Hands, no matter how you scrub them, are dirty. You dry them on the strip of old bed sheet or t-shirt turned cloth that hangs from the nail above the kitchen bin.

– You've opened that fridge four times. *Four fucking times*, Caleb. What's wrong with you?

It's always a good idea to know what is in the fridge before you look and to decide, before you look, whether you want it. My mum calls that common sense. Opening the fridge door means knowing what you want and needing to get it. After all, the fridge is not a cupboard; the fridge uses electricity.

– What are you getting now? What's that? Show me. Oh, No. No, Caleb.

There's no need to open a cupboard when there is food in the fridge. Always use fresh food before opening canned, freeze dried or packet foods.

–There's half a tin of mushy peas and half a tin of beans in the fridge need eating. I'm not having them go to waste.

I anticipate the thud of tins hitting Formica tabletop before it actually happens.

–There's some bread left. I froze it. You hearkened, Cal? Here, come see.

The larder door squeaks open. Mum keeps the freezer in the larder because there is seldom any need to open either. Freezer food is exactly that: a frozen asset.

I sit up, stretch, and reach for a smoke, timing using the lighter alongside the kettle boiling so my mum don't hear the flint scraping. Leaning on the sill, I aim the smoke and ash out the window.

At number sixteen, Chunk, Denise's youngest, is sat out in a plastic chair on the driveway, smoking and drinking beer, despite it being about 5 degrees Celsius out and not even ten yet.

Chunk's real high up in the army now, or so says his mum, Denise. He's back from Iraq. The fruits of his labour, a two-tone Scooby modded to the nines is parked on the drive beside him like some gargantuan pitbull that's rolled in oil and clad in an iron muzzle. It's one of two cars on the entire street, not including Phil's fish van at number twelve. The other car is a cop car. Someone probably complained about Scotty, Joan's boy, from number eleven; Scotty is the estate's one-man crime wave. That, or they've come for Josephine again, the madwoman at number nineteen, but the flowerbeds at number nineteen are looking pretty pristine, so I figure the madwoman is taking her meds, least for now.

– Layla?

Sometimes she shouts three or four times and then gives up, so I let my mum call till she's qualifying my name with swear words and I've smoked the rollup to the bone, before I dock it on the outer sill and reply.

– I've got work. There's some beans and bread on the table.

My throat is dry with morning, and smoke, so my voice cracks when I try shout thanks and either she don't hear me, or plain ignores me. Same difference, I guess.

— Caleb needs breakfast. Wash up when you're done and bring any cups down what you've got up there.

She pauses, no doubt counting the cups in the cupboard and on the drainer so she knows the answer before she then asks anyway:

— How many cups are up there?

Because she knows the answer, I know this ain't a question she'll let go unanswered. Still, I hold off for as long as it takes her to accuse me of ignoring her, before asking instead of answering.

— Why's it matter?

— 'Cause they're my fucking property is why and if you're telling me you ain't got them up there, well someone's waltzed in here and robbed the rest then 'cause there's a red mug with writing on it and two of them white ones what've got sunflowers on missing too. That's at least three.

That ain't *at least* three; it *is* three.

— I expect them to be in the cupboard when I get in, and don't leave the washing up piled on the draining board. There's no reason you can't dry up. And don't use the cloth to dry the crockery. Oh, and, Layla? There's washing out ont line, fetch it in if it starts spitting, and if Terry knocks —

Reaching into my bag for my blade, I hold it against my leg till the noise stops. All the while, I stare at the bedside table where there are two coffee cups with flowers painted around the handles, both holding dregs of rum and milk. Between them is a red mug with a needle like a spoon poking from it. My dad's mug. The only mug in the house not daubed with flowers or images of cats. Emblazoned on it are the words, *Same Shit, Different Day.*

Caleb is sat at the kitchen table, lacing his boots, when I finally surface. I put the frozen bread under the grill and pour the beans into a milk pan, giving them a stir. When he's laced his bovver boots up, slamming his heels into them so hard the kitchen tiles are showered in dried mud, Caleb leans over the hob, looking into the pan.

– Forks scratch the Teflon from the bottom of the pans.

When I hear Caleb parrot our mum it makes me want to remove my own fucking skin like Teflon.

– She also says not to wear shoes in the house.

– Floors can be cleaned. You gonna buy her new pans?

– You gonna clean the floor?

I pour coffee and put a plate to warm on the hob above the grill.

– You getting a taxi to band practice? I could use a lift into town.

– I'll be gone before you've washed up. There's last night's stuff too.

I look over at the sink. It's so full plates have spilled over onto the counter top.

— Mum says you've got to do them. Might as well do the floor while you're at it.

I ladle the beans onto the dry toast and push it in front of Cal.

— Anything else Mum says?

— Yeah. She left your giro on the side. She said you can buy some milk out of it seen as you drank all ours.

My mum leaves post-it notes to shout at me when she ain't around to do it herself. One is stuck on top of the envelope that mum puts the forty quid child benefit the Government pay her for saying I live here, and which she always leaves for me, seen as I'm never much here to cost her owt, least financially. I peel it off.

Get milk.

P.S. You ever smoke a cigarette in my house again, I'll take the cost of having the ceilings re-painted out your giro and change the locks. I will also tell Social Services you're vandalising the house. And they can have you. This is my home, not another doss house for you to come shit up when you've run out of money or welcomes elsewhere.

P.P.S Don't forget the milk.

I screw up the post-it note and toss it in to the bin. If there were a world record for the most amount of words fit onto a single post-it note, my mum would win it.

— She works at a supermarket, can't she get milk?

Cal is scraping beans from the now-soggy toast beneath.

– She said you have to. Didn't you even fucking butter this?

He stacks the uneaten plate of beans and toast on top of the pile of washing up. I watch the beans start to waterfall from the plate onto the counter while Cal ducks out of the kitchen to ring for a cab.

– Lay, where's the bacca?

Caleb and my mum always wait until they're at the opposite end of the house to me till they talk to me. So, even when I'm not being shouted at, that's how it sounds.

– What tobacco?

I ask quietly, just to prove there ain't no need to shout.

– Lay, I'm being nice and asking. You don't got to be such a cunt, you know?

Cal shouts back at me from halfway up the stairs.

From the sink, I hear the floorboards in the room that is meant to be mine creak beneath the pressure of Cal's boots and listen to him pour the contents of my bag out onto the bed, imagining my mum's reaction when she follows the trail of dirt from Cal's boots to the bits of litter and tobacco and gear and speed and grass residue, like confetti blown onto the bedspread.

Out on the street, a car horn sounds and Cal rushes back down the stairs with a cigarette in his mouth, slamming the door behind him. From where I'm stood at the sink, I watch him leggit up the path and jump in a taxi. I still haven't removed my hand from beneath the tap, which is running so hot now that by the time I feel it, my fist is swelling and throbbing like a heart.

★

I've a whole house to myself.

After meandering about, thinking of all the things I could do, I roll a cigarette and sit on the front step waiting for the school taxi to roll up, before realising they probably don't even know I'm here. I could still make it to Wayside, at a push, but somehow I just roll another smoke and get to watching the worms die.

Whenever it rains, a tide of worms appears in the concrete porch. Then the rain eases off and the water evaporates and they're left stranded and squirming about, their bodies turning blue like starved veins.

I used to pick the worms up and throw them back onto the front lawn, but when you try picking them up they writhe even more, until they get so thin between your fingers half of them clean snap in two. I know they don't know no better, that it ain't their fault; they probably figure my fingers are the beak of some bird about to devour them or regurgitate them into the mouths of their babies, but they just seem so desperate to escape any attempts to save them. At some point I can't recall, I just started figuring, fuck it.

I'm so busy watching the worms nut the concrete, I ain't noticed the rusty Mercedes pulling onto the drive. In fact, I don't notice anything until Terry, my mum's boyfriend, is kicking the toe of my sneakers and my eyes are level with the crotch of his two-ninety-nine jogger pants he buys in bulk off the Sunday market. Instead of 'Rockport' like the sports jerseys that local wannabes wear, Terry's jumper reads 'Rock*sport*', and the 'Addidas' label on his pants is a peeling iron-on transfer.

When I don't look up, Terry kicks my sneaker again, knocking my leg from beneath me. I jerk my head from my knees just before I fall face first onto the floor and join the worms.

– Your mother in there?

Terry kicks the sole of my sneaker a third time.

– Work.

Terry pushes past me, into the house. A moment later I hear his rip-off designer boots back behind me and hear him light a cigarette before he pushes past me back into the porch.

– When's she back?

I shrug.

– You don't know when she finishes work?

– You didn't even know she were at work.

Terry glances into the house again, then up at the bedroom windows, like maybe I have her bound and gagged up there. More likely he suspects some other guy has her bound and gagged up there.

– D'you hear me?

Terry kicks my shoes a fourth time.

– I said, tell her I called.

– I won't be here.

– So, write a fucking note then, genius.

I shuffle my feet aside so Terry can't kick them again, before asking him for some change to buy milk.

– Do I look like a fucking milkman?

– If you looked like a milkman I'd have asked you for milk.

Terry eyes me for a moment, before digging into his pocket.

– What's wrong with the fucking milk from where she works?

I take a final hot drag of my cigarette instead of speaking. Terry pauses, like waiting for me to give him an excuse to not give me money and to give me something else instead, before he pulls his wallet from his back pocket.

– You better not be trying to fucking fleece me, girl. 'Cause I'll tell you what, I'll know.

Except evidently, Terry don't know, at least not yet, because he passes over a handful of change without even counting it.

I spend Terry's change on the payphone through the ginnel and call up Miss and her mum, Dave, to pick me up. Mum has a landline, but it's restricted to incoming calls since Caleb started ringing sex lines when he were pissed, and leaving mum to pay the bill.

★

There are too many people to fit round the dining table and too much shit on the dining table to fit food on it anyway, so Dave fires up the half-keg BBQ in the garden and throws on whatever she can find.

Miss's twin, Jasper, comes back in time to eat, trailing six hooded kids that I vaguely recognise as Wyatt's and Gallows Hill 353 kids. They sit on the grass at the far back of the garden letting Jasper bring food to them and are gone as soon as they've eaten, taking Jasper with them.

The little girl from next door is over too while the plod get her dad out the house. When the police leave, her mum, Afiya, joins her kid, Dave, Pru, Miss and myself on the garden benches. The girl, Sanaa, climbs onto my knee to eat her butty. Her jet-black hair is braided into tight cornrows in a pattern like some language I cannot read, or map leading some place so far from here even my imagination runs on empty before I get close.

Pru empties a bag of kindling into the old fire drum beneath the white tarpaulin pinned up between the shed and fence to keep the patio dry, and we eat grain baps Jasper stole off the bakery delivery van during his

morning paper round and vegetable patties made from
a brown paper bag of turning veg Afiya's husband,
who has a fruit and veg stall in town, had left on the
doorstep. Before he came home drunk and got taken
away.

Moths have begun nosediving into the candles on
the bench. They are fossilised in the melted wax by the
time Miss and I take the dishes in and Afiya has bundled
her kid up in one of Dave's blankets like leftovers and
gone back home.

Out in the yard, Dave and Pru wrap themselves in
the remaining blankets. I smoke a joint and watch them
through the patio doors like a silent movie. Dave shrugs,
rubbing her eyes with a blanket corner. She counts
something off on her fingers, shaking her head.

Pru digs in her pocket, drawing out her mobile and
flipping it open, bluish light collecting in her wrinkles
and illuminating her frown. She says something and
Dave leans her face into her palms, nodding with her
face covered. Pru types something into the phone
keypad.

I figure Pru is texting a dealer but then Dave's
shoulders start shaking. She looks like she is laughing,
but when she looks up at Pru I see black lines of mascara
running over her face. She says something suddenly,
loud enough for me to hear her voice, but not to catch
her words.

When the sounds of pots clattering onto the draining

board stops abruptly, I continue the silence without taking my eyes off the patio. Miss is watching too from the window above the kitchen sink.

– Money shit.

I tell Miss, in reply to the question she ain't asked.

– It could be Jasper. He got suspended from school for –

– Pru's using a calculator.

I note from the corner of my eye the subtle tensing of Miss's shoulders, like the thoughts running through her mind are suddenly barbed.

★

This evening, after dinner at Dave and Pru's, Pru pushes a tobacco tin towards me, tapping the lid with her middle finger to tell me to hurry up.

Pru smokes white widow with cherry tobacco in liquorice papers, so her joints taste faintly like the penny sweets my brothers and me used to get from Old Bob's shop on Aldgate: him smoking cigars in the shop all day surrounded by open tubs of foam shrimps, jelly eggs and penny rings.

I light up the joint before passing it over to Pru who passes it on to Dave without taking a toke and flaps her hand at the tin again. Silently, Miss carries in a punch bowl full of Pru's gin-soaked strawberries. There's always dessert at Dave and Pru's, even if it's just canned rice pudding warmed outside on the burner, wrapped in a tea towel and eaten straight from the can.

I continue rolling joints even after Pru stops doing sign language at me, just for sommet to do while I wait for the bowl to empty so I can take the sweetened gin always left in the dish. But when the bowl is empty, Miss tosses her spoon into it so hard it breaks the silence and when I try to take the bowl Pru slaps my hand away, tutting, like I'm some bug. Miss and Dave continue staring each other out across the table.

– Miss...

– Mum.

– *Melissa* –

– *Mother* –

Pru and I follow Miss and Dave's blows like posh folk at a Wimbledon final.

– I said don't!

Dave shouts, slamming her hand down onto the table. Miss blinks at the sound, before turning her eyes to Pru, who stiffens, making the beanbag she's slowly sinking into rustle beneath her.

– Don't be looking to me. You heard your mother.

At that, Miss kicks back her chair and straight walks out the room. And Dave bursts into tears.

Pru leans forward, hugging her over the table and miming over Dave's shoulder for me to bring more booze. I pull two bottles of wine from the fridge, setting the white on the table and slip from the room. Taking the rosé and the punch bowl and downing the juice as I go, I reach the upstairs landing before I realise I've forgotten Sanaa.

By the time I've located Sanaa, who was curled up asleep in one of the dog's beds, and escaped the dining room a second time to put her to bed in Jasper's empty room, Miss has burned out to an indistinguishable lump beneath her duvet.

I pour wine into the empty punch bowl and put what's left of the bottle beside the bed. The lump stirs and the wine bottle disappears into it.

– Why can't she just be a normal mum who pays bills and –

– What, like my mum, you mean?

– Yesterday she came in with two tins of duck-egg emulsion for redecorating the lounge, the lump tells me.

– I'm sorry. I didn't know you felt that strongly about duck-egg blue.

– And then she opened the letters she's left all fucking month and started throwing packs of paint rollers across the room; we got a final notice, Lay. They're going to repossess the house.

– Didn't you get two final notices last month?

Downstairs, someone has turned the music up. I hear Pru and Dave singing, in turn, the wrong lyrics to a song which features the line 'fuck 'em' and laughing, when I hear sommet like glass smash.

I'm waiting for Sanaa to come running in at the

noise, so I can take her back to bed, curl up beneath the
covers and relive another story about Peter Rabbit's
escape from Mr McGregor's garden or the magic
porridge pot by torch light, but she don't. Probably too
hot-boxed to rouse.

Staring into the mirror above the desk, I imagine my
reflection standing up and walking out of the glass, like
somehow that'd be easier to accept than how it don't do
anything but stare back at me.

I reach out my hand so my fingers meet at the glass,
almost melting into each other except for the fact of the
mirror preventing me from bridging the gap between
my hand and my own reflection.

The bed creaks behind me. Via the mirror, I find
Miss's eyes amongst the pile of covers and cushions
tracing the scar like a seam running along my wrist and
up along the side of my thumb and across my knuckles
where my mum had shut my hand in the door.

– When I were li'l like Sanaa, my mum used call me
piano fingers.

Miss grunts, her voice muffled by the duvet.

– So, I asked her for piano lessons.

– Lay, what the fuck are you on –

– And she said I could have a grand piano soon as
Great Uncle Oswald's inheritance came through. Then
she laughed at me.

I swig what is left of the wine from the bowl. Miss
snorts, finally pulls the duvet down so I can make out

her face in the mirror.

– Great Uncle Oswald. I could use a Great Uncle Oswald about now.

– Soon as his inheritance comes through and I've got my piano, I'll buy a mansion, outright, and move Caleb and you and your mum and Sanaa and Jasper and Pru in too. We'll paint the whole fucking place duck-egg blue. And play piano all night. And drink posh wine and pretend we know the difference. And we'll build a moat and a wall and shoot cannons at any fucker what tries stop us. And we'll be the ones on the other side.

– What about your mum? You forgot about your mum.

– Forgot? Mate, what the fuck do you think the cannons are for?

I swig some wine, turning from the mirror to face Miss.

– And the moat. My mum can't swim for shit.

Miss's eyes, still full of tears, appear to burst when she laughs, as if something been lanced.

★

Bull ain't answering his mobile, so I take Miss to one of the guys I went to Aldgate Primary with, Stevie. Stevie's one of the 212 these days and can usually be found at the Place of Kings.

One of the old redbrick paper mills that made the
North West famous during the Industrial Revolution,
the Place of Kings is big, and derelict. Its doors are
all boarded up with them steel sheets that cops and
Councils use to keep criminals out, but which only keep
out the folk 'criminals' don't want to let in. We run
up the stairs round the back, which got added as a fire
escape back when Pok were used as a sofa showroom
in the 80's. Clit, who acts as doorman in return for free
shit, nods us in. The Place of Kings is about the only
place where the bouncers don't nod me in on account of
being Caleb's little sister.

Between the split left pupil his dad furnished him
with when we were kids and lack of front teeth (fuck
knows what happened to his teeth), Stevie's the sort
of bloke you can't miss – even if you want to, which a
lot of people do these days– unless you're in the Place
of Kings. He's also the sort of guy you can't imagine
ever having been a kid, or still being one, except if you
actually knew him when he were little.

We got married, me and Stevie, back in the infants'
yard at Aldgate Primary when we were seven and
actually still played during play time.

Here, he's sitting in a corner with a few guys I
recognise: his older brother, cousins, the kids who used
to kick around the green on Aldgate, back when I were
at Aldgate Primary School and used to wear birthday
hats and eat jelly and ice cream at their parties. Stevie

shows no sign of knowing me. Six foot now and got a kid with a lass called Claire. Back in the schoolyard, Claire had been in my class, and my head bridesmaid, while her big brother, Ray, had been my best mate at Aldgate, and is still the only guy I've ever slow-danced with, having asked me at a school disco once. Once upon what feels a real long time ago now, but is actually only a matter of about five years.

Ray's the first guy I ever gave head to out of choice. Ray's also now doing time in Strangeways for stabbing some mentally handicapped kid. Kid said he were rich, to try make Ray and his mates be his friends. Ray went round his house that same night. And when he found no money, Ray did the guy over and near-on killed him before anyone could prise him off the bloke. Everyone said Ray wouldn't have got such a long sentence had the guy not been handicapped already. Ray had no priors, not for violence. But then, Ray had debts, debts he'd not been able to pay off on account of refusing to work them off by being an enforcer for Stevie, 'cause Ray hated violence.

Claire don't talk to me either now. No bad blood or nothing. It's just there's nothing to talk about; we're not kids anymore. At least, we're not the kids we were. The kids who blushed at school discos asking each other to dance and bartered and haggled over toys rather than debts and gear.

Still, certain ties never break, so instead of going at

us for being dregs, Stevie tells us a name and the address
of a house in Kingsway, Heysham. Small favours being
all that gets passed between us now.

Me and Miss head back out. I'm aware Miss is eyeing
me like she's just realised I were someone, or at least
something, before I was just a dreg. And the thing I was
weren't just a kid, but a kid born and so belonging to the
Aldgate Estate and by proxy the 212.

We catch a bus up to Heysham Towers, cutting a
few stops early at Strawberry Gardens so I can brief
Miss without giving the old women sat in front the
satisfaction of thinking she's right: all teens are drug-
crazed delinquents.

When we reach the estate, I hand Miss the notes.
She waits just off the street while I go over and knock
on the door. I hear the familiar sound of dogs barking
and heavy chains, cage doors rattling, probably pit bulls,
fighting dogs, like they keep on Aldgate.

Some massive woman, wearing a velour tracksuit
and a high ponytail, opens the door.

– Stevie said I were coming. Boy knows.

She raises a drawn-on eyebrow, shouting back into
the house. A disembodied voice summons me in. I head
down the hall to an open door and enter a living room
full of competing voices: Boy, the guy Stevie passed me
on to, is sat at a dining table with two other guys. Eating
a full English and wearing a wife-beater, Boy looks
about my age.

– Sit down. We can't get owt yet.

Seeing as there is nobody else in the room, I figure there is a delay rather than a queue and sit down on the sofa. Junkies, shotters and the likes hate queuing for drugs in the same way normal folk hate sitting alongside a bunch of diseased and possibly contagious strangers in a doctor's waiting room, but at least you can see why you're having to wait at the doctors, and can raise the barricade of a magazine. A delay here could mean literally anything.

Boy carries on eating, his back to me while he talks in codes I know better than he probably realises, or cares.

On a muted TV some girls take chunks out of each other on some daytime talk show. The most vulnerable and most feckless estate folk hashing out their issues because the NHS has no money, and reality TV producers promise talk therapy and rehab to anyone willing to embarrass themselves to entertain the unemployed and those fortunate enough not to need to be, and reinforce the state of things.

Eventually, Boy clears his plate and comes over, sitting above me on the sofa arm and taking out his mobile.

– Two bars, yeah? You got the cash on you?

I nod.

– They're on their way. Some bollocks about family visiting; bairns couldn't get out till the relatives had fecked off. Fucking Sundays.

The dogs start up barking again just before the door to the living room opens. Boy takes about twelve bars wrapped tight in cellophane from some blond boy who's led into the room by the woman in velour. Looks like the Milky Bar kid gotten lost.

Boy makes a few more phone calls and people start arriving at the house. I stay sat at the sofa, my finger on the button to call Miss, who, like all the people now sneaking around the house, is lurking nearby trying not to look like she is lurking nearby.

– Got the money then?

– Got someone bringing it now.

I press the button and the mobile phone screen lights up. Boy's eyes shoot to the screen like a moth to a bulb. He don't say owt, but I know what he's thinking. The weed is here now. Suddenly it becomes obvious to Boy that I ain't 212, like Stevie; I ain't wearing gold hoops or the 212 regulation trackies tucked into high ankle socks.

It's funny. Folk, from clipboard carriers to cops to teachers to OAPs on public transport are always telling me I'm killing my chances of getting a job and a nice boy on account of having scars and dreadlocks and ink and piercings. Maybe, if I were *their* kid that much would be true, but I ain't their kid. My piercings and tattoos ain't some matter of rebellion, but confirmation, and *conformation*. Way I know it, I ain't ruining any chances I ever had, I'm just taking the only ones I've got. Least for now. The way I look means in ten years I might be afforded the luxury of being alive to regret my past trespasses.

I hear Miss's voice at the front door, saying word-for-word what I'd told her to say. So does Boy.

— Who you with?

— No one. Just an old mate of Stevie's.

— From Lancaster? Long way to come for two bars. Your people must be rich, or dumb... or tourists.

Boy twigs, finally pushing the resin across the table. Taking it from Miss, I hand the roll of notes over. Boy's mobile is ringing again. He counts the money, then gets up from the table as I'm ushering Miss back up the hall, shouting from the lounge as we head back up the windowless hallway.

— Oi, yous two, hang about. You heading back to Lancaster? I'm heading for Pok. I'll drop yous off.

In the car, I sit in the front passenger seat. Miss is sat in the back where she can't whisper to me. Boy offers me a cigarette, pressing a button to crack the window.

— You say yous are mates of Stevie's?

— We went to school together.

—Aldgate, for real? You ain't 212 though. Yous look like dregs.

Boy starts singing a bit of a heavy metal song. He grips the steering wheel as he headbangs to his own singing, or shouting, then laughs.

— People give you guys a hard time, innit, but yous

are alright, I know some of yous.

Boy asks if I knew Jim. When I don't nod, Boy does.

– Straightest gearhead going, Jimmy were. Heard what his brother did to the guy what run him down. Had been me, my fam would've set the pits on that gadge. Me, I grew up on the Range. 608, you know? Moved up here a few years back. Keep out of all that turf shit, you know? Just got my kin and that's it. Romani blood, innit?

Boy continues to hum the metal song he were singing and taps the wheel.

– So what's it like, being a dreg?

–What's it like being a gyppo?

Boy grins, and he actually looks attractive. Sort of.

– Us travelling folk is born into being hated, but yous freaks – that's them's words, not mine, that's what they all call you dregs people – yous choose to be moshy banging material. All that metal shit in your faces and fuck knows where else.

Boy gives my chest a side glance.

– And them massive jeans yous all wear, rain suckers, yous could take them off anytime. Be normal. Be anyone. Be them.

Boy nods out the window at the people on the street. I glance at the gold sovereigns across his knuckles as he swings the car into the car park.

– You headbang to Marilyn Manson?

– You live in a Conestoga wagon?

Boy laughs again, slapping the steering wheel.

— Yous are alright, you know. Your mate's a bit unsociable, like, but I get that broody goth vibe.

Boy twists in the seat to face Miss, and winks at her.

— I'm gonna give you my number.

Miss don't grin back but glares at me via the rear view then back at Boy, making Boy laugh harder: like, from a dreg, a dirty look is tantamount to a come on.

★

Polly, dropping her schoolbag over the sofa, leans down to me where I'm cross-legged on the carpet pouring fluorescent violet fortified wine between three glasses. Sam is kneeled beside me, sucking her infected lip-ring, her eyes batting about like pinballs between the front door and hallway.

— Your parents ain't going to, like, walk in or owt, are they?

Polly shrugs in reply.

— Pass that glass. I want that one.

Sam reaches for the fullest glass from between my knees. She takes the wine out to smoke by the front porch. I can see her through the lounge window, head darting up and down the street every time a car passes by. Polly takes the second glass, hitching up by me and whispering, even though there is no way Sam can hear:

— So, what goodies have you got in here?

Polly slides her cold fingertips into my jeans. I push her away and spark a smoke. Polly grins, running her tongue over her teeth. I look away from her as Sam reappears.

– Hey, I thought you weren't allowed to smoke in the house, you said –

– No. I said *you're* not allowed to smoke in the house.

Polly lights a cigarette of her own, removing her hand from my jeans.

Sam glances from Polly to me.

– Fuck's sake. I want some, what is it?

– Oh, give her some, whatever it is. Maybe it'll stop her whining.

Sam reaches for the wine.

– It were my money. Everyone just takes the piss out of me, it ain't –

– Fair? I know. Cry me a river, Sammy Doll, but first pour me another; I'm missing Maths this afternoon to sit about with you dossers. Whiskey, not that shit arse excuse for wine.

– Since when have you cared about Maths?

– Since the teacher's been fucking me in the store cupboard.

Polly rolls her eyes and downs some of the whiskey. Flicking my butt into the fireplace, I climb up and make for the hallway. Sam is still trying to work out if Polly is taking the piss out of her.

– I thought you were dating Flower...

– I am... Hey, where d'you think you're going?

Polly leans her head back over the sofa, extending an arm that can't quite reach me.

Laid out in the empty, freestanding bathtub, I don't know how long it's been till Polly's nails start scratching down the door. I'm about to get up when the lock clicks and the handle turns. Polly leans in the doorway, key hanging from her fingertips, and smirks. Sam is nowhere to be seen.

— What did you do to her?

— My mum's sleeping tablets.

Polly walks over and kneels down beside the toilet where I've left the wrap of coke and re-wrapped the gear in the foil, and shrugs.

— Don't play grandma on me; Sam was the one who thought to mix them with the wine, not me.

She sniffs at the burned-out brown on the foil.

— It's all proper admirable, how much you care about Sammy Doll, you know? Fucked up, like, but cute.

Polly slides from the toilet seat onto her knees and folds her arms over the bathtub lip. She leans her cheek onto her forearm so her head is tilted, clocks me sideways and blows the soot from her fingertips like kisses. I turn my face away and hear myself mutter:

— Caring don't make you fucked up.

— No. Caring don't make a person fucked up.

Polly places her mouth to my ear.

— The shit we do 'cause we care, though...

I feel Polly's lips curve into a smirk.

★

I smack straight into the bloke, a little too hard perhaps; the old codger stumbles. I manage to catch him around the waist just before he hits the floor. His flesh splays like a damp bag of bones over my arm. I set him straight, dazed at how weightless he feels and apologise for not watching where I were going.

Taking the route she's carved out through the queues before they can heal over again, I slide through the rush hour traffic of school kids and office monkeys, to sit beside Miss at stand 21. I lift the old man's cigarettes from my jeans and spark up, turning the deck of B&H in my palm and thinking on my brother, Dom.

I used to think of my brother Dominic like some Tom Sawyer character. Looking back, he were more like Dickens's Dodger, had Dickens not opted to provide Oliver with a couple of benevolent and wealthy grandparents that is.

In Britain you're under the age of criminal responsibility until your tenth birthday; the cops literally cannot prosecute you. You're the ideal tool: small, flexible, malleable, programmable, and untouchable. Cause a crimewave and, at most (and only if you're caught), you'll be referred to The Youth Offending Team who ain't much different to Social Services – and about as underfunded and overstretched.

It takes time and effort, a lot of fucking effort,

becoming an actual robber, though. So when my dad fucked off and took Dom with him, I quick enough threw out any thoughts of becoming a burglar along with the rest of my preadolescence and redirected my efforts.

For a while I'd beg money how Dom taught me, crying in doorways for bus fare some place I were never destined to actually go. But you can only pull the cute kid act for so long. In the end, you get tits. Then the piercings and tattoos start creeping in, like weeds and graffiti about some abandoned once-home. And then a whole new breed of folk start moving in on you. Puberty sure is a time of great change; you start out a charity case and end up an investment opportunity.

Dom left me a pretty sleight-handed pickpocket, as if he foresaw that I'd need it, but even now I cannot shake the Twist syndrome. Luckily, Lancaster's full of drugs, speaking of habits.

I started shotting on my own at thirteen. There's only one trick to shotting and that is to get addicted to money, not product. Few manage it though, at least at street level, or especially at street level. And the proof hides in plain view.

You see what's left of some one-time-dealers and punters and wonder how the fuck they even exist. Seriously, some folk look like regular people one day then six months later they've no teeth, no hair, no skin even, as if they're one big walking wound, like they're literally turning inside out. Most shotters ex them or refer them on. But you can't avoid them. They call from the gutters where they pool, begging to have the next bag emptied into them like dirt on a grave. A few months before they were in suits, driving swanky estate cars, playing at being parents, you name it; gear will take it.

The real scary bit is when you *stop* wondering.

When you first start using you rise from every nod like a phoenix reborn from the ashes. Junkies, meanwhile, they rise like zombies, leaving behind a little more of themselves each and every time, dividends for the ferryman. Not reborn, but undead. Junkies, they hit the nod not to rise, but to be returned to the grave, to feel the dirt hit, knowing what follows is to rest in peace. Over and over. Again and again. Till there ain't nothing left *to* give, but life itself.

It's no way to live and no way to die; being a junkie. It's the fate of all of us, when you think on it though – being eaten alive from the inside out. Dementia, cancer, AIDS, old age. Whatever. That's why there's heroin. And that's why there's junkies.

★

Giving up on the mangled card she'd been trying to cut into a heart shape with plastic safety scissors, Nicole starts telling Miss about her new boyfriend, Charlie.

Everyone says Charlie's imaginary. That's why Nicole's
here, at special school, 'cause she makes shit up. Least
that's what everyone says.

Scooping up the shredded pink pieces and moving
over to the kitchen area, I drop the scrap in the bin. I'm
not allowed to do Art anymore, but McQuaide still lets
me clear up the rubbish while the others work towards
a GCSE. It's meant to be a punishment, or an incentive.
All I know is it still beats another hour spent labelling
plant parts or trying to speak the national language of a
place most folk I live amongst couldn't even point out
on a map. I mean, folk actually benefit from not being
surrounded by mess and shit, y'know?

— Layla, what're you doing there?

I hold up the scraps to show McQuaide. The kitchen
area is off bounds to students, on account of the 'sharps'.
A few knives, and a single pair of non-safety scissors
I pass to Nicole so she can actually fashion something
heart-shaped from the battered sheet of pink card,
without getting caught. McQuaide nods curtly before
calling break.

McQuaide and Sue taking to the work-return
drawers to whisper to each other, I seize my chance
to follow Hazel out the fire door and through the
front garden, stopping short on the gravel path while
Hazel climbs into the bushes. It is raining lightly,
as per. Beneath the trees, big drops roll off leaves.
Hazel, hunches beneath them, being gobbed on by the

branches.

— McQuaide'll see you as much under there as stood here, you know?

Regardless, Hazel remains under the canopy until even her cigarette is soggy. We smoke and wait to be brought back in until we've finished full cigarettes. But nobody comes out to fetch us.

— Sommet's happened, Hazel says, skenning through the tiny window in the fire escape door. Inside, Miss signals that the staff ain't watching and we slip back in.

— No shit.

Miss, Nicole, Danny and Andrew are sitting about the tables in the side room staring through the doorway like it is a movie screen. Ryan is stood in the main room, his arms flailing like some scene from *King Kong*. Brenda is trying to console him, doing this funny dance forward as if to hug him then backing off again when Ryan's arms shoot out.

Meanwhile, McQuaide is trying to shout over them both and restore order through adding to the chaos. Hazel turns to ask,

— What's wrong with him?

— He spent all morning on that sculpture for his GCSE art submission and McQuaide just dropped the whole thing.

As Miss explains, I look to the mulch of card and papier-mâché at Ryan's feet. Even Nicole is shaking her head.

— Ryan told her not to move it until it had dried.

— I don't get it though. Why did she move it?

— Because she's McQuaide.

Nicole answers Danny's question, rolling her eyes and tutting. Hazel moves in front of me and Miss for a better view. We all stare through the doorway into the scene while Miss tells Hazel how Ryan had balanced the sculpture on the desk above the radiator, with Brenda's permission, and how McQuaide had tried to move it over to the allocated sculpture area, misjudging the weight and instability of the whole thing. Hazel looks on, frowning.

— What and he turned all them tables over?

Nicole nods at a copse of wire behind two upturned tables as she replies:

— He took out the chairs and a computer monitor too.

— We could calm him down.

Miss pulls up her hood and pulls the chord, as if putting on protective gear. Nicole snorts, staring into the mirror in her compact and preparing her make-up for Charlie, her made-up companion.

— Tell that to McQuaide.

Hazel puts an arm around Danny, who turns pink and goes quiet, for once. Nicole dares Hazel to do something, but 'course none of us do anything, except watch.

The more Ryan cries, the more McQuaide shouts.

She needs him to stop crying, to calm down, apologise and admit he's overreacting, that it don't matter, but he'd spent all morning on that sculpture, because McQuaide told him it mattered. And because he'd believed her.

★

On Clit and Mag's unlicensed television some charity-funded TV appeal is comparing the proximity of every British kid to a drug dealer to that of folk to rats. I glance out the window, or try to, except it's just a black sheet gashed up by a bare tree in front of a lamppost flickering as if choking on its own light. If only there *was* a drug pusher out there lurking down every alley.

– Turn that shite off, will you?

When no one pays any attention, Mag pulls herself from the sofa and flips the TV off. Then we are plunged into the silence everyone were trying to avoid and now no one dares disturb till Caleb and La quit fucking and come down stairs. The only thing worse than noise when you're coming down is silence.

– Who died?

Caleb asks, as he climbs over the people strewn about, to put a CD on. La drops down onto the sofa beside Mag, smiling, but Mag just scowls and turns away. Waiting for more drugs to arrive with a bunch of coming-down-people is like watching your mates getting old on fast-forward. Everyone becomes strangers in double-time. I plug my gob with a fresh smoke.

When Clit finally returns and we still ain't been booted out the house by Mag, I make for the kitchen. More important than getting my shit, I need to be the voice in Clit's ear, before Mag can start begging her fella in whispers and hisses to get these fucking wasters out of their house. Fucking wasters that were her best mates in the world only three hours earlier.

Clit splits the baggy open and starts pouring measures onto digital scales. Brushing past me and reaching for the wine as if a consolation prize, Mag storms back into the lounge. Flower and Polly linger in the doorway till Clit mumbles that he'll bring their shit through to them when it is bagged up, and they too withdraw, reluctantly going back to the big ashtray that is Clit and Mag's living room, where they can't see the powder, or see what percentage Clit reckons is owed them.

I rail my first line of the morning with the cupboard doors slamming in orbit round me. Cal slaps a final cupboard door shut over my head as I draw back on the last crumb of coke.

– Where the fuck do they keep the cups in this place?
– What cups?

Giving up, Cal dry-swallows a bomb of speed, and pushes past Clit on his way out, cursing me like I'm the reason Clit and Mag's cupboards are devoid of crockery.

Clocking me, Clit winks from where he's leaning

in the crux of the countertop and pulling on a crusted bottle of green juice I recognise as absinthe.

The post-nasal drip of coke in the back of my throat measures out the seconds like a leaky tap until the first ripple of muffled laughter reaches the beaded curtain in the doorway. The delicate chink and jostle of hundreds of glass fragments suddenly all alight shoot and scatter crumbs of rainbow. The sun has risen to peek through the kitchen window.

I move into the doorway, running a length of beads between my fingers and sucking deep on a smoke which tastes like a menthol on account of my mouth and cheeks being half numb.

Flower and Polly are huddled over the coffee table on bended knees beside Trix who's sat on small cushions of The Sun, cutting crude lines of fuck knows what. Ket maybe. AJ's pupils slide into the upturned corners of her eyes. Her tongue massages her gums as her eyes scan the room, no doubt searching out some newbie to lure into the cupboard beneath the stairs. Mag raises herself up on the sofa, her thin limbs unfurling out from a thick hemp robe. Her lips, stained with red wine, draw back to form a grin full of gaps and mossy teeth as she starts up, laughing suddenly at something I can't see, not from where I am standing.

★

— So, what's the dream, Layla?

— A state of mind in which someone is not fully conscious of their actual surroundings; an ideal; a fantasy.

— Ah, that's *a* dream, not *the* dream. Do you have a career in mind?

I cough, rather than reply. As if choking on the laughable idea that deboning battery chickens on a factory line, or washing shit and blood and abortions from hospital linen for minimum wage could even be described as a dream. That ain't a dream, in any sense. That ain't even a nightmare; that's just reality.

I stare into the empty seat Grace used to fill. Grace were this girl who'd left Wayside the week I had arrived, the girl who I replaced.

Miss told me Grace had wanted to be an archaeologist when she arrived at Wayside. After she'd seen the careers advisor and had her second review meeting, Grace were fast-tracked onto an apprenticeship in customer service. They set up work placement for her at the same supermarket where my mum works as a store cleaner. And when Grace left, it were to be a single mother.

— What do you plan to do after high school?

The guy repeats himself when I don't say nothing.

I frown. I were expelled from high school nearly two years ago; I know all too well what comes after. I weren't even out the school gates before I were learning that by the time you're being told you have rights it's already too late; they only tell you when the cuffs are already on. It were the cops that drove me out of school, after all, and it still took six months before the paperwork had caught up with my mum, and the Social came knocking, and threatening prosecution if she didn't get me in to another school. It took another two months after that visit before the cops caught back up with me and I ended up at Wayside. My mum says no local mainstream high school would accept me, not when they found out I'd been expelled from my last school for 'a violent assault on a teacher'.

Suffice to say, you can't tell clipboard people nothing though. You wait for them to drop the paperwork and actually face you. Meanwhile, they're waiting for you to drop the attitude and accept whatever they wanna do to you. That's the difference between kids and adults; minute you drop the attitude, they'll stab you in the fucking heart with their fucking pen. Minute one of them drops the clipboard though, you can bet your arse a kid will drop their attitude. You can't just say that though, because you're just a kid. So, every meeting, every appointment, every 'little chat' gets like watching a movie you've seen a hundred times and with someone new each time and someone new who each time thinks *they* know how it's all gonna' end based on having seen the trailer. All you can do is show them, let the scene unfold and wait for the penny – or clipboard – to drop.

I stifle a yawn, the comedown of all comedowns settling into the deepest parts of me; the parts of me I've been increasingly filling with gear. Someplace I don't wanna go, I know, I ain't coming down, I'm actually starting to rattle.

— You really have nothing? No idea at all?

The guy is cleanshaven, balding, with sticking-out ears. He's wearing a shirt with an ironed collar and a smile that makes him look simultaneously like a maniac holding a gun and a guy with a gun held to his head; he looks exactly like a young Tony Blair. Tony Blair in his first term. Tony Blair before the Iraq war.

— What did you want to be?

The guy blinks at me, smoothes his tie and tells me:

— I wanted to be a firefighter.

I look the advisor up and down.

— So, what happened to your dream?

The guy's smile starts to slide south like it's melting before he's even begun the sentence.

— Ah, well, as you can see, I became this instead.

★

Seems like everywhere, from a council estate in Lancs to a tenement in New York's Lower East Side has one: their own local nutcase. On our road, she curses at the mention of The Virgin Mary and holds loud Masses over her kitchen sink and eggs any kid who gets too close to the house, screaming *demon Jew, Jesus-killer* and the like at any kid with red hair.

This afternoon they came and got our madwoman again, after she threw a bucket of boiling water up the path at Li'l Patrick, Fish-van-Phil's boy, from over the road. She's called Josephine. But for all my life, she's been known as The Madwoman at Number Nineteen.

She don't look schizophrenic, most of the time; she goes shopping, waves her husband up the path from the kitchen window, spends Sundays on her knees in the dirt pulling weeds. She looks like any woman, like my mum, like all the women on the street. Better even; she looks middle class, posh; she's the only woman on the street who fills those binbags that charities post through the door, and she never stands around the cul-de-sac in her pyjamas at midday putting the world to rights like the sane women on our street; the women who say Number Nineteen can only go about being showy like that and acting better than everyone 'cause they don't have kids, and that's why they've got money to flash about. She's the oldest woman on the street and the only one on the street who don't have kids, and who made the vow 'for better or worse', and actually kept it. They say that's also on account of them not having kids. But then, from time to time, she starts pulling the marigolds out the flowerbeds instead of planting them, or throwing tomatoes at my mum's front porch, or screaming *cunting whore* and running round the estate in her knickers. And then they come take her away.

My mum ignores the tomatoes, furiously baby-wiping the windowsills, scrubbing the front step and washing away the crazy woman's crazy words before they can take seed and sprout, before the neighbours see that the madwoman spat her insanity all over my mum's front door like a curse or sommet. It's the same way, with the same wet rag in hand and same bowl of warm vinegar water beside her, that my mum erases my blood and dirt from the door too, after yet another attempt to break it down. Despite my best efforts, it stands, plain and white as a blank page.

It took her two years on a waiting list before the council offered my mum a place on this estate: the Dacrelands Estate. It's a good place; trees line the roads and the neighbours notice when you ain't cleaned your net curtains, and return borrowed sugar. And borrowed weed. It's an estate where people whisper rather than shout. And it's an estate where everyone ignores The Madwoman at Number Nineteen, except to remind us kids that her name is Josephine and she's got a sickness. And, being sick, it ain't right to put her windows through or throw paint on her flowerbeds or slash her husband's tyres when she directs her madness at your house, or at you.

Instead, everyone just watches while she does the job for them, slashing her own husband's tyres and stomping on her own flower beds and putting her own windows through. And nobody says or does anything; they just stand at their windows, waiting to sigh *they're taking her again*, so they can shuffle back out onto the street in their nighties to whisper to each other all the kind stuff none of them ever actually say to either The Madwoman or her husband.

Some, like my mum, have a condolence greeting-card on standby in their letter racks so that, when they don't bring Josephine back, they can be first in line to prove *they're* the good sort of woman, make *their* sadness, *their* feelings, *their* neighbourly goodness known. Not to The Madwoman's husband; to each other, through making that considerate and caring shuffle in their slippers across the street, card in hand.

Inside the card, the words already printed out: *Thinking of You at this Difficult Time*, saving anyone actually having to think up something to say.

★

Carol smiles up at me.

The Careers Adviser must've told McQuaide I hadn't displayed the expected behaviours at each individual juncture of time during our two-minute intercourse. So now I have to do the things I usually do in the centre of the room, exactly as I would usually do them, but from a desk in the corner, for a period of time reckoned by McQuaide's whim. That's supposed to make me think life choices have meaning and consequences. Or make me feel bad, or compel me to 'be good', or sommet.

– Layla, come on. I don't want you to get in trouble, chick.

Carol has pulled back the chair and is waiting for me to sit.

Behind me, Andrew and Ryan are studying *Hamlet* with Chris. Andrew is droning Hamlet's soliloquy aloud as if the words are some cold maths theorem, while Ryan groans into his hands, as if it hurts him to absorb their meaning. Not just because of what the words mean.

– Layla, turn this way, please. All you've got to do is answer the questions. You know all this stuff; we've been through it. Isn't your father Spanish? This should be easy for you.

I frown at Carol, who holds out a pencil. There's no pens, no crayons, no colour in the Naughty Corner. Like, the horror of not being able to colour things will compel us to repent, implore us to seek redemption.

– Layla. *Please*, I want you to get through this. You don't even have to say it out loud: *just write it*.

I stare at the page of questions in Ariel typeface, font size twelve and the words just look grey. Devoid. Swirling. Hypnotizing. Question marks that give the illusion of choice, but the letters quiver on the stark white paper when I try to focus on them, like they would erase themselves had they any choice at all.

At breaktime, Carol's warm, wrinkled hand touches my bare shoulder.

– Good girl.

She sounds surprised, and relieved. Around me, the others shuffle from the room in a single line, like a sentence written in yet another language I do not speak.

One of the special school classrooms' motivational posters is momentarily underlined by the queueing bodies that are slowly edging toward the narrow doorway. An Einstein quote, with a picture of him quizzically pointing above. My gaze drags, lagging over the ascending and descending symbols. Running the words through my mind feels like playing tug-of-war with barbed wire.

– Do you want to join the others for break? I'm sure Mrs McQuaide won't mind.

But Carol don't sound sure. I fold my arms onto the table and bury my head in them. A moment passes before I hear McQuaide approach the table and then walk away again, her high heels tutting like a clock.

When I next look up, the room is empty. And dark, thanks to the high window and grubby winter light. Just me and a bunch of faded posters, pinned to the walls and waving slightly beneath the aircon machine, like silhouetted bodies strung up to warn me.

I re-read the quote written in varying fonts like a ransom letter beneath Albert Einstein: *There are two ways to live: you can live as if nothing is a miracle; you can live as if everything is a miracle.*

Like I've just been told a joke minus the punchline, I'm left wondering. So, what is the other way to live?

Break over, Sue sits down beside me.

– I'm going to give you the work and then have to go over to Miss, Nicole and Hazel. While they're getting their trays, sit up and tell me whether you understand this.

I raise my head from my arms to glance at some science printout explaining fossil fuels and make the most noncommittal gesture I can.

– Wonderful. Call me over if you get stuck.

When the bell rings out for noon, it is McQuaide's turn to sit before me, gesturing me sit back down when I make to leave with the others.

– Carol and Sue tell me you've worked quietly all morning. That wasn't so hard, now was it?

★

Dregs arrive in tides. Sprawling out and riding each other's bodies, like dull pennies they litter the giant slot-machine shelves of hollow tombs in the Priory graveyard perched high above the Lune Valley. Below us, the Roman Bath House Ruins lie like a trampled novelty prize; and beyond, the city twinkles like a garish casino carpet.

From the highest tier of graves I watch DM scaling

the stones and people indiscriminately. To some people, somewhere, this would be no place for a kid. Some place, kids climb jungle gyms, not junkies.

I wonder if DM knows about those worlds yet, about bedtimes and mealtimes and story times, and all sorts of times he'll never have, not unless they come and take him away from here, from us, from his mother, Biddy, and from everything and all he does know.

In years to come, when DM is my age, I wonder what he'll feel when he realises it weren't ever Father Christmas sneaking round the house and drinking the midnight brandy. If he'll ever miss the idea of school fêtes, of sleepovers, of church Sundays. The idea of a dad. The idea of a God.

Calling to DM, Aberdeenie Jeanie scoops him up and prises an empty beer can from his little hands, tossing it on to the grass. AJ pushes dirty blond bangs from out his eyes, Kyle's eyes, the eyes of the dad he never met, on account of Kyle hanging himself before DM was born without ever knowing he were about to become a father.

DM rests his head against AJ's chest. AJ rocks slowly as she sits with him, whispering lullabies in his ear and humming the words she cannot recall, or never knew to remember, seeing as Aberdeenie Jeanie probably don't even remember Aberdeen, never mind her own crackhead parents.

– You guys want a hit?

Bull holds up a bright-pink bong from where he's sat cross-legged on the grass with Trix and his Mrs, Scraggy Mag. AJ slaps DM's bum. For a moment DM clings to her, so she has to peel him off her like Velcro. She stands him back on the grass and like a wind-up-toy DM totters across to Bull to fetch the bong.

AJ turns to me, laughing as she watches DM go, asking if Biddy told me what he'd gone and done at baby group?

– He only filled his dungarees with toys and started getting them all out afterwards in the fucking supermarket while Biddy were on the rob. Biddy says he had loads, all stuffed in his pants.

Returning, DM lifts the bong for AJ to take it and leans between us, chewing on a strawberry lace he didn't have a minute earlier. I put my hand on his head, untangling lengths of his hair and watch as his little head leans against my knee. Aberdeenie Jeanie watches me for a moment, before pulling a lighter from her pocket.

– Hit, birthday girl?

AJ leans forward, rubbing her nose against mine when I gesture for her to take it. She leans down to DM, but he pulls his face away, burying it into my knee and curling an arm around my calf until I can feel his tiny fingers dig in through my jeans.

AJ sticks her tongue out at him in response before bringing the bong to her lips. The stale water growls.

DM presses his back against my knee, looking out

into the group, the red lace hanging from his teeth. I wonder if the person he is waiting on is still waiting too, or if Biddy has already found what she went looking for. Where the fuck is she?

AJ exhales a thick stream of smoke, stifles a cough and says something about Biddy having gone to score. I don't know if she is speaking to me or DM. His heart beating warm against my shin, I consider scooping him up like Sam and AJ and the others do, but instead just put my fingers back in his hair and continue untangling the little knots in his blonde curls, picking out bits of twig and leaf and grass.

AJ sets up a second mix, packing her own store of grass in the gauze, and Clit kneels down beside me, a piece of bent cardboard in his hand.

– Happy birthday.

I rail the line straight off the card, DM ducking out from beneath me automatically, as if wanting to avoid me spilling powder into his hair. It tastes faintly like piss and numbs my cheeks. Speed, probably or low-grade MDMA mixed with a hefty cut of lidocaine. Pseudo-coke.

– Who bought this shit?

– Sammy Doll.

– Off who?

Clit laughs.

– Likes to think she can sort her own shit, don't she? You coming back to our place? Think your brother's coming over.

I search amongst the waning crowd, but Clit tells me that Miss is gone; she called a taxi to take Sam back to hers on account of Sam getting drunk and sick everywhere.

– Where the fuck is Biddy?

I feel Clit's eye on me as I watch Caleb and La, who are tangled up together on the gravestone slabs, staring up into the sky and whispering to each other behind cupped hands, absently pushing DM away as he tries to climb over Caleb and curl up in the nest of their bodies.

– Drought on, ain't there? Don't fret it, Lay Babes.

Scooping me into a one-arm hug, Clit rests his chin on my head.

– We'll watch DM, as per. And as per, Biddy will turn up. Like a bad penny.

He sighs, smiling slightly.

– She always does.

★

I can hear the crying from the end of the street. Letting myself in, La and Cal curled up like cats in the gutted fireplace don't stir. Leaning over the sofa, I find Clit and Mag laid out on it, eyes closed.

–Thought you were Biddy.

Mag mumbles, and then groans; Clit pulls a cushion over his head, and grunts.

Opening the bedroom door, DM is laid in the centre

of the single mattress, pupils wide and black as unhinged snake jaws like he's trying to swallow the night whole. He stops screaming when he clocks me, and just stares.

I lie down on the mattress and pull the lumpy duvet that DM has tossed to the floor up over my legs, and close my eyes. I can't tell if the mattress is damp, or it's just my own cold sweat. The sudden silence in the absence of screams hits me like blood washed from a wound that don't hurt until you see the damage. My gut is in knots already and my nose is running, salting my chapped lips till they burn. I try not to think about it, but my mind runs uselessly through my body assessing the damage like a tongue over a bust lip or yanked out tooth.

After a minute or so, I feel DM shuffle up the bed, pushing his bum into my stomach. His wet, heavy nappy presses against my navel. The back of his head works its way into the shaft of my collarbone. His tiny ribcage shudders in intervals, cut grass smell in his hair and that milky scent of toddler skin overpowering the stale, musty smell of the room. I pull my arm from beneath us and hold his warm little body to me like a hot water bottle. And he clings to me in the darkness as to a mouldy old comfort blanket that'd lose its magic if it ever made it into the wash and got clean.

★

I wake with a start at the sound of a flint on a lighter catching, and screw my eyes up at the sting of light suddenly hitting my retinas. Holding a hand up against the intermittent flashes of flame, I pull myself up, and the flashing stops.

My eyes are slow to adjust, but after a moment I make out Biddy, her skin the same jaundiced colour as the nicotine-stained walls.

Slouched in the corner, Biddy flips a Zippo closed and stares back. If she hadn't just done that, I'd seriously wonder if she were even alive; her eyes, the opposite of DM's, are constricted to hard, permanent full stops, and fixed on me like laser sights.

My vision fuzzes over again, when I climb to my feet. Careful not to wake DM, or stand on him, I step over his little body and onto the floorboards between the mattress and Biddy. As I do, Biddy flicks sommet over to me. It hits my sneaker. I blink down at the pebble-sized *fuck you* stopped at my feet. I can feel Biddy's eyes on me, not so much wondering if I'll take it, but waiting for me to take it.

I reach into my jeans and pull out a twenty, but Biddy shakes her head, and her gaze rolls from me to snag instead on DM's tiny body.

I scoop up the bag; knowing that even with her eyes fixed on DM, it's me Biddy's got her attention focused on, and shuffle out in the half dark. A twenty bag in one hand and a twenty in the other, I feel like the walking dead; as if my body just left my soul behind.

★

Rumour has it Trix and Polly were trying to complete the Bends up over the Heights. There's this bit of S-shaped road up near the army barracks. It's said that if you hit it at the right spot that you can cruise straight through the S without turning the wheel. That's the Bends. Fuck knows whose car it were, stolen most likely. Whatever. That ain't what everyone's talking about.

Polly got half-thrown out of it during the first revolution and chopped in half in the second. The car rolled three times in total, cleared the road and landed in a ditch. Trix somehow climbed free before the car blew.

The police found Trix two fields away. They had to follow the screams to find him. That's what I heard, anyhow.

– Just think about it, 'kay?

I reach for the ashtray, stifling a yawn.

– Lay, say you'll think about it, 'kay?

– I don't need to see them burn what the car didn't.

– Fuck's sake, that's our mate.

I pull myself out of Dave's rocking chair to cadge another tin from the fridge.

– *Was* our mate.

Miss only started hanging at the Steps four months back, after we met at Wayside. She's never had a mate die. Meanwhile, I've had enough.

– Shit happens. And people die.
I ain't saying you get over it. You don't, but, like anything, you get used to it. And, ultimately, you get on with it, you know?

– So you ain't going to the funeral and that's that then?

I shrug. What can I say?

– Lay, what the fuck is wrong with you? What's your fucking problem?

– Ain't nothing wrong with me. Ain't that *your* problem?

– My problem is that *Polly is dead*, Lay. She's dead.

Miss repeats herself, like it's me who can't accept it. I get up again, deciding to finish my beer in a room with a lock on the door. Miss starts sobbing.

– Everything is so fucked up, Lay.

– Death can't fuck up what already was.

I sigh.

– I need a shower. There's a few cans left. Help y'self.

– She were our age, Lay...

I think of Kyle. Kyle was sixteen when Cal found him hanging. Laura K was nineteen. Ain't even been six months yet since I prised her petrified corpse off La like a plaster, like the pain would ever scab over, like I could even abbreviate it. They were best friends. They were *my* friends. And some of them were far better people than Polly. I think of Mary, the White Keyring Queen. I think of all of them, and I think of how they were somebody's kid, somebody's friend, once upon a time. And I think about how it don't make no fucking difference, and can't; not now.

Now, even if it *could* make any difference, only difference is that it woulda been better if Laura K had offed it even earlier, at sixteen, before all the folk who didn't know her could shrug her off as *just another dead junkie*. Not nineteen, which is how old Jim were, too, when half us dregs watched his skull spill its shit at our feet easy as a dropped bottle of red. All the frenzied ideas and smartarse puns and barbed jokes, all the dreams Jim pretended not to have, and all the demons and nightmares he pretended not to have buzzing and blazing like fireflies inside that mad, dark mind of his – to just get spilt on double yellow lines.

– You ever even heard of Laura K, Bull's girl, La's best mate? Or heard of Kyle, DM's father? Not that he even lived to know it. Or heard of Jim? You ever even know Bull had a brother?

I begin pushing the empty cans together to take to the kitchen. Miss slams her hands onto the table, knocking the stacked cans so they roll, one by one, from the table and back into the space I'd just created.

– Look, what d'you want me to do? Tell me, Miss, what the fuck can I do?

Miss gapes at me, her eyes welling. Then, the tears just sort of break, like sommet inside her has imploded.

— *Nothing,* Lay, just... nothing.

And of course I know that. I mean, like, that's the whole point, ain't it?

★

Mag says Clit just found the purse, and that it were already empty, and then the police found it on him when they were just doing a routine stop-and-search. Whatever. Fact is, Clit has priors and there's an old lady with a bust lip and her bare cupboards to account for. Luckily, Clit has Mag; wherever he were at the time of the assault and mugging, Clit were at home with Mag.

La fills me in about it on the way back from a mish up to the Place of Kings. At the house, Clit is in the living room drinking a tin of Special Brew. La nestles down in the empty fireplace and starts poking at her arms. Mag enters from the kitchen without speaking. After chucking her handbag at Clit's head, she mutters something about him being a brain-dead cunt before disappearing back into the kitchen. Clit ignores her, tossing the witness report my way.

— Some woman witness identified 'the perpetrator' as being in his mid-to-late thirties, and bald.

I read her description in the witness report, and reason aloud that Clit will get off easy. Clit grimaces.

– He's pissed at being called bald and nearing forty, Lay Baby. Fuck the charge.

La laughs into the tracks on her right arm.

– No, fuck you, La. Aww, still not got a dig? What happened to getting clean, the methadone no longer scratch the itch, babe?

I clock the look that plays over La's face as she starts calling Mag from the kitchen, shouting about how she should come sort her man out. I put my cigarette out on the chair arm and bury my head in the witness report again.

I don't know how old Clit really is, thirty maybe, but I know his lack of hair ain't an age thing. Clit used to pull his hair out, like literally. Mag told me once when she'd done loads of speed and crack. She said he'd get mad or antsy or prang and just pull chunks of his hair out straight from the root. She said he'd done it since kidhood. That it got so bad his Dad used to Bic his head so he'd nowt to pull out.

Mag told me that when Clit first got sent to Stonerow as a young offender, they didn't shave his head no more so he just pulled all his hair out. And kept pulling it out until it just never grew back no more. That's how he came to get called Clit; he's bald as a clit and he's always got his hood up. That's what Mag said.

– Anyway, ain't describing you, is it?

I toss the report back to Clit, but he just shrugs. Mag never tells Clit the official story until just before the hearing, in case he forgets it. I've been witness to that.

— You coming tomorra? Think Mag and Bitchtits over there are doing a spot of shopping in town if you're interested? Y'know, they can always use an innocent face.

Mag wanders back in, picking up and downing what is left of Clit's Special Brew before curling up beside him. She tells me they're planning to liberate some makeup, aftershave and perfume so they can all get dolled up before the court hearing; make a good impression.

— Don't get Lay Baby in on nothing. Cal wouldn't like it. She's still a kid, y'know. If she got arrested again…

La's voice is slow and thick like blood pulled from a deep, sleepy vein, and it travels from what looks like a dark space between two arms draped over sockless feet.

— Be a'right. She's come before, ain't y'kid? It be a'right.

Clit shrugs. He gives up on the report, looking with narrowed eyes at La and then me, muttering something about how there's nowt worse than the shit La fucking started me on. But La has sunk further into the fireplace with the needle still in the back of her hand, and don't hear Clit, or just don't care no more.

★

La didn't introduce me to heroin. La just introduced me to needles, and not because she wanted to. She just knew someone would, after Jim died; La knew she couldn't stop me from fucking myself over, so she just tried to make sure no else could fuck me over.

The first time I did heroin, it were with Jim. Nobody blames Jim though, not now, not since Jim, Bull's kid brother became Jim *who was* Bull's kid brother.

Anyway, that's not why I remember that day; I remember that day 'cause it were the first time I ever heard Jim speak about his family. That's what Jim and Bull always got to fighting, more often literally, about – to talk about Jim's family was to talk about Bull's family, after all.

At thirteen, I'd never even considered that Bull must have a family somewhere, or noticed that when Bull referred to his family, he were always referring to the Steps, to the dregs.

First I saw of Jim was seeing Bull were on the ground at the foot of the Steps pinning some townie down and slapping him about a bit. Apparently Jim had come looking for Bull, and his arrival had come as a bit of a surprise. As I'd approached, I'd seen the two arguing before the fight got started. Drainpipe jeans, short-sleeved polo neck and prison white Adidas Superstars finished with a regulation throwback Perry Boy haircut, to match his regulation terrace get-up, this guy squaring up to Bull stood out and would have stood out whether he were hanging at the Steps, sat in the library, or doing just about anything except chanting 'Blue Moon' in Etihad Stadium or standing in the dock. I'd seen this guy throw the first punch, though I didn't know why. I didn't even know Bull had a brother, till then.

— Bull, he likes how everyone thinks he looks after you all. Tells it like it is. Dregs' own personal Jesus.

— He feels bad about leaving you.

— Never spoke about me though, did he? Or about our mum. Our dad. Our stepdad.

— Because he felt bad, not because he didn't.

Jim shrugged, and continued rolling out the foil and setting up the gear.

— Bull hated our dad, y'know? Our real dad. Wanted Bull to be his little right-hand man, our old man did, join him on the terraces, play footie and all that. Like I did. 'Like a boy oughta'.

Jim tore a sheet of foil from the roll.

— Bull wanted to, like, let his hair grow and strum guitars and write mardy tunes and run away to art college. And, when our dad died, that's what Bull did.

— Not until your stepdad got put away.

— I wear trackies and like footie, but I ain't no div. I know why Bull didn't go off to college till that cunt got banged up. Our stepdad? He ain't just into shanking kids, you get me? Even if that's all they put him away for. Guy's a fucking nonce, and Bull knew it. That's why he stuck around till our dear old stepdad got locked up, to protect his dirty little secret. Even from me. Not to protect me.

Anyone else were saying it, I'd have tried thinking up sommet to say in reply, something the complete opposite of what I were hearing. Sommet hopeful. When Jim said it, I just did what Bull wouldn't, what he couldn't. I just listened.

— I ain't royally fucked off about Bull effing off. I ain't even fucked at Bull for not warning me. I know our mum told Bull she wunt take the guy back. But she did. And I were still at home. But fuck all that. That's done. Over. Sorted.

I frowned, it were slight and automatic, but Jim caught it. Course he did.

— Lay, Bull believed our mum because he wanted to. He weren't trying to protect me. He were protecting himself. If my big brother had left when it were still going on, he knew the sick bastard would move on to me, fair do, but it weren't the thought of that what stopped Bull from leaving. It were the thought of me learning what the guy was. The thought of everyone finding out. Cause Bull knew, I wouldn't just fucking bend over and take it. That's the reason we scrap, when we do.

Jim slid the pen from the tin pipe he'd just molded around it, and handed it to me.

— Bull wears all that death metal get-up and writes songs about being judged by everyone else, he's a fucking hypocrite. I might dress like a fucking hooligan, buy the brands and all that, but Bull, he thinks like one of them, he buys their bullshit.

Jim bit the wrap open with his teeth and tapped a mound out onto the sheet of foil in his lap.

— Funny really, Bull hated our dad for trying to make him be sommet he ain't, sommet like me, but Bull hates me for the same thing — I don't wear the right clothes. I don't listen the right tunes. I don't say the right shit. I don't do the right drugs...

— You don't keep your gob shut.

Jim grinned at me.

— Aye, Lay Babes. I *won't* keep me gob shut. I won't be ashamed of what my stepdad did, like Bull is. And so...

Jim chased a line, held it until he looked about ready to clean pass out, and exhaled a thick cloud of smoke that smelled bitter, not like citrus-bitter, but faintly vinegary.

— And so?

— And so your Messiah, God of the fucking Steps, Lord of the Dregs, smites me like the hooligan he is beneath all that Father fucking Christmas beard and scratcher's ink.

Jim shuffled forward, held the foil sheet like a buttercup beneath my chin and positioned the lighter beneath the foil.

— I won't be ashamed. Not for what some nonce did.

Not even for my brother. If that makes *me* the devil, fuck it, guess that makes you the devil's advocate.

Jim winked, looking up at me.

– So why do this?

I asked, staring back, and living up to the role of being dubbed the devil's advocate.

– Do what?

– Do heroin.

Jim didn't wince, he'd never even wince when Bull swung for him, on principle, but I caught the flicker in his eyes and the tension in his jaw suddenly when I used that word; which Jim never did. When he did answer, there were no grin, even in his voice, which were suddenly low, not exactly a whisper, but low.

– Because knowing the past ain't my fault, ain't to say it ain't my problem.

Before I could respond, Jim had sparked the lighter. I heard the flint catch and corked my gob with the pipe.

And that were the first time I used, and when things get blurry.

The brownish powder melted instantly into a running tar-like oil, forming a line as it ran along the sheet at the slightest tilt of Jim's wrist, until it fizzled out entirely to a single black, smutty full stop at the edge of the foil sheet.

The last thing I recall before nodding out were the sound of foil tinkling in Jim's fingers like a wind chime caught up in a breeze and the trill of a Clipper flint cawing like a blackbird, like we were some old couple on a porch. The warmth kissed my bare skin like we were dozing beneath a midday sun someplace far far away from this place. Someplace like in the movies. Someplace where the sun gets warm enough to feel.

Roused amongst the debris of chalky concrete and mismatched sofa cushions, the next thing I knew were Jim's body pressed against mine as he half-carried, half-dragged me around Pok as if performing some bizarre, grotesque waltz in the haze of dust slow-somersaulting in the narrow shaft of light cast from the single pane window above us.

Jim said I'd to get the blood moving and my heart beating. He kept saying I had to stay with him. He said I'd been making this sound like a death rattle. I don't remember that, but I remember the urgency in Jim's voice. I'd never heard anyone call my name like that before; it hit me like a shot of Naloxone.

★

If you aren't making mistakes, you aren't trying hard enough.

I stare at the poster, trying like hell to make sense of the words, or just work out what the fuck gets me so much about them.

I'm stood there so long I walk in late and McQuaide bollocks me before even asking where I've been. I tell her the truth, but course she thinks I'm trying to act smart. Consequently, I spend the morning in the Naughty Corner, and am told at break to stay there and think about my actions.

I think about having not gone to court. I think whether Clit got sent down, about Mag and La being on the rob, and if they then got caught. I think about Polly getting chopped in half and Trix clambering from the car after looking to see if Polly were OK only to discover her lower torso sat beside him. And I think about Trix telling me about it after every time we fuck, like he only gets me naked so I have to hear it, so I can't just leap up and run away and scream, like he did.

I think about how Miss won't talk to me because I won't agree to go to the funeral. I think about the places I could go instead. I think about my mum, and how I've no fucking idea where she is, what she is doing, how she spends her days. What her and her boyfriend Terry do when they do go out together. What they talk about. If they talk. If my mum and dad ever really talked.

I think about where my dad is now, if he is anywhere. If he went back to Spain like he always threatened. If my brother Dom is still with him. If they talk. If they talk in Spanish. If they ever talk about me.

And I think of the first time Jim and me ever talked, the night after Jim first appeared at the Steps, looking for Bull.

I'd mished over to Bull's with my army surplus

backpack stuffed full of clothes. Bull had opened the door, a joint burning down in his teeth, clocked me – and the backpack – and rolled his eyes.

Just like every time I turn up at Bull's – even now – especially now – Bull let me in, assuming I'd had a row with my mum. I think that was the first time I'd ever turned up at Bull's and it weren't because I'd had a fight with my mum, or Terry, or Cal.

The black eye Bull had given Jim instead of a welcome hug less than twenty-four hours ago was just beginning to bloom. Sat cross-legged on the concrete-tiled living-room floor, he took the joint he had in his teeth and offered me it.

I took the joint, wondering if the fact the two of them weren't sharing joints like the rest of us always do – like me and my brother, Cal, always have – meant the argument weren't yet over. Bull left Salford when Jim must've been about twelve. Had they just never even smoked together before, never even shared a joint?

I sat down on the floor beside Jim so I could reach the ashtray. Meanwhile, Jim resumed gouging the clockface from an expensive looking watch. A 1980's Rolex, Bull told me, re-entering the room with three mugs of tea and looking royally fecked at what his little brother were doing to it, but making no effort to stop him.

I asked Jim why he was wrecking it; why not punt it if he didn't want it. I don't reckon I'd ever seen anything that were that small and worth that much money, except drugs.

Jim said he did want the Rolex; that it was his most prized possession. Later, after Jim died, Bull found it at his place and offered to let me have the watch, but if Jim had wanted me to have it, he'd have given me the watch. I held it until the metal had warmed in my hand and then I handed it back. I made Bull promise me that Jim would be wearing it when they buried him.

– My old man gave me this watch, along with the news he had terminal cancer. Sick joke, eh? I were only ten. A babby. Just about to start 'big' school. If dad had pulled that one on Bull, he'd have stormed off and gone written some whiny song about it. Then pawned the thing.

Jim shot the briefest glance Bull's way, not like to see if Bull had felt the dig, more to make sure the dig had hit its mark. It had, but Bull didn't retaliate, not that time.

I asked Jim, again, why then were he wrecking the watch?

Shaking the broken fragments of the mechanism from the bezel, Jim held the watch up by its strap. Closing one eye and staring at me through the emptied lug, he reached his other arm around and picked the joint from my mouth as I was mid-drag, put what were left of it back in his teeth, and fastened the watch on to his wrist, squinting through the smoke.

— The watch matters, because it was my dad's. And life matters.

I tried to make the connection between a family heirloom and life; something so small and specific and, well, life. I remember Jim taking a deep, slow draw on the joint, as if to give me time, or just for effect. In hindsight, probably both.

— That's why he gave me this Rolex. A guy being eaten alive by cancer knows better than anyone; time is all we have.

He exhaled the smoke.

— And all we don't have, as it goes.

Scooping the broken bits of mechanism, Jim opened his palm. Tiny pieces of gold, minute cogs and screws, glittered amongst the ash and concrete dust lifted from the tiles. Then, Jim blew a stream of joint smoke into his hand so the smoke ricocheted and glittered in the air momentarily, before dusting his hands off on his jeans.

I remember trying to figure out, even then, if this guy was a real genius, or just really stoned.

— But what time it is, what numbers those tiny little hands point to at any given moment, fuck that. Fuck sitting about watching life tick away.

I think all the fucking time about all the shit Jim used to talk. Mostly though, I think about if I'll ever talk like that again, to anyone, *with* anyone.

★

As it's considered only as someplace where the 608 hang out, few dregs ever eat in at Bally Ann's, and fewer still dare venture upstairs. Bally Ann's is a greasy spoon. Instead of serving fry-ups though, Bally's serves scraps baps and chip barms and dab butties and hot pot and butter pies and riddle bread and tater hash and pan haggerty. Pretty much everything is made of potato and is served up with a side of Manc caviar and bricky's tea. Pea wet is jugged and offered up like free coffee refills are in American diners.

Bally's balances on the edge of the town centre and borders the Range Estate in a sort of no-man's land. The upstairs area is always full of dolers, townies and fallout of the 608. That's how and why me and Flower got to coming here. The gangs, the ones usually chasing us, the thing to avoid, to fear, became the thing protecting us from all the bullshit on the Steps between noon and four, when the only dregs and crusties there are more likely hanging on the hope of a fix of some kind than offering one.

Being a real public place and always busy, as Bally Ann's is, the 608 never bother us for being dregs, or for being here. Even sitting on the back of the plastic bench in an open booth, spiking Flower's hair with pomade while he discovers the wonders of Malkin pie and fat rascals tying off the ends of my own unravelling dreads with the metal casing of cheap gas lighters, none of the gangs say shit to each other, or to us.

'Course, Flower were Polly's boyfriend, so when I hit Bally's I don't expect to see him sat in our usual window booth at the top of the stairs, not today, not when everyone else is at the crem, or more likely by now eating crustless butties cut into tiny triangles and banging on about how much potential Polly had back at Polly's rent's place.

– You OK?

– Far from it, Lay Babes.

Flower mumbles, toying with a lighter.

– They messed up my dole. I don't get paid till next week now. Broke. You go to school today?

I don't answer. I recognise Flower ain't taking an interest in my education, but is asking if I skipped Wayside to catch Polly's funeral like Miss did, and realise Flower must not have gone to the funeral either.

As if silence were the magic word, Flower unballs his fist and flashes a handful of bluish pills.

I follow him into the baby-changing cubicle where we each drop a pill. I bite the third into two crumbly halves we then crush and rail off the loo seat in an attempt to make what we've just dropped hit quicker.

Miss thinks I'm being insensitive, not honouring Polly's life, missing the funeral, risking my own taking this shit instead of taking *their* shit. Maybe I am. Maybe the right thing to do would've been to go watch strangers burn the corpse of someone I knew while people bawled and bullshited about Polly having been a real nice lass with a real nice smile when she spent her whole life priding herself on being a grade A bitch and had an average smile. But fuck maybes. And fuck what's right, if doing the right thing means forsaking feeling good to go watch folk chat sentimental BS while torching a child's body like a campfire marshmallow. Anyone can make their choices sound like the right thing; just got to say the 'right' words.

Reality is, funerals are put on for the living, not the dead, and if that's reality then fuck reality along with the rest of it. Hell knows, Polly would have.

★

— You weren't here in the nineties, Cal tells La, after La had asked why the estate is so full of cops over a bunch of kids smashing some windows.

I don't say shit. There's no way of making La understand. Cal's right; La weren't here back then. She can't get it.

When I were a little kid I used to see the numbers spraypainted on folks' doors and think they were like the crosses on the doors in the book of Exodus when the Pharaoh wouldn't listen, like they'd been put there to save the people from the plagues. When I was little and at Aldgate primary school I thought those tags of '212' were protection, even during the fires and the riots. It was only after that I learned that the numbers identifying house by gang were more like the red cross people daubed on condemned houses during the black death.

Mum and Dad were still together, just about, when the trouble started up back then, but they'd split up by the time the riots began in earnest. Cal was at high school by that time, and Dom, having gotten himself expelled from Aldgate Primary, were enrolled at a school in Morecambe a stone's throw from the flat where me, my dad and my brother Dom lived after the divorce. I still attended Aldgate Primary School in Lancaster though and kicked about with the kids from school who lived for the most part on the estate, even though my mum and dad hadn't lived on the Aldgate estate since I were a baby. After the riots they built a primary school on the flood plain of the Dacrelands Estate, by the river. Dacrelands, where my parents moved when they left the Aldgate Estate and before they split up, didn't have its own school when I were in primary school. Dad used to drive from Morecambe through Torrisholme village to pick me up from my mum's place rather than school so I could still play on the estate with my schoolmates – and to put off having to pick me up, I reckon with hindsight.

Consequently, I ended up seeing some of the shit that went down during the riots. Cal got it worse, though. I were an Aldgate primary kid; the kids knew me. Their older siblings knew me; I could still duck in and out of Aldgate Estate, no problem. When our mum sent Caleb onto the estate to fetch me away during one of the riots though, the 212 had seen him, jumped him and near on killed him. They had been the kids my mum used to make tea for when she lived there, the kids who played video games with Caleb, and had swung baseball bats at piñatas at birthday parties. The guys he'd spent seven years sat next to at Aldgate primary school. The big brothers and sisters of kids I still sat by and ate with when having tea at their 'rents houses.

But Cal had left. So when he reappered, they swung their bats at him. He wouldn't have stood a chance even if it had been just fists they were swinging; Cal's a dreg, not a fighter.

Afterwards, in the hospital, Cal still told the police he didn't remember nothing, he told everyone he didn't remember nothing. Cal didn't even tell me the details about that night. But then, he didn't have to tell me. Just like he didn't have to tell me to keep my mouth shut about it.

– Getting 'noticed' is about the worst thing that can happen.

Caleb reiterates this every time La asks how long he thinks the cops will hang about for, or when our mum will get back from Mon's place so we can leave.

– The cops will be here for days. Weeks. Go if you want.

Cal sighs again, rubbing his eyes.

– I just need to know that my mum gets back in the house safe.

La gets up to look out the kitchen window again, peering over to Mon's house.

– Well, how long will your mum be before she gets back from Mon's?

When Cal don't answer, La looks to me, but I don't even look up from the joint I'm rolling. I know better. I pass Cal the joint, which he sparks right there at the kitchen table, using one of our mum's saucers as an ashtray.

Mon, my mum's only real mate on the estate, got 'noticed' last night. Four other houses got noticed too, but ain't yet got hit. That's half the reason the cops ain't shifting, least for now.

Turns out the end house on Eve Crescent, one door down from Mon's place, there's been a crack house. Neither me, nor Cal heard nothing about it, but then Cal moved here, on to Dacrelands, too old to start hanging with the kids, and I mostly lived in Morecambe with my Dad and brother Dominic. We've always been outsiders, me and Cal, even if we ain't always been dregs. By the time I ended up back at my mum's place after my dad and Dom disappeared, Alastair, Mon's eldest, had set about getting his own crew together: the Dacrelands 414. It were more about fronting about on the estate than anything. Least, it were at first. Like everyone says, this estate is a good one. Seems now though, the 414 finally got themselves noticed. Literally.

When La goes to take a bath, which means do a bag, Cal fills me in, or tries to, on the trouble at Dacrelands since I left here for Miss's house and then Pok, where I've been since Miss won't speak to me for not going to Polly's funeral. Now Polly's gone and Sam's gone mad, my options are kinda limited. More limited. Whatever.

Alastair apparently has his hands in all that crack house BS, and the Wyatts and the Gallows Hill 353 were in it too. So, the Aldgate 212 had been watching them for a while, and warned them all more than once to shut it down, on account of the 212 losing custom their end. Then, some kid sister of a 212 ODs in the place, and two days later there's notices on all the doors of the houses whose kids have been fucking about at proclaiming themselves the Dacrelands 414.

When I got here, Cal had already arrived, La in tow, and calmed our mum down enough to get the story out of her before walking her over to Mon's place. Cal told me our mum called Terry, but he wouldn't come over on account of all the cops that are about.

From what Cal tells me, Mon were sat at the kitchen table that night. She's got diabetes and lost her leg to it last winter, so when the 212 turned up it were all she could do to keep them out. She had the door on the chain when they knocked, and she managed to get it shut properly, but another twenty or so came running, swinging bricks in tights and socks. They smashed out the windows and Mon got all cut up. Mon's youngest, Benny, was out and so was Alastair. They ain't been back, but they'll have heard by now. That's most likely why they ain't turned up here either.

Lately I've seen a lot of Wyatts from the 353 hanging about the estate, in the kiddies' play area and basketball courts by the Jehovah's church. I clocked a few with Miss's twin, Jasper, walking down the cycle track with Alastair the other week. They threw me some abuse – even Jazz – before Alastair said hey to me and they shut up.

Cal looks up at me sharply when I tell him this.

– Don't you go getting involved. Lay, I swear, if I hear –

– I won't. I ain't. Cal, I'm just saying –

– Just nothing. Just say nothing. Just don't.

Even with cops everywhere, in the end, the four other 'noticed' houses get done over and another catches fire after a shed full of paint goes up on the street next to my mum's.

Initially the cops figure that the 212 are responsible for the fire, but turns out that weren't the 212's doing; just Josephine, The Madwoman at Number Nineteen, who got a little excited when it all kicked off and lit the fire up.

The police pick Josephine up, while she's dancing on the shed roof barefoot and in nowt but her nightie, and we watch from mum's bedroom window, Cal

searching for our mum, La waiting on the cops to fuck
off, and me just watching them try drag Josephine off.
The scene's like out of *Jane Eyre*, when Rochester's mad
wife is dancing on the roof having torched the place,
but I don't say nothing. I know Cal wouldn't get it. He'd
probably think Jane Eyre was some member of the 414
and start stressing at me again about keeping my nose
out and my gob shut.

★

Perhaps the only upside of my mum's estate becoming
a fucking gangland is that Miss has finally forgiven me
for not going to Polly's funeral. Or she's just had to
contextualise shit. So I make it to Wayside the next
morning, Cal having rung for the taxi to pick me up so
La can cadge a free lift away from the estate.

Lea, our English Lit teacher, has decided to start a
family despite what she's learned from working here,
so Mr Ramsey, a substitute teacher used to teaching
mainstream school kids, comes to cover her maternity
leave. It's his first day.

Nicole is put in the other group with Hazel and
Danny. Anne takes them into the other room. When
we're alone, Miss says we should go easy on the new
teacher.

Miss always says we should go easy on them. Miss
means I should go easy. Andrew never gives an opinion,

he never has one; and seeing as Ryan always goes with the majority vote and I don't object, when Mr Ramsey walks into the room we are all sitting, quiet and patient, like normal kids.

Mr Ramsey instantly looks suspicious. Miss pretends not to notice Mr Ramsey eyeing us like our good behaviour is somehow a ruse, or trap. Miss also pretends not to notice what I have, what Ryan has, what even Andrew can't ignore.

– Why would you grow a titchy black moustache if you looked just like Hitler?

Ryan whispers behind his hand. Everybody shuffles in their seats, but nobody replies.

Clearing his throat, Mr Ramsey hands us all printouts of a poem and watches us as, in unison, our hands reach over the table and turn the papers over.

We are set the task of figuring out this poem by Gillian Clarke called 'The Babysitter'. After about ten minutes we are told to take it in turns to give our interpretations. I say I figure it is about postnatal depression. Not really into it. Not really into anything today. But apparently Mr Ramsey is into it. And is determined to get into it with me too.

He frowns, spinning the printout to face him and staring into the paper as if my comment could be the result of some typo or some shit. Confident there are no typos, Mr Ramsey asks:

– Didn't you read the title?

I re-read the title, upside down, like that could somehow reveal whatever he seems to think I've missed.

– Do you know what *babysitting* means?

I look to Miss. Miss gives a subtle shake of her head, but I weren't looking for approval.

I turn back to Mr Ramsey.

– Sure. Do you know what *metaphorical* means?

Straight up, as if he's been waiting for this, Mr Ramsey starts yelling. All of us sit there wide-eyed, while this stranger who looks like Hitler spits at us. Mad, sudden shouting like he spent the days ahead of his arrival deciding what would happen, and is now determined to prove himself right. Needed the money too much to turn it down?

– You know what really gets me? I mean, what *really* gets me about oiks like you? I'll be paying your dole one day! In a few years I'll be paying for you to be scum!

– Sir –

He ignores Miss, leaning close into my face and getting louder, despite being so close he could whisper and I'd still have to hear his bullshit.

– Scum! And you don't even care, do you? *Do you?* Answer me, you –

I'm midway through admitting I don't care, when Miss jumps back in.

– Sir, Lay just –

So then he rounds on Miss, pointing a stubby finger right in her face and exclaiming,

– And *you* –

– And what?

I ask, knocking my chair over backwards in the process, to square up to this guy.

Except, then Chris steps in, after hearing the shouting and stopping suddenly when she sees Mr Ramsey stood stock-still pointing at Miss. And me stock-still pointing at Mr Ramsey, and all of us looking about ready to start a fight like some mad Western, our fingers guns.

Ryan explains we're reading Gillian Clarke's 'Babysitting', laughing so much he half-falls off his chair when Chris replies, seeming chuffed rather than pissed at how animated a poetry class has gotten us all:

– Oh, really? I wrote a paper on Gillian Clarke in college. You know she had post-natal depression?

At that, I kick the upturned chair from behind me and walk from the classroom into the main room without waiting to get sent out.

McQuaide, as if she hadn't sent Chris in to us to investigate the noise, glances up from her desk, watches me walk to the Naughty Corner, and returns to her paperwork, without speaking.

Sitting down, I find my science workbook already placed on the table, a post-it note stuck over it instructing me to turn to page whatever. Above, the instructions:

Don't speak. Don't disrupt the others. Don't argue. And

don't move until the bell rings. And if you'd done that in the first place, you wouldn't be here now, would you?

★

Without a tourniquet, La slips the needle in, humming softly as if charming the blood that snakes up into the barrel as she pulls back on the plunger with her thumbnail. Plunging the solution and sliding the needle back out, La re-caps the pin and throws it like a dart into a corner.

– Cal told me about this.

Taking a pouch of bacca from on top of the notebook, La points at the blank box on the cover of the notebook.

– You haven't written on it.

Ignoring her and poking at the better of the two fattest veins in the ditch of my right arm, I feel first the slight pop where it breaks the skin and subsequently the pop and then subtle ache that signals I've hit a vein.

– Caleb said it belonged to Jim.

La asks, or just says. I can't tell. I watch her spread her hand over the blank cover, and look away. Drawing the plunger back, a thread of blood unfurls like a stem and blooms into the barrel like a rose trapped in a bell jar.

– They say there's over sixteen million books already in the British Library.

I tell La while depressing the plunger slowly, so the gear hits before the barrel is even emptied.

La laughs, so soft the sound issues like a purr. Maybe it is.

I slide the needle out, let my arm drop like a drawbridge and watch the pin roll from my hand onto the reel. La pulls a sheet of stained foil over the works, a polite gesture like a napkin on a plate but which somehow makes me think more of a coroner pulling the sheet over a corpse.

She leans back against the wall, her eyelids beneath yellow and lilac eye shadow suddenly fluttering. I tilt my head back against the wall, watching La's eyes struggling to stay open, like butterflies readying to fly from the otherwise-grey debris of some city levelled by an earthquake. She holds a cigarette loosely in her mouth, its smoke rising as if from ruins.

I know that if my own eyes shut they won't open again, least not till it's dark outside. As if she's thinking the same thing, La pulls herself up. She makes this simple act look like waking up to a job you hate, and stretches, saying in her Yank drawl, that makes her sound cool, even inflected with Lanky mannerisms and gear:

– All the words in all the world's libraries, ain't none of them your words though. And that book, it ain't Jim's, not now.

La yawns, spreading her arms so the flesh hangs

from the bone.

— It should be your name on the cover.

★

For days, weeks, Jim and me, we just read Baudelaire and listened to Patti Smith on old cassette tapes we'd picked up at Afflecks Palace or cadged on CD from the library.

Sharing one set of earphones, we'd crank the cassette Walkman Cal had handed me down or Jim's CD Walkman full volume and smoke till we could barely tell where our own bodies began or ended. Then, we'd fuck, half-dazed and gouging out on top of each other, unable to cum or care.

When it got dark, we'd shamble out for vending machine soup and coffees from the 24-hour taxi office. Sitting amongst guys in suits, loved-up couples and hen parties of pissed-up women in tutus, we'd listen to their conversations and their rows, the only folk there who weren't trying to go no place or waiting on a ride to take us elsewhere.

There were nowhere to go from there. We felt invincible. Like we were already dead. Nobody could touch us. Nothing could touch us. Not then. Weren't like we were in heaven, but it felt so fucking good to suddenly not feel like we were in hell either. Being nothing, but being nothing together.

But then people started looking for us.

It were the first day in fuck knows how many we ventured out and to Dalton Square, where everyone used to hang out before Jim's 'accident', before we all sort of crept away like murderers from a crime scene and began hanging at the museum steps instead.

Nobody gave us a hard time when we reappeared, or if they did, we didn't notice. I figure everyone were too sure that we'd scarper if they did. Now we had somewhere to scarper to. And a place they didn't dare follow us, and we knew it. And they knew we knew it. So, the atmosphere was a little charged, but nobody were about to draw on it. I guess they were just waiting.

Bull and Cal finally arrived, approaching as if about to go at us. We knew someone would call them. I stood my ground. Weren't like Cal would, or could, actually go at me, y'know? But Jim, seeing Bull, automatically stepped back, trying to evade his brother's reach, like. Ironic, really; it were the one time Jim weren't up for a scrap with his brother. The one time Jim was the one out of the two of them to back down, the one time he were trying to avoid being hit.

The car came like a black brushstroke smearing across my view. Like some masterpiece destroyed on an artist's mad whim just 'cause some detail or other weren't working out how they imagined it or sommet.

Our eyes just slipped from each other like hands and Jim was gone, folk swimming around me like half-finished, definitionless blurs you can't make out till you stand back, whilst Jim's head just poured out all this shit onto the cobbles. There were so much blood my hands couldn't contain it; like that mattered. Like, if I could catch all of it, I could put the pieces back together and everything would be OK.

They said it was instant and Jim died without even knowing it. I guess they were trying to offer comfort, but that's the bit that gets me most; the idea of dying so suddenly you don't even know it's happening and never will because then you're just dead. What a gyp that is, not death so much, but dying without even knowing it. I don't know why that gets to me so much, but it does; the idea death can just happen. That, and the BS people peddle about made-up shit like 'justice'. The fact people make up concepts like justice when you can die without even knowing that *this is it*.

Like they were desperate to convince themselves I were sloping off to grieve, people kept trying to console me for ages, tell me Jim was in a better place, his soul were at rest, he weren't in pain no more. When that didn't work, folk resorted to telling me it weren't my fault.

You really notice that when people die: the need to blame something, or someone. The inability to look death in the eye. Face it. Face everything. Face blame. People tell you what *they* need to hear. Owt, I guess, to arm themselves against the reality, and the only real truth.

People discriminate. Death don't. Dead is dead. It has to be. That's the whole fucking point. Concepts like religion don't give life meaning – death does.

★

Aberdeenie Jeanie cut sixth-form this afternoon to show us the letter. She took it to the library and had copies made so she could hand them out amongst us all. The cops are even giving out twenty-four hour bans and eighty quid fines for people loitering on the museum steps. How they plan on enforcing that one is anyone's guess. I suppose we'll see, anyhow.

Dear Parent or Guardian

As principal of Lancaster Girls' Grammar School, I am increasingly concerned for the welfare of a number of students who consider themselves members of an organisation calling itself 'The Dregs'.

The school feels any student's participation in gang behaviour is intolerable and that the organisation known as 'The Dregs' is a negative presence in the community, compromising the reputation and safety of the school as a whole and the wellbeing of its pupils. Because of this, I, and the staff at Lancaster Girls' Grammar School, wish to make it abundantly clear that pupils affiliated with this gang will be dealt with accordingly. Any antisocial, violent or disrespectful behaviour either directed towards staff and/

or students at this school will also be treated as serious.

Parents and guardians should be aware that a number of the members of the gang known as The Dregs are known or convicted as paedophiles, drug dealers, and adults with criminal convictions which include violent crimes. These are individuals who are regularly at the heart of antisocial behaviour within the community.

Incidents that staff and students at Lancaster Girls' Grammar School have become aware of involving the gang known as The Dregs have, in recent months, included: drug abuse, violent acts, theft, criminal damage, vandalism and threatening behaviour. Lesser offences have included vandalism of the museum itself, which is a Grade II listed building, blocking the entrance of the museum and gift shop, skateboarding in the city centre, public drinking, and verbal abuse both of police officers attempting to remove the gang from the city centre and members of the public attempting to shop in the area.

Due to the seriousness of this situation, the administration at Lancaster Girls' Grammar has come to the decision that any student seen to be congregating at the Museum's steps or socialising with known members of this gang while wearing school uniform stands at risk of instant suspension.

While the school is unable to enforce punishments for students while not wearing school uniform, any crimes committed outside of school time may result in investigations into those pupils' behaviours during school hours, which may result in pupils being disciplined or even permanently expelled from attending Lancaster Girls' Grammar school. The behaviour of

*a minority of students, which jeopardises both the overall excellence
of the school and the safety of the many students who attend to
pursue an education, will not be tolerated or ignored.*

*Finally, a PTA meeting is being held to discuss the matter
further and the school urges all parents to attend and make their
voices heard. Concerned parents and guardians are asked to please
meet in the Atrium at 6pm on the 22nd of November. Until that
time, any parent or guardian concerned that their child may
have ties with a member of this gang or has experienced abuse
or bullying from gang members is urged to contact the school
administration board, and the local authorities.*

Yours sincerely,
M. K. Burton

– So where's the letter for the effing 212 or the 608?

Cal furiously screws up the copy of the letter AJ passed
to him.

– Like anyone's dumb enough to write that.

– They ain't sending letters about the 212 or 608, Cal,
'cause no kid off Aldgate or from The Range goes to
Girls' Grammar.

– No one off Aldgate goes anywhere.

AJ laughs at Bull's reasoning.

– It all comes down to territory, Cal, and you know it.

Bull pauses, as if to afford Cal the time to realise he
knows it. And then remembers it's Cal he's talking to.

– The 212, the 608, all the gangs for that matter, they

all have their own estates, turf, schools. We're dregs. We're the scum on the surface. Course it's easier to target and chase us out; we ain't got no estate to call our own. We ain't got nowt and nowhere –

– We've got each other…

The older lot laugh at Miss, tossing each other eyerolls. Except for Cal. He just looks at Miss incredulously, and then tosses me a scowl like she is somehow my fault.

★

On account of Christmas, Pok is full, not just of junkies, but of those on their way, the not-yet-junkies, all the kids and drunks and general human detritus who have a mate's place to stay but, this time of year, been cleared out to make room for artificial trees and strings of cards that go on about the essence of Christmas spirit.

It gets like a refugee camp at Pok around Christmastime.

I wake most days to new faces, and wonder how many of these will become familiar faces, old faces. How many of these kids will lose the last bit of themselves here, or sell it. How many of these old guys, sleeping rough for decades without giving in, will give in this Christmas. And I wonder how many of them look around and think the same about me. If anyone would even notice if I just disappeared.

The ones who keep their shit tight by them, never talking much and never fully unzipping their rucksacks, multiply at Christmas too. Everyone hates them for the way they go about looking like they've something worth beating them for. Sometimes even I want to scream at them: take a look around; what have you got to lose at this point? Bit late to start taking precautions now, ain't it? It creates a fucking atmosphere. Feeds the crack paranoia like pre-storm electricity in the air and makes for rows and scenes. But even here, I'm a fifteen-year-old kid, and there are rules.

Sometimes, usually when arguments kick off amongst my mates, or some shotter or whoever storms in shouting and shaking people awake looking for So-and-so, or I wake with someone's hand rifling my pockets, or worse, I think of leaving. I think of the guys, of the dregs. And I think of my mum.

I know if I turned up and laid the sob story on any one of them, they would let me in. Even my mum. If I cried or something. If I just said what they wanted to hear. If I told them I was sorry.

Sometimes I even imagine it so much I actually end up standing in front of their houses, like I've magicked myself there or something, but I guess that's where the magic runs out: the point at which imagination and reality meet, so next thing, I'm right back here again, like it were all just a dream. Sometimes I don't even know if it were just all part of a nod.

★

Miss takes the packet of cigarettes I offer without looking up and shakes out a smoke with one hand, texting with the other. Resting the mobile on her thigh, we both watch the screen dull then light up again.

I lean forward off the seat, resting my forehead on my palms.

– Fuck's sake, grow up, Miss, will ya?

Miss turns from her mobile to look at me.

– What the hell do you think I'm trying to do?

– Sulk?

– Then maybe *you* need to grow up, Layla.

Miss returns her eyes to her mobile.

She won't speak to me 'cause she found works in my bag, but she'll still shot with me 'cause she needs the money to pay for her own habits – and her mum's. So, we while away the time, waiting for the bus, in silence.

I'm left to turning the deck of pickpocketed smokes over in my hands.

We didn't always pickpocket, me and Dom. We started out on the straight and narrow with a paper round. But Dom shotputted the whole bundle into an alley-O one day, after finding out Dad hadn't been saving our wages for us as he'd said, but were instead blowing them in the pub as we earned them. That was just after the divorce, when we'd both been sent to live with Dad; when Dad realised my mum was serious, this time.

Turned out, so was the newsagent; he prosecuted. Dom got a suspended sentence – out of leniency, they said. Dad were less lenient. He knocked so much sense into Dom that time that he near on knocked his grey matter straight out his ears. Dom spent two weeks in Preston Infirmary with swelling of the brain. I thought Dad had killed Dom that night. Seeing Dom punched out like an alarm clock and then just lying there silent and broke like that, I reckon that's when it first hit me that one day sommet would have to give. I just didn't know then what or when or who, or how.

It never occurred to Dom to change though. After all, what could we change, except gigs? When Dad moved us to Queen Street and three big high-street banks bought out some of the derelict real estate on the promenade, Dom got a new idea.

I'd sit on the freshly-cleaned limestone steps of each bank beside the cash points till someone clocked me. Then, I'd begin to skryke 'bout being abandoned by my so-called mates and having no bus fare. If a stranger offered me a lift, I'd point out that innocent little girls don't just hop into strangers' cars. And innocent grown-ups don't ask them too. They'd usually pass over a few quid and back off, and I'd make my way to the next bank, Dom catching up with me and taking the money in the cobbled byways behind cheap hotels and pubs in case any of the other kids saw my game and tried robbing me between spots.

It seemed like easy money, till some drunk couple our dad knew collared me and threatened to tell our dad.

That's when we began robbing from Dad's local, The Rising Sun. We'd been doing odd jobs for the landlady; used to take her pit-bull, Mossy, for walks down Morecambe prom and stuff. Were like she felt obliged to keep us out of trouble seen as she got our Dad pissed enough to guarantee we'd be in trouble no matter what we did at kicking-out time – a time which had its own meaning for the kids of the pub's patrons.

Eventually the landlady got to letting us take the trays from the till upstairs, to cash up at lunch, and after hours too if we hadn't got bored and dribbled back into Morecambe's alleys already. For months we filched a twenty, sometimes thirty, never more than forty, from the trays, noting who was working what shift. We either exploited new bar staff, taking more on their shifts only, or balanced smaller amounts over the course of the week. That gig went tits-up when Dad, in a withdrawal-fuelled rage (the only thing worse than a drunken rage) turned our room over hoping to find contraband booze and instead found wads of notes counted out in bank-change bags.

If we'd ripped off a bank Dad would've been proud, but we'd ripped off a pub. Worse, we'd ripped off Dad's pub. Dom nearly lost an ear that time. The doctors saved it, but it weren't ever the same. A boxer's ear, Dad used to say, afterwards, roping Dom into a hug more like a headlock and giving him a noogie.

Hell, we did all sorts after that. I used to wonder sometimes if our dad hadn't bust something inside Dom's head afer all, some of the ideas and plans he came up with, and we carried out, too.

For years we shotted for the lady downstairs, when we lived in Tuppence Passage down by The Battery in Morecambe's notorious West End. She'd catch me and Dom on the stairs, poking her head and a bony finger out of her apartment like Hansel and Gretel's witch and offering us cigarettes, purple sweets that tasted like cheap perfume, tins of cider, and eventually money when Dom realised how desperate she were.

When she was out hooking at The Cat House or one of the other 'massage parlours' in Lancaster or along 'slut strip' on the Bay above Morecambe's rock and candyfloss shops, we broke in the flat a few times, but there were never anything worth cadging.

The whole place was littered with white Narcotics Anonymous keyrings, coiled KY tubes and pop-bottle crack pipes. The flat always smelt of sour milk. She even invited us in once when she were high and gave me one of the white keyrings. Its silver-embossed lettering like a joke I weren't in on, least not then.

She said they dubbed her 'the white keyring queen' at Narcotics Anonymous, and told us that once she'd saved thirty up, and then enquired at the next meeting if she could cash them in for an orange keyring? Laughing till she were wheezing and had to get up to hock back a load of gob into the kitchen sink.

For nearly two years, even after we moved to a new building above a Bargain Booze offy in Strawberry Gardens in Heysham, me and Dom would trek the three miles to pick up for the White Keyring Queen at the weekends, right up until Deano, this kid who lived nearby and used to shot for her during the week, went in one day and found her all bloated and naked and purple on the sofa with her legs spread, slumped over her genitals which had somehow prolapsed. Deano took a picture and showed all the street kids. I didn't even know her name until Deano passed me the Polaroid, asking if I'd seen what happened to old Mary? I only looked to see who old Mary was.

Her lips were solid black. Her stomach looked like a ripped-open sack and her flesh was mottled with purple veins and sweat, like some mouldy, rotten smelling cheese posh folk would spread on crackers.

You can become desensitised to almost anything, no matter how horrific, but somehow that image of old Mary, it haunts my mind like she did that flat.

★

The last day of Wayside before the Christmas holidays. I only came 'cause I knew lessons would be benched in favour of festive stuff. Sure enough, McQuaide springs a 'Christmas treat': we all have to make Christmas cards out of this glitter stuff you blow with hairdryers onto card so it sets like plastic. Ryan's already throwing a tantrum, wanting those novelty scissors that cut in zigzags, while the rest of us cut zigzags with safety scissors, which being plastic, never cut straight, anyway.

I make a card with a red sparkling Virgin Mary on the front of an ivory card, because that's the only stamp no one else bagsied and the only colour card no one else wanted. Blank. I then spent twenty minutes staring at it, trying to figure out who I can actually write to.

★

I ain't seen Sam since Polly died. Don't even know if she went to Polly's funeral. Perhaps that's why Sam's mum is reluctant to let me in. Maybe she thinks I'm a shit mate for not coming sooner. Maybe she is still pissed at me for that bottle of bourbon I took from hers last time me and Polly were up here. Maybe she's just being a mum.

I hand her the Christmas card, then follow her up the hall before she can tell me not to, to where she shuts the lounge door and shuts me out. After a minute, the door reopens. I briefly catch sight of Sam on the sofa, chewing the sleeve of her jumper, her eyes reflecting scenes on the TV, and I try shouting her name, quick, but Sam's mum shuts the door.

She begins shooing me out, not even bothering
to make up an excuse or even just *ask* me to leave the
house. Sam's mum is herding me up the hall, and so
quick I don't even have time to turn and instead sort
of reverse, tripping over slippers and cat toys until
she actually pushes me backwards over the front step.
I almost land on my arse and automatically grab the
doorframe at each side to try prevent myself from going
arse over tit onto the driveway.

Staring up at Sam's mum, as if to ask what the hell,
I see her eyes fill and brace myself for her shouting or
hitting me or whatever, but she just lets go this tiny sob
almost without sound, and the door shuts between us.

I hear her set the lock and I kick the door. Imagining
her jumping with fright behind it, I kick it again and
start shouting madly through the letterbox:

— Who's *my* mother meant to blame? Your kid? You?

I hang about a while before giving up, pointlessly
turning a few circles on the drive and kicking at the
gravel and spitting obscenities.

From the street, I glance back at the house and see
Sam watching me from the lounge window. She don't
look mad I've just cursed her mum. She don't even look
real. More like one of the white plastic dolls that crowd
her bedroom. Her eyes are unflinching, glassy. And we
just stare at each other until something moves behind
her and suddenly the blinds drop down.

★

I slide my finger over the kettle switch, close my eyes and hold my breath. The kettle shakes beneath my grip, like how I used to imagine a portkey from the Harry Potter books would sort of rev up, filling with magic like an engine flooding, about to suck me away and let me drift like an ember gently down into some other reality, some place a million miles from here.

Reaching boiling point, I don't even jump at the switch when it flips out no more. It's like I'm watching someone else react, like I have gone someplace else already and now I'm just watching what's about to happen.

In my peripheral vision, my mum's powder-pink dressing gown flashes past the kitchen doorway. From the corner of the Formica countertop I pick up the coffee jar. I'm uselessly twisting the lid, trying to get it open, when my brother storms in, grabs my shoulders and yanks me out, twisting me to face him.

– She's fucking insane. She's in my goddamn room!

My voice rising in me feels like sick, so I gag instead of speaking.

– She's up there wrecking all my stuff. Lay, for fuck's sake, go stop her!

Next thing, I'm standing dumbly in the bedroom doorway, like how dreams move from one to the next without reason or explanation. Somehow I'm still holding the coffee jar in both hands and think stupidly I'm like one of Baby Jesus' Magi holding out an offering. My mum pauses when she notices me. She frowns at the jar and then at me. When I don't say owt, my mum just returns to screaming, at me now, not Cal. It's the usual tirade on how there ain't nowt I can do except Get to Fuck. She shouts about how I roll in at stupid o' clock, use the house like a hotel and how that's all anyone does, how everyone sucks her dry. How sick and tired she is, of everyone.

Cal shouts up the stairs something about how he pays rent and has rights and our mum stops crashing about the bedroom and rushes out onto the landing, ramming me out the way. I don't even put my hands out. I feel my feet leave the carpet and just close my eyes, wondering where this next dream will drop me.

Reality resumes about me like when you wake suddenly and grope for the bed, feeling as if you're about to fall off the edge of the world.

The coffee jar, suddenly loosened, spills over me in one black wave. My back hitting against the handles on the chest of drawers and my skin wet suddenly with sweat, I feel my heart beating in me like an alarm bell, metabolising up the gear left in my blood. I have to get out of here.

– Thirty quid? You eat more than that, you selfish bastard! And who cooks your meals, eh? Who irons your shirts? Well, not no more, oh no.

Mum charges back in to snatch at the bundle of Cal's clothes she'd thrown onto the floor, hauling me then from the room and throwing me out. I fall a second time, arse over tit onto the landing, shifting my back against the wall to stop her from landing on top of me.

– I'll take the fucking keys. You ain't throwing my stuff out!

Cal screams up the stairs, still safely out of her way.

– Then I'll throw everything out the fucking window!

My mum tries to step over me to get down the stairs with a handful of Cal's clothing. Cal has started on about the neighbours and it being the middle of the night, but Mum has turned on me.

– And you, coming back here for nowt but fucking motty and fucking off again soon as you have it. Do not even get me started on you, madam, 'cause y'won't be here when you're old 'nough to be out that door for good. I'm telling you that now. I've done my bit and then some far as you're concerned.

I hear the keys jangle in Caleb's hand at the foot of the stairs.

– We ain't done owt. You're fucking wrong in the head. Look at her, what've you done to her?

Mum looks at me where I'm curled foetally at the top of the stairs, throws Cal's clothes in the air, lets rip this huge wail and starts back towards the landing just as I've climbed back onto my feet.

On account of her being only 5'2", her forehead butts me straight in the nose. Blood runs down over my lips instantly and my mum runs into her room, slamming her bedroom door shut behind her.

Taking the stairs three at a time without feeling where my feet are landing, or knowing if they have, I make it to the hall. Grabbing my leather jacket and bag from the banister post, I make for the front door. The bangs coming from mum's room, like contractions, intensifying the whole time. Then, I realise: foil. I need foil. I dart back into the kitchen, pulling the whole roll from the drawer and turning to really get out, but Cal still has the key and stops me in the kitchen doorway.

– Go and make her stop, Layla.

Me and Cal both pause, hearing the bedroom door open. Clothes start raining over the banister.

– Just let her go. Here, she can take all your shit with her!

Mum is leaning over the landing banister. Cal screams up at her.

– Go to bed, you fucking maniac! What, you going to headbutt *me* too now? You're a psycho, you know that, a fucking psycho! You ought to be locked up!

Gathered up amidst the clothes, the cordless telephone handset hits Caleb on the head like a brick and makes him reel back.

– So ring the fucking police! Have me locked up, you ungrateful bastard!

Somehow, I pull the back door key from its hook on the hallway wall and make for the garden, realising only when I'm in the garden that Caleb is shouting for me.

– Layla, please – just go back and make her stop – sis, you can't just leave me.

And when I ignore him:

– I swear it, I'll tell mum. I'll tell her everything! I'll tell her what you are and she'll put you in fucking care like she always meant to. I fucking stopped her. You can't just fuck off. You... you... you fucking selfish junkie bitch!

But I am already gone.

★

In a cubicle lit by halogen, I swing my legs from a bariatric bed. My toes just catch the linoleum. I could be three years old again. Everything seems so big. The plastic-covered foam mattress crackles beneath my arse like a baby-changing mat. Except where the doctor is stood, having pulled my trousers from me, ten-inch snap on side rails surround me like crib bars.

– Can you lie back on the bed, please; your leg needs to remain elevated.

I'm wondering, if I lay down, whether I'll end up on a ward in paper knickers, or get whisked away to the Tate Modern. A new installation: The ASBO Generation.

– Are you on any medication?

The doctor gives a sideways glance while inspecting

the knife wound. I make some noncommittal gesture and she writes something on a clipboard.

– When did you last eat?

I frown, trying to make days out of the last knot of time I've just worked my way out of. Giving up, I shrug. I genuinely do not know.

What I do know is that this lady has the power with a signature to unlock the medicine store and pull free Valium, codeine, morphine, fentynal.

– Lie back, please.

I fold my arms, leaning back into the bariatric crib, catching sight of my trousers in a pile on the floor, and glance away from this stranger, who I know has the power to have me sectioned with a signature. My ribs stand up and jut forward. Beneath, my stomach dips and the skin pulls taut to my hips. I don't know how all my insides can even fit into a space that small.

– You haven't eaten today?

I catch sight of the food trolley abandoned outside the cubicle; a label on its titanium steel side-plate reads 'regeneration unit'.

– I could use some pain relief...

The doctor hears me, and ignores me.

– Any alcohol or drugs in the last forty-eight hours?

I shake my head, looking down at my white slab of thigh and the black stitches she's just tied off with a small black bead. The whole thing looks absurd, like a sentence from a page half-torn away.

– Did you do this to yourself, or...

I nod, and the doctor don't go on to finish her question. I nod so that the doctor don't bother finishing the question. And so that I don't have to do more than nod in reply.

It's pointless trying to explain to a medical professional that I hadn't meant it to happen. That I hadn't thought on how I were still holding the blade when I'd punched my thigh. That I hadn't even meant to punch myself, nevermind stab myself; that I'd just spilt a whole bag of gear and weren't punching out at myself, but more generally at the whole thing.

When I nod, I know she won't ask me why or if I meant to stab myself either; when you're a teenager with more piercings than facial features and half your friends' initials – some dinged with once-'ultramarine' Indian ink – scarring your arms, doctors rarely do ask if you meant to stab or cut or burn or whatever yourself when you shuffle in through the curtains.

The doctor insists again that I lie back before disappearing through the curtain divide; like, if I lie down while she's there, there's more chance I'll still be there when she returns.

I slide from the bed and pull my jeans back on over the undressed wound. The small beads scabbing over catch, and I feel the warmth of fresh blood spreading beneath the denim before I've even got the fly zipped. I glance about the cubicle automatically, like after a one-night stand, making sure I've left no evidence. Or, more like, as though there's going be a bottle of diamorphine or oramorph or pethadine or fentanyl – or, fuck it, anything, left out for me like morning-after coffee or money.

All I see is the magnetic suspension system curtain rail and read the brand label embossed along the smooth, plastic light fittings. Clit says that flat light fixtures and magnetic blind rails are used in prison to avoid suicide attempts. I wonder if every cubicle is equipped with anti-self-destruction fixtures, or is this just the cubicle cases like me get brought to? Beside a light fixture, a yellow Sharps bin with its toybox-red lid hangs from an exposed nail on the wall.

Hearing the doctor, I fasten my jeans button and slip back into my unlaced sneakers. My left shoe sole is wet on the inside where the blood had run down my leg into it. I edge over to the curtain divide so I can catch sight of the doctor as she shakes her head, leaning at a small nurse's station.

– Fifteen. No parental contact. Underweight. Stabs herself with a four-inch blade. Pupils like pinheads. I can't even get a name out of her...

Hearing her say it, like out loud, the reality of the situation wells in me; there's no chance this woman is going to write a painkiller script.

An older, fatter, male doctor beside her shrugs, preoccupied filling in a script for whoever is sat beyond the roller wheel curtain divide in the next cubicle.

Slipping from the cubicle, eyes searching out a green exit sign, I hear a patient behind the curtain divider through which the older fatter doctor disappeared.

– Thanks. I need these... no, no, just to sleep, of course. It's my psychiatrist, he said I'm neurotic. Can you believe that? I just can't get over it.

★

The light drops from the sky like hourglass sand.

Soon, the only folk left and not in doorways will be as drunk as those who are. Some will be more drunk. On more drugs. All flocking to bars like moths to artificial light.

Till then, cross-legged on one of the benches out front of Lancaster Bus Station, I watch folk pour in to the depot as if night is a shadow cast by some great leering monster that's about to swoop down and lock its jaws around their heads and carry them off.

Sometimes I think that's the only real reason people rush about doing anything. Out here, things just *are*, till they *ain't*; in the meantime, there's just what a person can do and what they can't do. Out here, people don't sit about saying they'd die to have this or that, they just get on with dying for it, whatever it is they need in order not to die or feel like they're dying. The streets at night hold the secret truth of every city.

Like mirrors or the picture of Dorian Gray, nobody wants to face people in doorways because nobody wants to face themselves, not really. The reality that every gutter tramp framed by a dark doorway is someone; someone's kid, someone's ex, someone's fault.

It's too scary. So, when we can't smile, we just paint one. And so nobody tells the world what they are. All anyone does is tell the world what they want. That's why most folk refuse to meet eyes with the homeless. That's why those who do kneel before them, as if to gods, offering money and food and gifts. And that's why folk get indignant when homeless people refuse what's being offered; them doing the offering ain't offering mercy, they're begging for it. We all are.

Any fucker who says otherwise wouldn't last a day out here: the truth would off them at a glance.

*

The bus stutters through midday traffic as it approaches Galgate.

It has begun to rain, but softly. Dampness fills the air fluffily, like clouds. I recall a time in my Dad's truck when we drove so high up this hill, in Scotland, somewhere, that we literally entered the clouds. I wound the window down to cut through the fug of whiskey and cigarette smoke. It were so cold, but I stuck my whole body out into the haze until I were so far out my Dad looped a finger into my jeans to prevent me from falling from the cabin as we reached the apex and he flung the lorry into neutral to defy the speed inhibitor. Then, we plummeted back down to earth, pretty literally.

I watch my reflection in the bus window blur and melt like a late Monet along with the memory as the fixed pane begins to condensate.

– Stop kicking my seat, Lay.

– What would you spend the money on, if you didn't spend it on grass and shit?

I ask the back of Miss's head.

– What makes you think I'd be doing this if I didn't need the money to pay for 'grass and shit'?

I shrug, not that Miss sees it.

– Me and my brother, Dom, we once spent thirty quid on gnomes from the local Garden Centre and arranged them round the lounge. Scared the shit out of Dad when he woke after a sesh with Uncle Keith, who weren't really our uncle, course.

Miss shakes her head, but I clock her misted reflection; in the pane, the corners of her smudgy lips upturn into a reluctant smile, but only for an instant before the condensation begins distorting her face, so it begins to melt before my eyes, and I'm reminded of Mary the White Keyring Queen, and her bloated dead flesh and knurly face. The gnomes had only lasted an afternoon before my dad and Keith had lobbed them from the window. From two floors below, people crowded around, picking up shards of rosy cheeks and slithers of moony eyes and looking up at the flat, trying to piece together what the fuck had happened. Maybe that's why Mary had nailed her windows shut. Maybe she weren't just trying to keep folk out, after all, but keep whatever were in there with her from pushing her over the edge.

Someone had called her Mary though, named her, loved her. She must've had parents, once. *Someone* made her. Someone spent nine months creating and carrying her. Still, perhaps no one had ever loved her, never not given up on the White Keyring Queen, never believed anything of her from the start. I wonder what sort of kid she'd been. If Mary had dreamed of some sort of career, of being a mum, of being anything, before...

If there was a before.

Maybe Mary were a mum. I wonder if she had mates. Someone she once called her best mate. Where they were when she'd ODed and needed them. How many people she said 'I love you' to in her life. I wonder if it is possible to go through life without ever saying those words, without hearing them, without meaning them. Why it was some kid who found her. Some kid who only found her 'cause even he was looking for money.

Usually, we spent the money hitting the penny arcades along the promenade, betting on those mechanical horseracing games in order to hear the guy who did the commentary from this little side box; or playing Space Invaders, checking out who had the highest score each Saturday. Dom loved the arcade. All the kids did. The lights. Everything being in 8-bit and two dimensions. The sound of winning.

Miss sighs, rubbing a circle clear in the opaque window and staring through it. She gets up, reaches over me to press the button so the driver will know to stop on the corner of Archibald Road, and then puts out her open hand to me. I reach to take it and she draws it back, raising her eyebrows.

– Lay, the money. I need the money.

★

The more money me and Miss make the less time we spend together lately. Miss splits the bus at the station, heading home. I split for Pok.

This homeless guy travelling through, asks us: what's the difference between us, between humans and animals? That gets a pretty decent bit of gab going up at Pok, stirring up the overhanging atmosphere without spilling blood. The sort of banter Jim used to always get going, making you suddenly see all whole new sides and dimensions to folk; crackheads getting philosophical and smackheads resiting nodding out just to chat to each other about supermassive black holes.

It sort of became a thing, our thing, trying to shock each other, but Jim were into shocking anyone, everyone. He used to jump up and start reciting Larkin or Oscar Wilde sometimes just to get a rise out of Bull or the guys at the Steps. And it worked, every time. It were like watching someone acting possessed in church. Everyone would prang out, not least because if a guy in 80's Perry Boy garb starts mouthing off at the Steps, it usually means trouble. All you had to do were quit telling him to pipe down, and he would. But no one ever did. Someone always gave Jim the reaction he wanted. And it were usually Bull.

I've never seen anyone square up to Bull like Jim used to. It were always Jim on the floor, pinned under Bull, when the two would call quits. Jim always started it and Bull always ended it, but Bull was always the one who looked broke afterwards. So long as *something* was happening, Jim was grinning. Jim weren't scared of nothing, except nothingness. I guess that's why Jim were known at Pok for his gab, and why no one at Pok ever sparked him out for it, even when it were obvious they wanted to. When it came to fighting, Jim wouldn't be the one who got hurt, even when he were the one who ended up with a shiner or limped away rather than walked.

Without Jim here, the only time any actual talking gets done at Pok now is when some newbie or flyby waster happens upon The Place of Kings. Even then, the quality of the gab seems lacking somehow.

When this latest crusty starts up on asking what separates 'man from beast' as he words it, folk just roll their eyes, or roll over muttering about love, and war. Love and war though, I mean, they're secondary. Get to the real heart of it and the answer is *nothing*; except we have this thing we call 'consciousness': the power of language; the power to call things *things*, and so to deny what seems true and articulate that denial; say: I am not an animal, until we convince ourselves; this is not what I am; not who I am. Not really.

I can look in a mirror and say: this is me, or: this is just a reflection. Animals don't know they've got a choice. So, they don't have a choice, y'know? A cat will box its own reflection in a tumble dryer window every day for all its life without realising it's fighting itself. Humans, they realise they're fighting themselves and do it anyway.

Consciousness imposes onto life this goal, to be not just free of hunger or fear or threat for *now*; but to be *never* hungry, *never* in fear, *never* feel threatened. We don't reproduce to create life, but to fulfil our own life. Consciousness don't open up life. It reduces and shuts it down.

Are you free of hunger? Are you free of fear? Are you alive? Reduces down to: are you happy? Are you happy? Are you happy? And, if the answer ain't yes and yes and yes? Suffice to say, you got to be saying 'yes' all goddam day, cos it only takes one 'no' to have this whole apparatus clatter down on top of you. Least, that's how it gets to feel.

★

Cal brings his decks over and sets them up in Clit's and Mag's living room. La, Clit and Mag nip out for pharmaceuticals and beers, though the house is full of booze. The house is always full of booze. Alone with him, then, I realise I ain't seen Cal since I ran out when mum had tried to throw all his stuff out the window.

He don't say nothing about the peroxide-stained Sex Pistols tee Mag lent me and I've been living in the past week, or the fact it's all I'm wearing. Besides a pair of Clit's boxer shorts. I wonder if Cal knows why I look so rough is 'cause I ain't been using, or if he just accepts I look like shit because he thinks I am using.

In silence, we wire up the electrics and get the place pretty much all set up till there ain't owt left to do except put together a loose playlist.

Cal slides a CD over the carpet to me.

– Remember, I taught you the lyrics to this and mum got a letter from your reception teacher saying you were going round the playground at break getting all the kids to chant 'lager, lager, lager!' – remember that?

I trace the crack along the front of the CD case.

I remember racking my first line of ket on it not long after I'd been sent to live at my mum's, and, not knowing what the fuck I was doing, I'd gone at it too hard and almost shattered the case.

I remind Cal that I was only five years old.

– Four, you were four. You'd just started school. It was just before your dad got pissed and came in with them knock-off clippers he bought in the pub, and woke you to shave your head 'cause he mistook you for Dom. Your hair were still long. You were four.

Cal laughs then stops, glancing at my legs which are bruisey from having gone at the door and gone at Mag, and gone at Clit and gone fucking crazy at being shut upstairs with nowt but a handful of Paracetamol and Valium the past week. He stares back down at the CD, his reflection warping in the plastic.

– She spent Christmas with Terry. Mum, I mean. She went to him.

I wonder why I am being told this, and why Cal sounds so surprised. Course she chose Terry; Cal chose La.

– What did you do?

– Went to The Hammer and Sink with La and Bull. I thought you might be there.

Crusty Don, the owner of the Hammer and Sink, is a mean bastard, but he never throws anyone out Christmas morning. Last two years running, me and Cal made sure we got trashed enough to pass out at the Christmas Eve party. We ain't the only ones; it were Bull's idea, originally. Crusty Don let Bull stay a few years back, get pissed, listen some tunes, get fed, and now there's a whole bunch of us to clean up after Christmas Eve and help organise the annual Boxing Day feast in exchange for someplace to spend Christmas Day.

— La told me you were at the house with Clit and Mag. Saw Clit at the Boxing Day Banquet, too. He asked me to bring my stuff over for tonight. Said you were... here.

Cal and me share a few joints, running over some of his set list like old times as we wait on Clit, Mag and La to get back with the MDMA.

I'm aware Cal is looking at me, and I'm aware that the question he's about to ask ain't a question with any fucking answer, least not one I can give him.

— Is it really bad?

I try my best not to make any sort of gesture, to do nothing, and say nothing.

— La says it is the worst thing in the world. The worst thing a person can go through...

I instantly wonder what La's comparison is.

I know I'm supposed to make my big brother think I am OK, but how? How can I sit here and show him a kid like me can do gear, do turkey and be 'OK', and his girl can't?

I know how I can do turkey and not slither back down into that black, hopeless bliss; it ain't about gear, not for me. If it were just about gear, if I felt that way at all, if I saw shit how Cal or La do, and thought things can get better or worse, not just different, hell, I'd *be* La. I'd be on a fucking methadone script and still fucking using. I'd be lying, robbing folk, saying shit and meaning it and then doing the total fucking opposite; I'd be nodding right now, and in both senses of the word.

As is, I ain't. I ain't nodding in any sense of the word. Fact is, I ain't La.

I spark a smoke and think of telling Cal about Mary the White Keyring Queen instead of actually telling him about Mary. 'Cause I also know, my brother ain't really asking me if I'm OK; he's asking me *how* I am OK.

And there is no answer to that question; no truth, except *that*. I can't make Cal understand, just like Cal can't make La understand and just like La can't make Cal understand; I guess, the only truth is, you really can't tell a junkie nothing.

★

Biddy and AJ come over looking for a babysitter for DM. Finding a party instead, Biddy shuts DM in the spare room, where I've been holed up with my demons the past week like Scrooge with the ghosts of Christmas, being force-fed soup and rationed Valium, along with words of advice wrapped up in expletives by Mag.

I've been holed up since I came here looking for La,

having found no one holding at Pok, and found Mag instead. Mag saw my bloodstained jeans and saw that I were 'holed up' and decided sommet had to be done. 'Sommet' being to confiscate my shoes, bin my jeans and shut me up, literally.

They say it's like flu. I ain't ever had flu. Still, I reckon what matters is what's different between clucking and having flu, not what makes the two similar. All the physical, and literal, shit that goes with kicking heroin, that's the easy bit.

That's what folk don't get, and can't get without getting a habit and getting over one. Folk tell junkies to try see beyond gear, beyond the rattle. But junkies ain't junkies 'cause they can't see what lies beyond being strung out. A junkie's sight is forever fixed on that next fix, 'cause they know *exactly* what lies beyond it, and beyond being a junkie. It ain't the fear of rattling that keeps a bag rat from kicking. It's the fear of life, of having to actually live it, rather than just survive this moment, every moment – 'just for today'.

When you have a bad cold, the idea of an afterwards is a dream; in a week the pain will have begun to ease and you'll start to feel better. When you're rattling, the reality of an afterwards is a nightmare; a nightmare you choose to realise if you consent to cluck; when your body stops hurting there ain't even the pain left to distract you from living the nightmare. The nightmare of life without gear, that's the real pain and it don't kick in till the gear's sweated out and the physical withdrawal is over.

People who do heroin 'cause they love the feeling of being on it, they're the ones who don't become junkies, not the ones who do. A junkie is someone who falls in love with the hustle, not the high. Every junkie or soon-to-be smackhead knows it ain't when you plunge the needle that the relief hits, it's the moment before, when you pull back the plunger and the blood plumes in the barrel. The ritual, the routine, the daily rigmarole of getting and using, always something to do, always somewhere to be, always some*thing* to be. The fear of rattling is the perfect fucking motivator, but that's all it is.

Fact is, having a broken body don't compare to having a broken psyche. That's why all the patients doped up on medical grade heroin in NHS hospitals don't walk out a week or month later reborn as insatiable gear fiends. The realisation that one tiny injection can cure everything, even the desire to be cured, to be anything, that's sommet you only realise if what's broke about you *is you,* rather than just a part of you, like a leg or hip or sommet.

Sure, it ain't been the merriest of Christmases, but if it's been the worst, it ain't on account of sweating out the smack; that ain't why I've been climbing the walls. I just don't like walls or being this side of any locked door when I ain't the one holding the key. Suffice to say, I'd rather be locked out without gear than locked in with it. That's the difference, and the only difference that makes any fucking difference in the end. And that's why La can't get clean and why I can, why I am. For now, at least.

Trix is showing me the earlobe piercing he's stretched big enough to hold a camera film canister. He takes it from his ear and is popping it open to slide a twenty-bag of grass from it when I make to get up, and meet the gaze of Mag, from across the room where she's sat by the front door. Wordlessly, I gesture over to where Biddy, cross-legged on the floor, is playing poker with La and some tourist kid called Rich. If I wanted to score, the goal is two feet across the fucking carpet. Mag, instead of accepting the futility of playing prison guard, elbows Clit in the ribs for the second time tonight. The first assault being on account of Clit having let Biddy in the first place.

Unable to get out, at least without turning the party into some fucked up intervention held by drugheads rather than for one, I retreat back upstairs to escape the countdown, and the tension.

Miss is trying to get DM to sleep, rocking him on her knee while Bull, Sam and AJ chat on about the end of the world.

– It's World War Three. And it's already begun, AJ shrugs, stubbing a joint out on the floor, like that's that.

– If y'right, God help us. Tony Blair leading a world

war? Not that no fucker can stop him trying, like.

Bull snorts. Miss points out:

– Two million people marched in London against
the Iraq war.

Our eyes meet and she hazards an almost smile. I
don't return the smile, but I do resist the urge to tell her
to fuck off.

– Aye, and might have well rolled their eyes at the
TV. Saved the train fare, and the hassle. We could do
owt and it wouldn't mean nowt, and don't, except
handcuffs; we're the fucking ASBO generation. Owt
we say or do, it's antisocial behaviour, long as it's not
in agreement with them. The system's devised by
Oxbridge cunts done courses in how to fuck over every
fucker what ain't one of them.

Bull pauses to spark a cigarette.

– Hell, don't even gotta be a colour or foreign no
more. Just young. Or poor. And us kind, we're both.
You wanna march, you march all you like, Miss, but it's
their tune you'll be marching to. And all it'll get you is
slapped with a fucking electronic shackle. You might
end up a poster girl, but you can bet it'll be to peddle
their agenda. Cool Britannia, what a gyp. All we won
were Eurovision. Folk like us, we've more in common
with Iraqis than them posh cunt politicians; no fucker
cares about either lot of us, 'cept to kill or kick us. Or
wind us up, set us on our feet and laugh as we bumble
about killing each other.

AJ is laughing. Sam, leaning her chin on her knees, ain't.

– My mum says I'll look back in twenty years and laugh, that everyone does.

– What, like folk laugh about The Holocaust?

Aberdeenie Jeanie shoots back, laughing even harder while Sam just frowns even harder. Bull rubs his eyes, shaking his head.

– Even if we do find it all some lark suddenly, Sammy Doll, what's that tell about us anyhow? Laugh, we're the fuckers. Don't laugh, we're just the fucked.

Downstairs people begin howling and whooping. At the sound, AJ flips her mobile open. I see the tiny fluorescent digits light up: 00:00. 2004. Bull glances at the screen too, lifting his can in silence. To the next twenty years.

★

Inside smells of piss and Special Brew and every character in here could be a possible version of myself in ten years' time. I never imagined how I might spend my sixteenth birthday, and, looking at where I've ended up, that's probably for the best.

In the seating area, a kid is trying to rub sommet brownish and sticky from under his nose onto a woman's t-shirt. Oblivious (or just used to it), the woman, who has deep lines like scars giving her mouth a permanent downturn, pushes the toddler off her, over her fat like over conveyer belt rollers. The kid reluctantly slides out from between her open legs onto the stained linoleum. The woman ignores the toddler's attempts to climb back onto her lap, frowning into a Disabled Living Allowance leaflet.

The bloke beside her rolls smoke after smoke in his yellow fingers, a can of ale tucked behind his left boot. A girl in the corner, scrawnier than me even and vaguely familiar somehow, is sat with what looks to be Mr Bojangles. He wheezes at the skinny girl that she needs a bra for those eyes. The look she shoots him don't make it any clearer whether they are here together, or just together, here. Her eyes, red and glassy, lean forward out her skull like eyes that've spent too much time peering from a high-rise balcony.

Me and my mum zigzag through the steel queue dividers like cattle in a slaughterhouse. In front of us, a mother and son are having some hissed argument. The son, say, late twenties, is almost crying, shushing his mother, who keeps grabbing his arm.

– Don't be so pathetic. You're happy enough to call me 'Mummy' when I'm dishing up your dinner or bailing you out of whatever shit you've got yourself in. Don't try act the hard man now.

My mum and I stay silent, staring in opposite directions like our heads are working via opposing forces. His mother glances over her shoulder at me, giving me the once-over before turning back. When I turn to face her, she glances away, and my mum elbows me.

– Mum, seriously. I'm leaving if you don't stop –

– Stop what, Davy, doing your paperwork or wiping your arse? Just shut the fuck up will you. Nobody gives a shit.

The mother and son get beckoned forward. Mum and I edge forward in synchronised, slow steps.

We pass a woman whose words bubble out loud and coarse and black; how I imagine cancer cells grow. Even her hair seems to be trying to jump ship, twisting from her scalp like barbed wire.

At the counter, the girl absentmindedly rocks from side to side from a swivel chair whilst dealing with my mum's request. She hands over a booklet without looking at what she's picked out, like we're at some funfair lucky dip stand. Behind the counter, it's like a library for the down and out. I bet there's a different booklet appropriate to every person I know filed in those little metal cabinets.

My mum sits as far removed from every other case in there, pulling her handbag close by her and looping her arm into the strap. She sits straight, shoulders down. Each lumber of her spine pokes through her cardigan, like a perforated edge. I imagine reaching forward, taking both her arms and pulling her until she splits clean in half, tearing up not just the papers, but this whole damn scene.

— You better effing appreciate this, Layla. I could be relaxing on me day off, not here, not doing this.

I wonder if anyone has ever felt appreciative to be here, if appreciation is even possible in a place like this.

Opposite me, a fat man with stains down the front of his pastel lilac shell suit, a ginger shaved head and face like it was embossed onto a Scotch egg, shoots me a shifty look before returning his gaze to his knees.

— Sit up, will you.

I draw myself up against the chair. My spine hits against the back of the hard plastic seat. I hunch forward, leaning my elbows on my thighs.

— You're serious, then, about this?

— What, you think I'm here for the good of my health, am I?

— I just thought like we were meeting for a brew or sommet, like, to talk, is all.

— Talk about what?

My mum's eyes don't move from the small black print.

My mum had always said to me: they can cut the leccy, stop the gas, send the bailiffs, but long as you got a roof over your head you've a place to crawl back to at the end of the day.

Translated: my mum thought it were a practical idea to get the estrangement papers signed while I'm still at school so I'll not have to wait as long for a place to live when I finish school, when I am an 'adult'. I'll officially be 'of no fixed abode' then. 'Officially' being the operative word. I think of home, of what a home is, and I think of someplace I have a key to. More, home is some place *only* I have the key to. But to those with clipboards, it's what's on paper that matters. And on paper, my mum's place is my home, for now. So, for now, I'm pinned to my mum's place like paper to a clipboard.

Apart from pregnant women, foster kids and mothers (ones who still have custody of their kids) I'll be a priority case for council housing. They'll probably put me on Aldgate, and I'll finally be able to once again walk through the subways and paths near the train tracks without being chased or threatened by the 212. Maybe they'll even welcome me back and let me into the crew and I'll embark on a glorious career in petty crime, be the first in my family to afford a car and house insurance...

– If you're going to fucking ignore me though, I'll walk out them doors right now. I'm telling you, this is my only day off, you hearkened, Layla? You want me to walk out them doors? 'Cause I'm telling you, when I'm gone I'm –

– Gone. I know.

I sign my name on the last page of the form without reading any of it and try to ignore the fat sweaty Scotch egg-man who's started rubbing himself and winking at me.

Back at the desk, my mum hands over the papers and I hear her start explaining how I'm still at school and how she's agreed to house me until I complete my GCSEs. I sigh, pushing myself up from the counter. Mum shoots me a 'don't start' look, turning back to the lady and putting on her most polite, least Yorkshire-inflected voice, the voice she saves for social workers, bailiffs, and the people at the YMCA furniture shop.

Back on the street, my head seems instantly clearer. I spark a cigarette, thinking on how many people I've seen crying in them waiting rooms struggling through housing benefit forms, working tax credit forms, Disabled Living Allowance forms. And yet, how easy they make it to become estranged, to get rid of people, to write people off.

Walking toward the city centre, I try keep pace with my mum, who rushes even if she's not going anywhere. I catch up with her down Bashful Alley where she is forced to stop at the traffic lights at Town Hall Corner.

I am about to ask how her how her Christmas was, when she turns on me.

— You going to follow me round town all day then? What is it, money you want? You angling for fare someplace?

We stand for a moment, neither of us speaking. I look to Bally Ann's café. My mum sighs, glancing up at the shabby, sunbleached sign, and then digs in her coat pocket. She tries to hand me some change without opening her fist, like she is purposefully trying to hide how much money she is offering to pay me to go away. Like there's a chance I might refuse it simply on account of how much, or how little, it is.

Like she knows what I am thinking, my mum suddenly winces at me, her eyes rolling over my laddered tights, mismatching grey boot socks and the snapped, knotted laces of the cracked bovver boots La had told me would look 'smart', and which suddenly feel like clown shoes. I pull my brother's old hoodie tight round me and beneath it, the duct tape AJ wound round my chest and said would do in place of a bra pinches at my skin.

I want to rip everything off, do something, anything. I want to scream, but I know my mum will just run away from me (instead of walk away), so I apologise, even though I genuinely don't get what I'm supposed to have done.

She pulls my fist from within my hoodie pocket by the sleeve rather than grab my arm, like to drag a wily toddler along. My hand opens instantly. I step forward, like wondering where we're going, and almost collide with my mum, whose feet ain't moved. In the confusion, she shoves the money into my open palm, turning and crossing the street before the lights have even changed and getting honked at by some guy in a van who has to brake to avoid clipping her as she darts through the traffic.

By the time I've looked up from my palm, my mum is gone. My mum is gone and I have three quid. I count and recount it, like there is any significance in the amount.

The local bus routes flash through my mind. Where is it she thinks I am heading? Where can three quid take me? Not enough for a train ticket, but more than enough to take any bus to its final destination, and what's more, get back. Ultimately though, not enough to get anywhere I can think of wanting to go. Not even halfway to a fix.

★

The Steps has just been served a 48-hour dispersal order in accordance with new legislation. Any group of youths or persons understood to be engaging in antisocial or potentially criminal behaviour, or just causing a public nuisance, can be ordered from public places, and prohibited from returning for a set amount of time. Consequently, everyone breaks up into groups of three or less and tapers off into shops, byways and the likes with the secret intention to regroup at the back of The Priory behind Lancaster Castle.

Ducking down into Market Gate precinct, I pass an electrical goods shop I've never noticed before, and stop to roll a smoke out of sight of the cops and PCSOs still loitering about in place of us in the town centre.

On a display TV through the shop window, I see American girls pouting at the cameras and hanging from their fathers' arms, laughing and sucking gloss from their lips as fitting-room staff pull debutante dresses from a long line of one-offs. The camera zooms in on a price label on a pair of shoes that apparently cost $1677. I try not to convert the figures into pounds sterling.

Pulling the lighter from my pocket, I clock a security guard approaching. Reaching me, she gabs something into the walkie-talkie fixed to her jacket at her collar and then points at a sign.

— This is a no smoking precinct. Please, move on.

— It ain't lit.

— I said, please move on. You've no need to be standing there.

I glance about where other folk are, equally, stood about, some of them stealing looks my way.

— What about them, then? What reasons do they got that means they're allowed to stand there?

— I'm not speaking with them. I am dealing with you. And I won't ask again. You need to move. *Now*.

I light the cigarette, pointing with my lighter to the sign below the one that states, 'This is a No Smoking Precinct', to the sign that states, 'NO DOGS', and stare out the security guard. In reply, she reaches for her walkie-talkie and my arm simultaneously. I make to duck, but she grabs me and twists my arm hard behind my back, drawing my wrist towards my neck, so I double over and drop the smoke.

— Move on how, go where?

I growl back at her, but I'm facing the pavement. Turning my head to face her just makes her yank harder on my arm.

The security guard's eyebrows drop into a frown, loosening her grip so I can at least stand straight again, despite the fact she's still got hold of me.

— Anywhere. I don't care. You just can't stay here.

She's already dragging me back towards the precinct entrance and out into the city centre, where I've just been moved from. As if he's been waiting for this moment, a copper clocks me instantly and walks over, telling me as he approaches that I've just been removed from this area and I'm about to be arrested if I don't shift arse.

I ask him, too, where I am supposed to go, and he too frowns at me, as if trying to figure out if I'm being funny, or trying to be. He points down Penny Street towards the crossroads and The Range Estate and tells me that beyond Horse Shoe Corner will satisfy him.

— What, for forty-eight hours?

I know I wouldn't probably last forty-eight minutes if I went too far in that direction.

— Look, I've been civil with you...

He tries reasoning, like I should be grateful for not having been clubbed with a truncheon or some shit.

— But this is getting silly now. Just walk. Just go.

Down there. Now. I don't care where, just go until I can't see you. And before I arrest you.

– For what?

The copper raises his eyebrows reaching for his belt, not for a walkie-talkie, but cuffs.

– Last chance, kid. You've had more than enough of them already.

So, I begin walking towards Horse Shoe Corner, stopping only to avoid knocking some little kid who nearly collides into me as he runs, laughing, to step on the horseshoe fixed into the pavement, a good luck charm cemented into the concrete by the local council.

★

I prise Miss's grass out of Sanaa's small fists while she wriggles on my knee, humming 'Happy Birthday'. When I pour the grass into the L-plate, Sanaa blows the whole mixture onto the floor, laughing and telling Miss to make a wish. Miss looks at the grass now littering the tiles, looks back at Sanaa, and seems to decide to pretend neither thing just happened. She continues emptying the basket of meds onto the dining table.

– I'm off the meds, Lay. I've had enough. Like you say, the doctors are qualified but that's just semantics, right? I'm an adult now. I make my own choices.

I lick the gum strip across the fresh joint, holding it above Sanaa's head so she can't reach to blow it from the skin and roll it over, twisting the end and turning it in my hands to push in the roach.

— I thought you'd be happy; you hate meds. And doctors.

— What, like I hate stairs 'cause people fall down them?

Miss lifts an eyebrow, like she does at Sanaa when she's larking.

— And I don't hate doctors either; it's just a shit system, is all. You ever noticed how the people telling you to take responsibility rattle when they walk? Everyone's a fucking pillbox. I ain't about to condemn one junkie and seek redemption from another.

— So, based on that, you sit in a chair drooling all day off heroin?

I wish the heroin sold round here were as powerful as Miss makes it sound.

— As opposed to drooling all day off Prozac, or clozapine or sodium valproate or lithium or Seroquel?

I shrug, taking a pull of the joint, and notice as a seed bursts in the cherry and lands in Sanaa's hair. I give her head a pat, just in case it's still burning.

— Prozac don't make you drool —

— What, so it's the thought of drooling, specifically, that stops you from doing smack?

Miss sighs instead of answering, and busies herself with separating the meds into piles.

— Then what's your solution, oh wise one?

– Remove moral duality, any notion of good versus bad, and there's no searching for a solution; there's no fucking problem.

Miss laughs.

– That's your 'solution': bin morality? Sounds like junkie logic to me, Lay. Y'know, that's how serial killers think?

– Maybe. But then, what logic has you treating drugs like any are panapathanogenic?

– Quit trying to out-clever me with big fucking words, Lay. It don' make you clever; it makes you an arsehole.

Dave moves into the room like a moped driving through a washing line, dragging a trail of socks and vests. Dropping what she ain't already into the ironing basket, she whisks Sanaa from my lap by her arm and literally swings her into the front room and onto the sofa. She shuts the door on her, dragging the bolt across and shouting (through a hole in the panel Jasper put there with his fist the last time Dave tried shut him in the living room) in reply to Sanaa's protests.

– You know you ain't to be in the back room when the grownups are smoking, baby girl.

I lean back in my chair, lobbing Miss a book of Will Self's journalism from the pile of un-returned, unstamped library books behind me.

– Panapathanogenic; to treat drugs like they're somehow inherently evil.

Dave's eyes follow the trajectory of the book until it hits her daughter, then she turns to me.

— Good book, is it?

I nod in answer to Dave, as I tell Miss to read the damn thing. Dave rocks back and forth in her chair, at intervals reaching to turn the radio down, and back up as she waits on Sanaa to give up on screaming and slamming herself into the door to be let in. She growls suddenly when Sanaa lets go a particularly high-pitched shriek at the same moment Dave has once again turned the volume down on the radio.

— Fucking kids. Lay Baby, I swear, never have kids. Speaking of, where's Jasper?

I pass Dave the joint and shrug.

— I haven't seen my own son in three days.

Dave shakes her head in wonder.

— Four days. Three nights and four days.

Miss corrects her without even looking up from from the basket of meds.

Without standing, Dave reaches over me to grab something, then starts prodding the ceiling with something that looks like a long hoover attachment. Her calls for Jasper to fetch his arse into the dining room teeter-totter with Sanaa's screams to be let back in the dining room.

I take two boxes from the basket, reading the labels.

— Miss, you've tamazepam and codeine in here, you know that?

– Check the expiry dates before you pocket owt.

I pull open the untouched boxes. There are three full blister strips of codeine phosphate and I also find two more boxes of tamazi in the basket, along with some Tramadol in a bottle. What's more, there's also a sizable quantity of co-codamol, containing 8mg of codeine and 500mg of paracetamol, probably due to the fact Miss has enough plain codeine to have never bothered with the co-codamol.

Extracting codeine from co-codamol ain't difficult, just arsy. It requires a method of fractional crystallisation that involves kitchen equipment and a basic understanding of the difference in solubility between over-the-counter analgesics (like paracetamol) and opiate-derived drugs (like codeine), which provides broke junkies and bored kids the world over something to do with an afternoon. It's a real basic technique, used in chemical engineering. Most folk with enough motivation to start dissolving, precipitating and filtrating chemicals usually have at least enough motivation to get off their arses and just go buy some drugs outright, but there's enough co-codamol here that I figure it could be worth hanging on to. Just in case, like.

– Lay Baby, what're you going to do with all that stuff?

Dave, having given up on calling through the ceiling to Jasper, eyes me. I put the bottle of pills in front of her, turning it so she can read the label.

— Oxazepam has anticonvulsant properties and an average four-hour half-life.

When Dave just stares at me, I tell her that it postpones *delirium tremens*, adding that it has the added bonus of being less toxic than most other benzodiazepines, such as Valium.

Miss throws the last of the empty packets into the bin before pulling a final, half-empty bottle of Oxazepam from the basket, and rolling it across the table to me.

— Meaning, Mum, drunks pay more for oxazepam than tamazepam or Valium 'cause the chance of OD off oxazepam ain't as high and mostly not fatal if you mix it with drink, unlike with other benzos.

Dave's frown hardens with a new kind of misunderstanding.

— I see.

She gets up from the table and leans over her 'to do' list, asking Miss:

— You wanna end up like your uncle Tommo?

— What happened to your uncle Tommo? I ask Miss.

— Nowt, Miss mumbles with a shrug.

— Exactly. Nowt. He does nowt, and he's a drunk pain in the arse to everyone what knows him, and will never be nowt more.

— He reads a lot...

Miss reasons. And Dave tuts.

– Only 'cause he pawned his TV and can't get no real money for punting library books, not like he ain't tried, and not like I ain't told him this house is full with quite enough pilfered library books – thank you very much, Lay Baby.

– If your daughter would read them already I'd return them.

– I will read them.

– When?

– When I fucking feel like it.

Miss throws a final box of pills from the basket at me as I get up to take the drinks out to the car.

In the back of Dave's VW, my legs lodged between Sanaa's bright plastic debris and the bottles beside me rattling, Miss and Dave sing like crazy in the front. I pass single-skin joints over the seats and Dave floors the Bug over the long, bucking country roads how the boy racers use them on the weekends, like rollercoasters.

Miss and Dave sing louder and the car labours to pick up speed. Every lurch has me groping for the bottles like some pisshead, while Sanaa's toys lap and stab at my ankles.

Whenever I'm in a car, I imagine I'm someone else. Sometimes, I am some rich kid being driven home from another term at private school to spend a lavish Summer Holiday with Mammy and Papa. Sometimes, I'm some Beatnik hitchhiker setting out on my own exploration of The North, like Kerouac did across North America in *On The Road*. But whenever Dave drives over The Heights and through The Bends singing 'Bat Out of Hell' as we go I am just me, hitting my head against the window, dropping lit cigarettes and clutching at bottles.

We jump out of the car at Dalton Square and cut down Grab Lane, through Bashful Alley and past Horse Shoe Corner on our way to the Steps, evenings being the only time the cops don't bother to scatter us.

Not everybody has arrived yet. Making the most of the impatient brood already assembled, Miss and I set about trying to shift some of her meds off on the crusties. Recognising Flower, or, rather, hearing DM and looking his way, I go over to ask if they want to buy any tranquilisers, mostly for something to say. Shaking DM by his dungaree straps while DM twists and hisses like a feral cat, Flower asks:

— Tranquilisers? What sort? You seen Biddy? She was meant to be back by now and — ouch! DM, for fuck's sake stop being a dick, *please* — she's got the house keys.

I pass Flower a strip of the oxazepam, realising I ain't seen him since the day of Polly's funeral. I'd heard he'd been crashing at Trix's place up Gallows Hill way since Trix turned eighteen and his foster rents threw him out — foster kids get to skip council housing lists. Last I'd heard, Trix's landlord had thrown them both out and Flower had taken to sofa surfing. Nobody had told me he'd taken up with Biddy.

DM is pulling at a hole in the knee of Flower's jeans.

Flower is trying to ignore him, but when DM jumps on his feet, Flower jumps too, and I see his feet are bare beneath his frayed baggies.

Flower gets shifty after that, curling his toes back beneath his jeans and deflecting any questions I pose. It don't take GCSEs to know Flower's bare feet ain't the result of some misplaced Eastern philosophy though, like when Trix had gone through this phase of wearing hemp and going barefoot. Seems so crazy that I'd ever been suspicious Flower might be a cop. No one would question the guy being here now, except the cops.

The group finally begins the trek up to the Castle. I follow, leaving Flower soleless, tranqs in one hand, shaking DM by his dungaree straps again with the other. As if holding up a bag of bait, hoping something will swoop down and take it.

Sitting on the flattened gravestones at the back of the castle once Miss's birthday party has begun and haggling with Clit over the going rate of oxazepam, I try to remember a single actual conversation me and Flower have ever had. I think of gelling Flower's hair while he ate fat rascals in Bally Ann's. Mostly we'd just chat shit and get pilled up.

I remember Flower asking Bull about The Place of Kings when Polly first brought him to the Steps. I wonder how long it'd taken him, after that last afternoon in Bally Ann's on the day of Polly's funeral, before Flower found his way to Pok, or just into Biddy's bed. If he'd even made it up to Pok yet, or *just* Biddy's bed. If she fixed his first needle for him. If he's the latest guy on babysitting duty for DM already, he's hustled pretty fast. That'd explain why I've never seen Flower at Pok, though. Not once. Course Biddy wouldn't want Flower buying his own shit, then she'd have to pay for hers, and not get to skim his before handing it over. I think on the New Year party at Clit and Scraggy Mag's and what might have happened if Flower had have turned up. If that's why he hadn't been there: if Clit and Mag had told him to keep away from me in an attempt to limit my access, or Biddy had in an attempt to limit Flower's options.

Bull pulls out a guitar. Clit and Mag hand out tambourines and obscure musical instruments, wooden rainmakers and the likes. AJ starts playing didgeridoo and La shakes a tambourine. I take a harmonica, a standard diatonic, and play some twelve-bar blues while Miss improvs lines between riffs.

Within the hour there is about thirty of us, including my brother. Me and Miss have Wayside in the morning and I have my second review meeting. While Miss drinks enough whiskey to knock herself out by midnight, I cadge two bombs of speed from Mag, drink the snowballs Dave mixed up for us and try talk to Caleb about Flower. Caleb gives me a dab of MDMA, kissing my forehead and wishing me Happy Birthday. I teeter on reminding him that my birthday were in

January, that the party is for Miss, but shut up, when, as he leans over to kiss my forehead I notice Cal's wearing Flower's boots.

★

My Mum don't show to the review meeting, which means two things. 1. McQuaide can't share her suspicions that I still ain't taking the meds. 2. When the bell goes, I don't.

McQuaide keeps me back, interrogating me on where my mum might be, like I've any idea or could have. McQuaide has me sit there all morning and what feels like half the afternoon, supervised by Brenda while they try to call my mum.

Course, nobody answers the phone. I wonder if I'd even told my mum I had a review, if they send letters out to parents or sommet. I try to remember if my mum works Tuesdays and try to imagine what she might possibly do on her days off.

– You must have some idea where she might be. Don't play games, Layla. What did you tell her about the Review Meeting?

– Nowt, I admit, wondering if my mum purposefully avoided the review meeting on account of having had me estranged.

★

When Sam and Bull arrive at the Steps, me and Miss automatically follow them before the cops can come move us on.

We take refuge at The Priory, sitting in a circle on one of the flattened graves, passing the joints clockwise, like always.

After a few joints, Sam tells us how her mum's got her in counselling and AA and she's being referred to Royal Ash, the inpatient youth nuthouse in Galgate.

– I'm on a waiting list for a bed. They think I'm going to kill myself.

Sam passes the joint over to Bull who snorts and takes a drag.

– Evidently no time soon, then. Fucking waiting lists before they'll let you be crazy...

He passes the joint on to Miss.

– Yeah, what if you kill yourself before you reach the top of the waiting list?

Miss takes a drag and passes the joint back to Sam, who takes a long, slow pull and then shrugs.

– Then I'll be dead.

She leans across the grave of the forgotten stranger we're all sat on, to pass me the joint.

– Won't have to care about what-ifs no more, will I?

I take a drag and try think of sommet to say as the joint, like a fuse, burns itself down in my fingers.

★

– It'll just be a glorified fuckfest. If AJ was a bloke, she'd be on a sex offender's register.

Miss is whining like there's a chance she ain't going to come along.

– Glorified? Don't get your hopes up.

I toss Miss her jacket.

On our arrival, Scraggy Mag greets us at the door. She is wearing a satin top hat and has a moustache painted on with what looks like black eyeliner. Ushering us in, she tells us how lucky we are to be so young, and how she wishes she'd saved some of her own virginities for tonight.

Sure enough, everyone is already wasted, painting their lips black and kissing AJ's Grandma's bedroom walls. Couples and groups wrapped up in duvets keep rolling and unravelling past the lounge doorway. When Miss sits down on the sofa in the back room, two stripy-socked feet unfurl themselves beneath her like the witch's from *The Wizard of Oz* and Trix's flushed face appears, cursing and swearing at Miss for sitting on him.

Leading Miss into AJ's bedroom, 'cause she says she's having an anxiety attack, we find Bull and some girl naked, playing with a gerbil on the bed, taking it in turns to dangle the rodent over each other's navels and thighs and tits. The TV is on, but muted. On the screen, Tony Blair looks like he is trying to seem solemn as he speaks, but it is as if he can see right into the room, see us, and is trying not to gape, or laugh. Next to him on the screen, but far away, cruise missiles rage across what looks like a model village in a sandpit. Black words unfurl below: 'BAGHDAD', then 'LIVE'. The footage cuts again. Soldiers load more missiles. The words rolling along the screen now read: '09:00 Iraqi missiles hit Kuwait'.

The naked girl picks up the gerbil, dangling it over the bed. When its tail falls off, the gerbil scurries to safety under the divan. Miss looks like she is about to burst into tears. The naked girl, I recognise now, is Sasha, the girl from the club, who Miss had bollocked me for bringing back to Clit and Mag's place last year. She laughs and throws the tail at Miss, telling her she's stupid, gerbils' tails always fall off, like, that's what gerbils do for a party trick or something.

– It's a survival mechanism. Everybody knows that.

We leave the bedroom when Bull drunkenly suggests a foursome, and I find Miss a beer. Sam has just kicked Miss in the face while trying to spin on her head in the dining room, coked up and insisting she can breakdance. Miss pulls her hood up, trying to hide that she is really crying by now.

Sam squeezes into the sofa and turns her puffed-up eyes on me. Before I can get up and free, she starts gushing how Polly were the only person who ever told her the truth, and now she's dead and she don't understand anything anymore. How can she? Like she ever did, and so I find myself sandwiched between two crying girls at a party.

— Weren't it Polly who convinced you a brothel is a soup kitchen?

I make an attempt to provide a context. Sam hisses at me.

— When you weren't there. When it were just us. She was different. When we were alone. You don't know. We —

— Sam, Polly fucked everyone. If Polly had been a bloke 'stead of a fifteen-year-old with a fanny, she'd have been fucking hated, not admired. What Polly did was rape, not love.

I think about the set-up me and Polly had, and qualify:

— Paying for it, at best... Just 'cause some girl dies don't suddenly make her an angel, Sam. Not even in God's eyes, if you want to start believing in all that lark. Even then, she'd have had to repent. And Polly weren't sorry for shit. Least of all your shit.

Sam glares at me like I killed Polly or something. Maybe I just had, in a way; in Sam's eyes. But I figure, Polly's already dead, so if giving her the actual truth of it stops Sam killing herself, fuck it, y'know? And if it don't, least she'll die having been respected by someone enough to be talked to straight, even if it kills her. After all, sommet kills us all; might as well be the truth.

Aberdeenie Jeanie finally appears, her lips blackened with lipstick. She sees Miss is upset and pulls her from the sofa and onto her feet. Miss tries to resist but seems to realise her attempts are futile against AJ's. Miss weighs more, but AJ don't quit, ever, so Miss gives in.

AJ leads her from the room and up the hall to the bathroom. And I follow, leaving Sam to experience my first three-way kiss with AJ and Miss, eyes open and staring into Miss's ruined make-up, her eyes tight shut and still sobbing all the while she has her tongue squirming about in my mouth like she's searching desperately for the words or something.

After Miss finally gives up crying, AJ sits her on the toilet seat and sets about sorting Miss's mascara out with her Grandma's wet wipes, giving Miss her first bump of coke and all the time making these babyish *shhh* noises.

Pulling across the shower curtain, I sink lower into the empty bathtub and smoke the bag I scored at Pok after my mum's no-show at the review meeting the other day: the first since leaving Clit and Mag's. Cold water from the tap drips down my arse crack as I chase lines, making me shiver until the gear kicks in.

The greyish forms through the curtain merge and separate into different shapes like a Japanese shadow play, only the shadows are more abstract, like ink blots bleeding into each other as if in some crazy monochrome kaleidoscope thought up by a shrink.

Back in the front room, searching for some place to vom, I eventually throw up over the back of the sofa. Sasha, still naked, asks Sam if she's ever done it doggy style as she drinks something that smells like cider out of a mug. I try to be sick in the washing-up bowl that is being passed round, but Sam snatches it away, telling me it is her turn next and to get my own fucking bowl. I put my head back over the sofa, wiping my mouth on Sam's jacket afterwards, and hear Sasha ask Sam if she's ever got fucked in the arse, soon as Sam lowers the sick bowl from her face.

Sasha takes another pull of the cider. Sam, face blotchy and swollen and her eyes still wet from crying or just puking, shakes her head slowly, like you can be unsure whether you've been fucked in the arse.

– If you ain't done it in the arse, you ain't done it doggy style. Everyone knows that.

So that's what Bull had told Sasha.

I think of Polly and how she'd have hated to have missed this party.

★

AJ shakes me awake.

I instantly chuck up again, this time hitting the bowl Sam had left on the sofa, before AJ literally drags me out into the hall, where Miss is stood waiting to inform me that Sam's gone into AJ's Grandma's bedroom with some bloke.

I follow AJ, who is pissing Miss off by giggling and pushing at us to get a better view of what Sam and this guy are doing. I open the door ajar, and, sure enough, Sam is laid there, with her legs up and folded over some guy's arms on AJ's Nana's orthopaedic mattress, making awkward little noises beneath some guy whose bare back is covered with what looks like acne.

– Hell, stop them.

– Shhhh.

Aberdeenie Jeanie puts her finger to Miss's lips, muffling her own mouth and trying not to giggle. I shut the door on Sam and the whole scene while AJ tries to reason with Miss.

– We'll be there when she needs us.

– What, when it's too late?

Miss appeals to me.

All the parties before Miss and I met last year. All the closed bedroom doors we've all walked past. I reckon there ain't one of us here tonight who ain't been on both sides that door, except Miss, who ain't been on either side of that door, until now.

– It's already too late.

Whatever it is that's happening in that bedroom, to rush in there and start dragging Sam out, it won't do nothing, not now, not for Sam. Everyone says every choice they make for Sam is *for* Sam, but what a person does for somebody can seem a lot like doing something *to* somebody when you're doing it 'cause *you* want to feel better. Fact is, you can't rescue no one unless they want rescuing. That's the problem; half the time it's impossible to know if someone is waiting, hoping, needing, to be saved. Sometimes, the best you can do, *all* you can do, is be there, and hope, and wait.

Deny a person their autonomy, which includes denying a person the right to fuck up, and you're denying a person any opportunity to do owt but fuck up. The only thing worse than no one coming to make it stop would be if someone did. Every lass here knows it. Every lass here's lived it. Every lass, but Miss.

– But, Lay –

– Everybody loses it somehow, Miss.

– She probably won't even remember.

– Like that makes it any fucking better–

Miss hisses at AJ, who shushes her again, and whispers back.

– Better she don't remember losing her V 'cause of being pissed, than she remembers 'cause her mates ran in and tried to haul her bare arse out the bed mid-shag.

AJ is still giggling as she pulls Miss away from the door. And, albeit reluctantly, Miss lets her.

★

Miss is sat hugging Sam at the kitchen table.

Aberdeenie Jeanie rounds up what is left of the drink, swigging from bottles and groaning when she discovers the smouldering remains of a shop-bought quiche Lorraine in the Aga, still in its cardboard box.

She calls to the room at large, quiche in her hand like a neon clown about to hurl a custard pie:

– Everybody get the fuck up and get the fuck out!

Three guys I don't know file past and leave through the back door. One is the guy who fucked Sam. Still shirtless, I recognise the constellation of sores pocking his back as he passes me, followed by AJ who pelts a lightbulb over our heads at the guys, shouting as they disappear out the yard and into the cobbled alley beyond.

– Meth? *Seriously*, what the fuck! This was my Grandma's house, you sick cunts!

When the house is empty but for me, Sam, Miss and AJ and Cal, La, Clit and Mag who're still asleep in the living room, AJ sets about making breakfast pancakes, served with lines of coke and glasses of warm Bucks Fizz in place of sugar and orange juice

Sam is complaining she hurts. She's been bleeding. Miss is complaining her nose has been bleeding. AJ, still dressed in dayglo Lycra, but now wearing her grandma's floral apron and sunglasses as well, stops flipping pancakes to reassure Miss that it's just the coke and nothing serious, and comforting Sam like some wartime nurse from a dystopian sci fi movie.

– Sammy Doll, it's just your hymen. It won't hurt soon, sweetie, I promise.

– But it's foaming, should it foam? I'm foaming. Its fizzling and foaming, and –

– Sam, honestly, it's normal, you – wait, *foaming*? What's foaming?

Sam had come into the bathroom this morning while I were raiding AJ's Nana's medicine cabinet and whinged to me that she burned and itched. I'd given her a thrush tablet I found in there. I hadn't given her the Directions for Use leaflet; I thought it was obvious to swallow the pill, what with all the pills she'd dropped last night.

– I didn't know she'd shove it up her fanny.

– Hell, Lay Baby, what the fuck?

AJ snarls at me. Telling me to finish up the pancakes, she steers Sam from the kitchen. Taking a strategic position by the sink, I flatten a piece of foil on the draining board to smoke the last of the gear, perfectly angled to toss my guts down the plug hole without letting the pancakes burn. With my back to the room like this, I can't see who's coming in or out, so don't realise Cal's come to fetch breakfast for La, Clit and Mag till I hear him behind me.

– AJ says there's breakfast?

He leans over me to look into the pan, his chin on my shoulder. I try shrugging him off, nodding to the plate by the kettle that's already stacked with pancakes but Cal's already clocked the foil. I feel his body tense, and wait until I can smell the butter in the skillet burning. Pinned against the counter, I think he's reaching for the foil and try again to free myself. Instead, Cal takes the pan from the hob and slams it down onto the counter so hard hot butter spits back, peppering my bare arm.

— Shit.

Cal releases me. He glances at my arms.

— Sis, shit, I'm —

Somebody shouts through from the lounge asking why breakfast is taking so fucking long.

— I'll clean up. Just take the plates.

I run the tap, rinsing the blisters freckling on my arm in the cold water.

— Sis —

— Bro.

Shutting the tap off and wrapping my arm in a towel, I take a deep breath and turn from the sink, but Cal ain't there. Nobody is there, not even Miss, just the faint halo where the plate of coke had been, and the stack of untouched pancakes.

★

AJ wants to trek into town with us at midday ahead of her Gran's funeral, but has just discovered the dried up pool of sick behind the sofa. She tries to rope Sam and Miss into helping her clean it up, but Sam says she has this meeting with her mum and shrink she has to be at, otherwise they'll threaten her with an inpatient stay again. Miss agrees to stay behind, but only to clean up the sick. Clit, Maggie and La have already gone, so Cal and I head out together to catch the train from Bare back into Lancaster.

On the platform, Cal and I grab coffee and take to a bench.

– I thought you were writing in that book Jim gave you?

– Jim never gave me it. Bull did. He just found it amongst Jim's stuff.

Cal mutters something about me 'splitting hairs'.

– If I could just say it, any of it, all of it, there would be no *it*.

– Great, well then, we can just sit here in fucking silence. Perfect.

I can feel my eyes burning in my head.

– You're going to wake up one day, sis, and get your fucking wish, y'know that?

People on the platform have begun to edge away from where Cal and I are sat. I watch them, catching eyes with any who dare to toss a glance our way.

– And I won't be sat beside you then, not in no fucking gutter, that I can tell you.

– Save it for your wife, bro.

– Fuck my wife. And fuck you and your bullshit. 'Cause it is bullshit, Lay. You act all like you don't care what no one thinks, but if you really didn't give a shit, you wouldn't be doing *that* shit. And fine, if you can't admit it to me. But if you can't even write it, if you can't even admit it to yourself, then you really are fucked.

★

The Visitor has a fixed smile, just like all the Visitors who come insisting that they're not here to test us, and insist on writing down our answers to the questions they ask us.

– It's just regular school, except there's fewer pupils and no uniform.

Except, if Miss has to say 'except' after likening our school to regular school for The Visitor, if you have to say that other schools are regular, then your school ain't regular. Regular schools have uniforms and classrooms and yards. Regular schools have school trips. We ain't even allowed in the garden without a one-teacher-to-two-pupil ratio. And no one, except us, would get the crazies we get, either to visit or teach us.

McQuaide and Brenda pull Andrew from the room after The Visitor starts playing pan-pipe music, through a boombox covered in smiley-face stickers she's brought with her, and Andrew starts screaming and hitting himself. Hazel smiles at Carol, who always gets upset when we forget to act civilised. Miss usually comforts Carol, but Miss is preoccupied this morning, sat in a swivel chair and wearing two hats and her hood up and refusing to do owt.

Carol smiles her little rosy old-apple face back at Hazel, losing her place on the page of my Spanish vocabulary book, and making no effort to find it again.

Instead, she seems intent on maintaining her smile, glancing from the door Andrew is sat beyond, probably being restrained and Miss, who's fashioned her own straitjacket by having folded her arms inside her zipped up hood-up hoodie and turned her back to everyone.

— Miss was normal in the taxi...

Nicole rolls her eyes at Danny.

— Danny, that were an hour ago.

The Visitor shuts herself into one of the rooms we're usually split between, telling us she'll be back soon, and winking. When she finally opens the connecting door to the room we've all been crammed in together, there is a collective sigh of relief. Fifteen minutes together and even the teachers are ready to fight for a corner and assume the foetal position.

We all turn to face The Visitor, except Miss, who is this morning really committing herself to being, or, least, *seeming* crazy. 'Disassociated', McQuaide calls it. McQuaide, who's never disassociated in her life.

The Visitor claps her hands together, making her bangles jostle on her thin arms.

— What I want, after break, is for you all to take it in turns to go into the other room. On the table you will find a picture, a piece of paper and a pen. All I want you to do is replicate the picture you see, then place your paper, face-up, on top of the one you copied and come back in here. OK, guys?

Brenda translates these instructions during break.

— Just go in there, sit down and have a look at the picture, all parts of it, then copy it as best you can. Take your time and don't worry if you make a mistake. There are no mistakes. It isn't a test, guys, OK?

After break, while The Visitor finishes her cigarette outside, McQuaide returns with Andrew and takes the opportunity to reiterate the instructions, her eyes fixed on me.

— Go in there, draw what you see and come straight back out. No dawdling, no messing about and no wise ideas. Is that clear?

One by one our names are called and we get sent into the other room. After fifteen minutes, McQuaide has to go in to fetch out Nicole, who I spy leaning back in the chair pretending to talk on her mobile to her latest imaginary boyfriend.

Back in the main room, and with Nicole in tow, McQuaide moves Andrew from the newly designated Quiet Area so that she can sit Nicole in there and reinstate The Naughty Corner.

When I go in the room, there is a childish black and white drawing of a tree with a single branch. There is an owl perched on the branch.

I look about the room, first setting myself to thinking up ways of remotely detonating the guys in the other room. And then I just start thinking up possible escape routes: smashing the chair through the glass panes, and pegging it, arms flailing, through the dying tulips outside. But the open windows ruin the daydream.

So, eventually, I replicate the picture and return obediently to the main room.

Half an hour before the taxis are due to arrive, The Visitor has McQuaide end lessons and everyone sit in a circle. She put the pictures on the floor at our feet and has us look at them.

– So, what do you see?

The cat on the first tree, on the picture drawn by The Visitor, has become an owl by the last picture. The branches have sagged and contorted into a single, crippled bough. The tree itself has sort of petrified and lost its leaves along the way, and the sun in the upper left corner has disappeared entirely.

When no one offers an answer, The Visitor clocks my sticky nametag. We all get made to wear nametags on Visitor days.

– Layla, is it? What are you thinking?

– I'm thinking a two-minute game of Chinese Whispers would've got the point across.

McQuaide instantly shoots a warning look, the sort of look you shoot a dog when secretly you want it to growl at the neighbours.

– The sun's gone, Hazel says pointing suddenly and leaning forward in her chair. McQuaide tells Hazel to calm down, but The Visitor smiles encouragingly.

– Well spotted, um, Hazel. I've never seen that happen before.

I frown, turning from McQuaide to point out that if you see an owl you don't look for the sun, but everyone has already begun trying to work out who lost the sun.

Ryan, actually getting onto his hands and knees to take a closer look, breaks the circle and breaks the spell. Suddenly, everyone is talking, then shouting, over each other and leaping up out of their seats to point out which were their picture and prove it weren't them, that they hadn't lost the sun, like it is some insult or crime.

The Visitor tries to restore order without much success, looking to McQuaide who is smiling at The Visitor in the same way she smirks at us kids, and doing nothing much else.

— It was you!

Ryan suddenly shouts out loud, pointing at me.

Order restoring itself with the realisation, The Visitor quits pleading with us.

McQuaide, meanwhile, remains arms crossed and silent, her eyes stuck on the clock. Brenda's shoulders relax, having hunched almost high enough to muffle her ears and she too leans in, looking from the picture and then to me as though inspecting a photo-fit. Even Miss turns in her swivel chair to look at the picture until I flash my eyes like headlights at her and she pulls the cords of her hoodie tighter, disappearing back behind her makeshift veil.

The Visitor blushes, looking at us like the proud mother of a kid who for the first time had drawn a picture with the crayons and not just shoved them up its nose.

Appealing to McQuaide, she asks if we have time to try the spaghetti exercise? But we did the spaghetti exercise last Visitor day, when some guy who Jesus had apparently sent to try and save us passed Miss a single strand of dry spaghetti and told her to snap it in two strands, then five bunched strands, then twenty bunched strands; eventually telling us that the point's meant to be: if we stick together, it's harder to break us.

That last Visitor day really had got messy after Andrew had pointed out that there were only eight of us here; it's easy to break eight strands of spaghetti. But last Visitor day had been Ryan's turn to get real crazy, and Ryan does it best. He'd even flipped the desk over, screaming.

– That was the point? That were the whole fucking point? We're already in special school, how much more broke can we get?

*

Everyone, for the most part, does their damnedest to ignore me, except for Terry, my mum's boyfriend, and the one person who has no place shouting about me, or at me.

After my dad, my mum never got with another guy till Terry. She got rid of my dad, but she still keeps her wedding ring in a little trinket box in her room. I found out when Caleb hocked it once and I had to pay to get it back from the pawnbroker before my mum realised it was gone. Course, Terry don't know about the ring.

– Exactly.

Terry is sneering at me, leaning in so close I'm backed up against the hallway wall while he's spitting whiskey bubbles in my face.

– You do *nothing*. You're a spoilt little shit what don't do nothing.

I automatically try to parry his weight and free myself. Terry responds, taking a handful of my dreads and twisting them round his hand like rope until it feels like they are about to rip from my scalp. Keeping a tight grip of my hair, he drags me outside and up the driveway, telling me he'll effing well make sure I go to school and learn some fucking manners. Not Wayside though; not some fucking special school. Terry says he's taking me to a '*real* fucking school'.

We hit the gravel drive at lunchtime, so the classrooms are empty. Terry gets out. Storming around to the passenger side, he unlocks the door and pulls me from the car so I go knees first into the grit in front of the reception area. I half expect him to march me up the steps too, but Terry just spits at me and kicks up some gravel my way, and I figure his courage evaporated at that long wait at the traffic lights where he'd paused when the light had turned green.

I pull myself up. Terry swaggers back to his car, and I stumble, following him, to stand in front of it, daring him to let the brake off. He revs the engine. I lean in on the bonnet. I can feel the car pulling against the handbrake. The bonnet moves from beneath my hands as Terry swings the car into reverse, wheelspinning back out onto Morecambe promenade.

I spark a cigarette, ignoring all of the first years who have crowded, like readying for a fight, till one of them dares laugh and I turn and backhand his face so hard and so fast he puts his fingers to his cheek and runs off crying. And the others back off somewhat.

I am suddenly aware that Sam is there, leaning with a girl I don't know against the pillars. They are eating ice cream sandwiches. Seeing her in her school uniform, thick woollen tights and ballet flats, ice cream wafers pinched between her fingers and red hair in French plaits, is like entering into a parallel universe.

Some woman rushes out the main doors with the kid I'd backhanded. The woman's screaming like some disaster has just happened. That mad screaming people do to try get themselves heard, the sort of screaming that ensures no one gets heard. I don't move. It ain't that I want her to call the police, like she's threatening, I just don't know where to go from here.

The teacher, or whoever she is, turns back through the doors, running from me when running at me don't work.

Sam, meanwhile, descends the front steps, linking her arm through mine and pulling me away. The lass she'd been stood with is speaking now into a pink mobile. I consider walking up to her and slapping it out of her hand, but like she knows what I'm thinking, Sam keeps pulling at me.

– Is it your Mum's bloke? Were that him in the car?

I warn Sam to let go of me.

– Listen, just walk to the gates with me, they can't do fuck all then. Lay, seriously. They're calling the cops in there. Walk, Lay. *Walk*.

I pull my arm from Sam. She tells me to think of my mum, but I am already; I'm wondering if she is waiting beside the phone to hear from, or about, me or waiting beside the door, for him.

Reaching the school gates, Sam pushes me over the drive back out on to the road.

– Just go, Layla. Seriously, just fuck off, for your own sake. I'll see you later at the Steps.

From the iron railings, I watch Sam walk back up to the school realising for the first time that Sam has this whole other life, a life beyond the Steps, beyond *us*. Sam ain't just a dreg.

★

Some people cry and look like they've been crying forever; I spend one night on the street and look like

I've been on the street forever. Suffice to say, I didn't need to tell Caleb I'd slept rough.

– Why'd you do all this to yourself, to me, to Mum? Why didn't you just go home?

As far as good advice goes, telling a kid to go home is like telling an asthmatic to just breathe or, failing that, to hold their breath till the attack subsides; the last thing any fucker needs is someone beside them who hasn't got a fucking clue how to save them telling them to 'go home'. Especially when that person is their own effing brother. Or telling a kid to sleep in the open, like Polly once tried to convince me was 'safest', like, with all her brood of old, posh relatives, she had any clue or had ever had to spend more than half an hour at a bus stop after dark. Advising anyone to sleep out in the open, that's like telling an asthmatic to exorcise their lungs with crack. The only thing worse than someone who ain't got a clue is someone so clueless they can't even see how clueless they are.

Sleeping out in the open means public: fact. Public means people: fact. And if no one is there then nowt bad is going to happen: fact. You need to find someplace people-less and corner-less; 'cause if some fucker does find you and no one else is around, the last thing you want to be is cornered: fact. Sleep out on the street and you will get pissed on or kicked silly when the pubs empty: fact. Those blokes who'd chat you up if you were stood at the bar will stomp on your head if they

see you bedding down in a doorway: fact. Homelessness
changes people, whether you're homeless or not: fact.
And everybody's an expert at surviving, until they have
to – fact.

★

Dividing the clubs and bars studding the West End from
the tourist-trap trinket stalls of the east (chippies and
penny arcades all garrisoned east as if to keep the day
folk from the local drunks), there is the supermarket:
the only one to brave the flipside of the promenade.
There used to be a Wild Western-themed amusement
park here.

The husk of the old big dipper is all that remains of
the theme park now. It dwarfs even the supermarket.
You can only really see what's left of it at ground level,
from the rear of the supermarket, and getting a load of
that view involves vaulting two ten-foot mesh fences
tinselled with barbed wire, to get to the loading bays
where industrial fans blow hot air throughout the night.
Sometimes, when the wind gets up or there's a storm
blows in from the Alley-O you can hear the structure
groan and creak like some huge beached sea monster
slowly starving on the shore, while folk crawl about and
around it like Lilliputians.

The longest period of time I spent out here were
the winter Jim died. I'd mish out to score or for sugar

and energy drinks, making sure I weren't seen, and slept here, the gear I kept devouring just to stay warm only kicking in in earnest when I were someplace warm and my blood would get to actually circulating. When I finally got picked up by the police, that time, caught nicking pic'n'mix sweets from the market stalls, I hadn't taken my shoes or socks off for days. It were so cold, I didn't even notice that I couldn't actually feel my feet. So I stumbled around stubbing my toes, feet bumping together like dodgems without my realising, for near on a month. At the police station, when I did first have to take my shoes off, in case I were hiding drugs or about to try hang myself by my sneaker laces or sommet, my toes reminded me of the rows of bodies that wash back to shore when the cocklers drown in the bay. I had to shake my socks out to retrieve three full toenails that had shed somehow, or been pulled off along with my socks or something. I were so cold I couldn't even bleed.

Living here, where the country crumbles away like a sandcastle, you get to wondering how the jet stream of the North Atlantic ain't washed this whole sorry rock away already. As it grows dark, I get to shivering. After a while, I just sort of jerk and lurch. Even after a dig. My knuckles and fingers swell and balloon until I can't even roll a cigarette, or hold a pen. The only time I can feel my fingertips is if I place a flame beneath them and spit roast my hands like campfire sausages. But I still can't feel the warmth. Just numbness, and then pain.

The worst thing in the world ain't anything a human can do to you, it's getting so numb and cold that you can't even feel where you begin or end no more. You get so cold you give up on even looking to get warm again. That's the sort of shit that no one tells you about. Last time out here, before the cops picked me up – which ended up in me ending up at Wayside – I began avoiding going indoors because the heat just burned me after a while. I'd swell up and flush and get mazy whenever I went indoors, scouring for forgotten change in the fruit machines in the amusement arcades, or on the rob in the shopping arcade. I got hives and itchy blood when I ran hot water over my skin in public toilets.

Most of the time, I just sort of sat all day, watching parts of myself I could no longer feel peel away like I was literally falling apart. Even the fear dried up like a scab. It didn't feel like I was dying, but like my whole body were sort of shedding from me like a chrysalis, like I were experiencing some Kafkaesque metamorphosis in reverse, and in the end, I'd somehow climb free of everything.

*

The first of the pissheads and junkies are already out. Clit and La are sat with my brother and Bull at the Steps, seen as the cops have grown bored with the dispersal order already and don't usually start moving us until the complaints have stacked up around lunchtime.

Clit wrinkles his forehead, passing me a smoke and telling me there's always a room for me at his and Mag's place.

– She's got a room *at home*, Cal says.

Bull don't say owt, just hands me what is left of his cider, grimacing when Cal's voice rises.

– Why would you choose to sleep rough? Hell, I don't get you at all sometimes, Lay. It's like you're asking to get raped, you know that?

– If you ask for it, it ain't rape.

I point this out, mid-swig of the cider.

– Easy, guys. Fuck. Ain't even noon, bit early for domestics and rape. Let's keep it light, yeah?

I know Clit ain't trying to calm Caleb for my sake, least not wholly. Mag has stood up at Cal's mention of rape and looks about ready to give the cops reason to disperse us.

In contrast, La's lashes are rising and falling like gills, as if she's breathing through her eyes. She looks ghostly almost, her skin greyish and bloodless. I wish I looked like that right now. I imagine if I kissed her I could somehow inhale her whole, like a blowback.

I ask Cal what he's been up to, trying to neutralise the air a little, and trying to distract myself from the ache in my bones and my stomach, which ain't cramping yet so much as burning with warm, flat cider.

Cal says he and Bull scored some bling and

consequently he ain't slept yet. He says he's on his way back to our mum's place. He asks if I'm coming. I say I'm going to stick around town and Caleb tells me to walk with him as far as Bashful Alley.

Hood over his head and his hands buried in his pockets, Bull walks ahead to give Cal and me space for whatever Bull thinks we need space for. From the back, and with that swagger only Mancunians manage to pull off, like a visual accent, Bull reminds me a lot of Jim.

Cal liked Jim, or he liked the idea of me and Jim, at first. While Jim were staying with Bull, Cal pretty much always knew where to find me, when I weren't at my mums, Jim even convinced me to turn up to school, most of the time.

Bull and Jim's mum were an English high school teacher at the school they'd both attended in Lower Broughton before their dad got cancer. She never went back to teaching afterwards but that were why, Jim had said, he'd stuck school out and ended up with nine GCSEs, despite everything. He used to read, at first, because then he could speak his mum's language, he said, but I guess school had also seemed an escape for Jim. In the end though, I guess even books ain't enough, not alone. Not for Jim's mum, who took back her ex the same night he got let out of prison. Not for Jim, who six months later came looking for Bull. And not for me.

The big clock above the Steps chimes out for nine AM, as we near the arch over the alleyway.

– Listen, sis, please. You know what I think of Clit
and Mag and all them lot...

I stop short of the alley.

– You don't have to act like them, sis. It's stupid. You
don't belong with them.

Bull has realised we've stopped and is loitering in the
alley a little way down, just out of earshot.

– Listen, just come with me, yeah? I'll put some
tunes on. We can chill, just you and me, like old times.
Crack a few tins. Mum will be at work...

When I don't reply, Caleb tries again.

– I've got some speed left –

– What about La, is she one of them?

Cal sighs.

– La's got problems, Layla.

We stand for a moment, silent till Bull, still waiting
further along the alley kicking a can, kicks it a little too
hard and makes it ricochet off the alley walls. Caleb
flinches. I glance down the alley in time to see an old
woman suddenly pick up pace to scurry past Bull.

– You're not coming?

I don't offer Cal an answer. I don't have to.

There's no explaining to someone who don't
get it, and no need to explain to anyone who does:
giving a person a house don't mean that they ain't
homeless. Suffice to say, homelessness would be called
'houselessness' or 'abodelessness' if having a place to
sleep made any fucking difference.

★

It's raining and everything beyond me seems bloated and vivid, how the grass and all things natural seem to bloom and swell when it rains. Everything except people, who just shrivel and grimace.

I stand at the foot of the drive, droplets dripping from my eyebrows and the wind cooling the rain on my cheeks till it's so cold it stings, and I try to imagine going to class. Imagine saying 'Yes, Miss!' when the register is called, and colour-coding printed-out sheets of the human eye, and feeling proud of being able to explain phenomena like rainbows.

My throat is so dry my tongue is stuck to the roof of my mouth, as if it's been so long since I've spoken the two have somehow fused together like the scab of a wound. I watch the rain burst on impact with the earth and rush over the leaves like palms, leaking through the branches above me like parted fingers, absorbing into the cobbles and wending down the hill, racing and beating the human fallout gushing from the railway station. I put my own hands out and the rain runs over and off me like I'm artificial and plastic amongst the dull foliage, unable to disintegrate into the natural order of things.

★

When there are no more crisp packets, bottles, lolly wrappers and chippy papers on the footpaths to pick up, I let the junk, as La calls litter, push me off the council-laid concrete pathways onto the grass and through Dalton Square Gardens where old knots of yellow police tape blow like ribbons from the rusty iron railings.

I trace each desire line, chasing frilled metallic strips of packets, neon sherbet tubes and shards of coloured glass, my thoughts punctured by the odd syringe until the curve of the pavements and railings filters me back into town as if a pinball hitting the gutter.

I wander round with the pigeons, pecking cigarette ends from the ashtrays in the bus station until a security guy asks what I am doing.

– Nowt.

He asks which bus am I here for.

– None.

He asks, am I meeting someone.

– No one.

Folding his arms and staring down at me where I've sat at one of the stands to roll a smoke from the dog ends I've collected, he asks:

– Well, what exactly *are* you waiting for then?

Good question, I concede, as we walk side by side, towards the doors which part automatically.

★

People moving off the Aldgate Estate commonly describe it as 'getting out', like they've just done a stretch at Stonerow Head or Strangeways. Which, as the whole estate is surrounded by prison-like ten-feet high walls of red brick, ain't so much a metaphor, perhaps.

Entering the estate and seeing the peeling paint on the grocer's mural, I'm surprised it's still there, as if I dreamed my childhood rather than lived it. I won a community competition to have that design – my design – painted onto them shutters. My brother Dom stole me a set of oil pastels from a real art shop so I could capture the intense colours of the fruit stacked in crates outside of the greengrocer's store in town. The shop on Aldgate itself didn't actually sell fresh fruit. Just artificial fruit flavoured pops, ice cups and condiments for seasoning potatoes, which were the only vegetable it did sell, pretty much – canned mushy peas aside.

Now, black steel shutters slash up the reds, yellows and oranges – literally, the fruits of my labour. My mural has been ruined by the people trying to stop the people who they say ruin the estate, ruin the lives of the law abiders: junkies, thieves, delinquents, people like me: the one-time mural-maker and budding artist.

Being an artist were what Cal dreamed of being really. Him and La and Bull and Laura K used to gab about how they were going to move to Manchester after art college and set up a stall in Afflecks. I just liked the idea of being owt but a dinner lady, or cleaner like my mum, or ending up on the wrong side of the bar at The Hammer and Sink, like Netty.

Bull's new ground-floor flat faces Aldgate Green in the centre of the estate and overlooks the block of flats I was born into. The way the net curtains hang lopsided in the kitchen window and the two front-facing upstairs windows are positioned make the block look like it is smirking, like it knew I'd end up back here, sooner or later.

Bull is sat about in the flat playing Texas Holdem with some guy who says his name's Tomba. I pour drinks and roll smoke till we're running low on stuff to plug our gobs with. I take up a 12-hole diatonic, scratching the dried crust from it before going over some bars to fumigate what is otherwise silence.

AJ turns up within the hour, with dinner in her rucksack. Her Grandma never used to buy nothing in the supermarket which didn't have a sell-by date that weren't at least a year away, so since she died AJ's never had to go shopping once.

– Grubs up!

I watch AJ unpacking tins of vegetables, packets of Cup-a-Soup and all manner of freeze-dried foodstuffs.

Bull won't hook up the fridge to the electric for food, but grudgingly OKs it when he realises I need it to accommodate the solutions of distilled codeine settling in there. He even provides stolen pint glasses from The Hammer and Sink so we can more accurately gauge the water ratio. It takes around eight hours to distil codeine, so we all eat instant ramen and play video games in the meantime.

Lounging on the concrete floor, I roll a few joints from dog ends and Bull hands out pudding: Valium and black tea in rinsed-out vending machine cups. Looks like a scene from a horror movie nuthouse: Bull doling out meds through the kitchen serving hatch.

Around midnight, Bull pulls the cushions from the sofas and armchairs and fits them over the concrete floor like a spongy jigsaw so we can sleep. AJ has already been out for an hour or so off the Valium; Bull lifts her onto the cushions with no effort, like some fairytale giant. He's so gentle, Jeanie don't even stir.

I bed down under the curtainless window, where it is darkest. My back against the cold smooth slab of wall, I think of Bull's old bedsit and the one room that were Bull's bedroom and living room, and then Bull and Jim's bedroom and living room, and then Bull's and Jim's and my bedroom and living room, as I watch Bull magicking nicked hospital blankets from cupboards. When the blankets run out, Bull drapes his army surplus coat over me.

Crouching down beside me, he carefully takes my head in one huge hand to slide a pillow beneath it. His mouth close by my ear, I can feel the warmth of his breath on my cheek. I close my eyes and pretend the Valium has wiped me out, and then nearly flinch when

I feel Bull's fingers lifting my dreads from my face. His beard prickles my cheek as if he's about to kiss me. I tense. He's so close I feel the heat off him and feel him hesitate when I tense, before he whispers, so only I am able to hear.

– Even if Cal is a bit of a div as it goes, he is your brother, Lay Baby.

Bull sighs right into my ear as is if trying to blow the words into my brain.

– I know.

I whisper back, without opening my eyes.

– Do you?

– Jim loved you. Whatever you were, you were his brother.

– Aye, I *were*.

Bull's beard tickles my cheek as he raises his head again. He climbs up from his knees, but reaches down to brush my cheek dry with his thumb.

– Jim is dead, Lay Baby, but *you* ain't.

★

My eyes stammer open at the sound of sirens shrieking past the pane and through Aldgate. The blue beacon lights beat like gigantic, neon ghosts against the far wall till the whole room is lit up intermittently. It's like I'm being spun inside a huge zoetrope.

The window jambs slice the rotating beams of light

into charged blue figures, which dash about the grey walls in a confusion of flashes, as if they're trying to find a way out. Ironic that the police should wake me rushing past to some elsewhere emergency.

I'd never seen the guy's face when he'd been at AJ's, but I recognise the hushed grunts and remember the constellation of his acne-covered back over Sam. Guess that's how I hadn't recognised him until now. And now it is too late to matter.

Tonic immobility, that's what the folk with clipboards call the last-ditch defence mechanism of rabbits in headlights; the inability to flee, fight, scream, even shake your head, say no, say stop, say anything 'cause life has already taught you reacting or saying anything either makes no difference or just makes things worse, that things can get even worse. That there are worse things, even worse than this.

Dried sweat crusts my mouth. The corners of my lips are sore and chapped and taste tinny like blood. Needle stubble grazes my cheek in swells. It strikes me more than the actual thrusting.

I watch the scenes play out about me. Lowry-looking shadow folk climbing the walls, as if set free from one of Cal's old art college books, until they plain run out. Or the light does. Some cross. Some meet. Merge. Fade away. Some melt only a couple of inches from my reach.

It's a funny thing, how sometimes the only way you

realise you are hurting, or just how hurt you really are, is when you feel the sudden absence of the reason, like a knife being pulled from your side, or the weight of a body lifting from on top of you.

★

– All I'm saying is that we arranged to meet in town at noon. I rang you and we arranged it. Then you turn up here looking like death at five in the fucking morning. So, I text you and you never reply. So, then, on my day off I have to get up at five AM because you didn't keep to the arrangement we made. I asked you when we spoke on the phone if noon in town were something you could commit to and –

– Mum, please, I know this; I was there.

– That's the point, Layla: we make an amicable arrangement, and then you're just there, and at five –

– Because –

– And even when I text, you don't reply –

– I tried explain, Mum; I ain't got my mobile. It's in my bag. I left my bag at –

– And I'd been at work all day. I'd been working all damn day and then you start fair shecking the house. Capable of hammering at the door in the middle of the night and yet can't even reply to a text message –

– I haven't got my mobile, Mum –

– *But I didn't know that* –

— *But you do now*. If you'd've just answered the fucking door then you'd have known that —

— It were five AM! Who answers the fucking door at five AM —

— People whose kids are hammering on it?

— Anyway, you didn't have to sleep in the fucking porch all night.

— I guess I just don't see your fucking issue here —

— *That is the fucking issue*, Layla: I'm just trying to explain what happened —

— Mum, *I was there*; I know what happened —

— And it wun't have happened had you just stuck to what we arranged! You said you would be —

— I didn't foresee the fucking night I had. I'm sorry, Mum. *Jesus* —

— I'm not angling for an apology. And don't expect Jesus to save you. I just want you to stop fucking interrupting me!

I bite back the urge to say owt. My mum glares at me, asking eventually:

— So, what, now you're playing dumb?

— Hell, mum, you said I was interrupting you.

— Well I'd finished then hadn't I? I'd explained. I tried to explain and you kept interrupting —

— So I shut up.

— See, there you go doing it again, interrupting me. If I'd have known you were going to be like this, I wun't have let you in —

– I slept in the fucking porch. You didn't let me in.

– Oh, what, so you ain't sat at the kitchen table right now? Hallucinating now am I, Layla? Skenning Scotch fucking mist, am I, eh?

– You ain't seeing nothing, you never fucking do!

– Oh, boo fucking hoo, Layla. Being fifteen is *so* hard and I'll never understand, will I...

– You don't try!

– *I* don't try? Who clothed you, who raised you, who didn't fucking do a midnight flit? I could have let them have you when y'dad gave up. Did I though? Did I? I din't have to pick up the fucking pieces, yet again. But I did, yet again. If you just took some fucking responsibility... *I* don't understand? I were trying to understand. I were trying to understand why you said a time, then come knocking me up at five fucking AM to apparently inform me your whole fucking shit tip of a life so far is my fucking doing. Easy to blame the parent who bothered to stick around, ain't it? Course you're my fucking fault; I'm the only fucker still daft enough to be here.

And that's the crux of it; my mum wants the world to know it ain't all her fault. Meanwhile, I want her to know what 'it' is, not because it's her fault and I need some apology or want to hurt her, but because *she's my mother*.

My mum takes a deep breath.

– I won't have you coming back here whenever

partying gets boring, waking me up at all hours, and I won't sit here so you can try hurt me 'cause your night weren't as fun as you'd hoped, and if that makes me the world's worst mother –

I let my arms drop from holding my head onto the table, but I guess it looked like I'd slammed my hand down between us, because my mum flinches, and it's only then that I actually want to hit her, or shake her, or just squeeze her so tight I melt back into her flesh somehow, so we don't have to be two very fucking separate people.

– Look, Mum. I *am* sorry. Mum, I'm... last night, I were –

– You're not sorry, you're not sorry for owt. Look at you.

Mum looks me up and down, tossing me the same expression she usually reserves for Caleb's girlfriends.

– Layla, there's a big difference between being sorry and *being* sorry.

– Hey, sorry I'm late, I missed owt?

Caleb slides into a chair beside our mum and across the table from me, wearing last night's eyeliner and our mum's pink dressing gown. He reaches between us, taking a biscuit from a stack neither me nor Mum have touched.

– Mum, I've got sommet I need to tell you. La – Sarah, I mean – wanted to be here, but she's, well, she can't, but... Mum, we're getting married.

★

Taking to the street is like entering a cinema and being handed 3D glasses. You see the same stuff that's always there, but you see with different eyes. You think the same dumb stuff, but somehow your thoughts take on new depths. There ain't no better place to go, if you need to figure out what really matters in life, than a doorway. If anything matters.

Still, I watch whole families going about their lives, stopping to lean down to their lagging kids and administer a kiss or a slap, and I don't get it.

Even here, I've never been able to reconcile how at some point my parents' lives crashed and intertwined, or how just about any couple ever think a relationship can be so pure, so solid, that it'll outlast the time it takes to create and raise a whole human being.

It's like a foreign song got stuck in your head. No matter how much you replay it in your mind, or get told what the song means, the lyrics stay foreign.

Seems the only thing my parents ever agreed on was naming me Layla in homage to the Eric Clapton song: 'their' song. When they finally split up 'for good', I asked my mum what made them have a kid together, and she told me: pregnancy.

– I were five months gone already when I found out you were on the way.

That's what she'd said, as if anticipating my next

question, and simultaneously suggesting I owed *her* an apology.

★

I finger the wrap in my pocket and get up, making for the toilets.

The blue lightbulbs fixed behind thick shatterproof Perspex ceiling tiles in the bus station are supposed to make it difficult to see your veins to get a hit. But if waging a 'war on drugs' don't put folk off, it's probably safe to say coloured lightbulbs ain't about to. Anyway, drugs have no agenda; how you meant to win a war against something that don't even care whether it wins or not? War's a reason to use drugs, not a way to stop people doing them.

The blue bulbs just mean disorganised junkies leave trails of blood and the organised ones leave spectacular, fluorescent graffiti in the cubicles along with their used needles.

From the doorway the block letters appear senseless: black fragments smashed up by the ultraviolet scrawl of some crazy or junkie who sometime passed through this place: *I'm scared this is the only mark I will ever leave on the world…* is emblazed on the only mirror which ain't yet had a fist through it. I've seen the junkies at Pok highlighting their veins with light-sensitive magic markers before heading out in the mornings, the way

businessmen fiddle with their watch-straps or cufflinks.
When me and Jim used to hit Pok so we could smoke
our gear without Bull's beady eye on us, I didn't
understand what they were doing with the markers.
Feels like a lifetime ago, but in reality it were only last
year. I think of if Jim were here, where I'd be, where
we'd be. Of being a 'we'.

Above one of the cracked basin mirrors, a peeling
sticker dully instructs the raped *what to do next*. Only, the
sticker has been half-ripped off to reveal nothing but the
capitalised demand of the previous sticker beneath it,
so the whole things reads: *Have you been a victim of rape?*
WASH YOUR HANDS NOW!

I sit on a lidless toilet seat in the corner cubicle and
pull the shoestring taut in my teeth till my pulse rises in
the best vein on my right arm. I can't see it, but feel it
well enough to hit it, and plunge, without even pulling
back, without even thinking of pulling back. Then, cap
the pin and slide it into the overflowing sanitary bin
beside me, and, after replacing my sneaker, I lean back
and stare up at the blue, fluorescent ceiling tiles till my
eyes give up trying to keep any handle on what they're
seeing.

The air smells disinfected. Everything is literally
blue, even the atmosphere. Made this way to keep the
junkies out, the toilets are almost always empty except
for junkies who're about the only people desperate
enough to resort to using them.

The lights give the whole place an uncanny quality.
Everything in here seems dreamlike and unreal,
even without drugs. The scars along my forearms
phosphoresce like they're cracks in the ultraviolet light,
like, if you chipped the mosaic of my flesh from me,
beneath, I'd be made of nothing but pure light.

★

I'm smoking my fifth cigarette by the time Miss wakes.
She raises her hand to hush me without even looking
to see if I am about to speak, leaving me wondering
mutely what I might've said. Then she begins scribbling,
going back over the pages, adding details, re-wording
paragraphs.

I wait until she pauses to concentrate, and ask her:

– What's the story, morning glory?

Miss shushes me, screwing her face up. I slam
my empty coffee mug onto the dresser so she jumps,
dropping the pen.

– Great: it's gone now. Thanks a bunch.

– Anytime. Cigarette?

– Why don't you like me writing my dreams down?

– Why do you like writing them down?

– Because I forget them if I don't write them.

I begin rolling Miss a cigarette.

– Just because you don't dream don't mean you can
ruin mine. And don't laugh at me.

– Don't say funny shit then. You think I don't dream?

– OK, Lay, so you dream. So what's your problem?

I light the cigarette instead of offering it to Miss. Miss pushes:

– Did you dream last night?

– I were cunted last night; I didn't even know I were alive till I woke up, Freud.

– And you're telling me I've got a problem because I write my dreams?

– Loads of people always do loads of stuff.

I shrug.

– Yeah, because *that's life*, Lay. Deal with it.

Miss throws her Dream Journal to me.

– You fucking deal with it.

– Deal with what, Layla? For fuck's sake, I don't know what the fuck you're trying –

– This is not life.

I shake the Dream Journal by its pages. Miss just watches, and then sighs.

– Whatever, Lay. It's too early for this shit.

She pauses in the doorway, without turning to look at me.

– I go to sleep at night and write about my dreams in the morning because it's more interesting than sitting up with you these days. And because I'd rather write my dreams, rather *have* dreams, than be a fucking junkie. Is that what you want to hear?

— If that's the truth. But if you really want to hurt someone you've got to have the bollocks to face them when you deliver the line.

I stand up, doing nothing to stop the ashtray which slides from my lap. It empties itself onto the carpet. Miss turns then to look at it, as I move into the doorway and stop, inches from her, my breath in her make-upless face.

— You write in that journal every morning to focus on anything, *anything* that stops you from focussing on the day ahead, from facing it. You try to find meaning in your dreams, in *this* (I push the Dream Journal into her chest) because you can't accept that there just might be no meaning, no reason why you are what you are or where you are, no reason why what's happened to you has. You believe in your dreams 'cause you *can't* believe in nothing... not because you do.

Miss's eyes fill up as I speak, like I am literally pouring the tears into her.

— No, fuck *you*, Layla. Don't you ever dare tell me about what I've been through; you ain't the only one with scars.

I step around her, flicking my burned down cigarette into the pile of ash on the carpet.

— Lay, what is this really about? If this is about —

— Don't say his name like you knew him; you didn't.

— No, I didn't. And I won't. I can't. Not now. Not 'less you tell me —

– Jim were nineteen. By the time the ambulance arrived, I were glad they couldn't save what was left of him. His eyes were pointing in different directions and I could feel the broken pieces of his skull in my hands. It were a fucking mercy he died in that gutter. That is all there is to know; that is life, mate.

– No.

Miss whispers, more as if she's defying a voice in her own head than mine.

– Mate, that's just death.

★

They're taking Danny away. He don't want to go. Like that makes any difference.

Everyone's been singing Danny Boy, teasing him. *Oh Danny Boy, the pipes, the pipes, they're calling, every morning, summer's gone, and all the flowers are dying. 'Tis you, 'tis you must go…*

And that's the deal. You come here a wrong 'un, delinquent, thief, junkie and you leave a schizophrenic, manic depressive, autistic, borderline. Cured? Labelled. Tick a box, two, all of the above. Whatever. There's only two labels that really matter: psychotic and neurotic.

Miss is a neurotic. Her diagnosis is depression with a side of anxiety, but they don't try send her back, 'cause they're neurotics too – and they're scared of her mum,

Dave. They let the diagnosed psychotics stay here, safely medicated, but the neurotics have it hard; they're threatened with 'recovery'. The neurotics are made to take therapy where every week they rip them open, reassemble their contents, seal them back up, wind that tape tighter this time, and deliver them by first-class post back into the mainstream. Try get them to go wherever it was they were headed for before they got lost or broke.

For Danny, that means returning to Boys' Grammar where he tried hanging himself off the pipes in the toilets, and they burst and there were too much water to see he'd pissed himself, not at the fear of dying, but at the thought of surviving.

The only other ways out are, firstly, Stonerow, which is the prison on the hill that'll take anyone over twelve – girl, boy, man, woman, child, paedophile, or pregnant like Grace and now Hazel. Or, secondly, well, finishing the job Danny fucked up the first time round.

So everyone keeps singing, like a dirge or a dumb animal call to something already dead: *the pipes, the pipes are calling…*

McQuaide tries hushing us, but even Brenda starts humming the tune while she waters the window plants. McQuaide tries hushing her too, but she says she can't help it, she says, it's been stuck in her head 'all bleeding morning'.

★

Everyone had complained about the wedding being in the morning, but on account of the short notice it were the only slot Cal and La could get, or afford.

When I finally arrive at The Hammer and Sink, my brother and La have already been married for about three hours, and everyone has been wasted for about six. I watch the scene unfold like a soap opera.

They've done a good job. It looks like a real wedding. La is the only sober person there. Even my mum is pissed, pulling me to the dance floor when 'Build Me Up Buttercup' comes on, which Cal had played just to please our mum, who kept shouting over the music:

– That's what you get for rushing; a shitty registry office, shitty gifts and a shitty turn out.

Gripping my arms while we dance like otherwise I might escape, my mum laughs and hollers at me along with the music. I can't figure if she's just pissed or taking the piss.

As if he realises, Caleb leaves Trix holding down the decks and jumps in between us, making our mum cry and hug him and apologise for throwing a cup at his head when he were just a baby, her fingers searching out the smile-shaped dint in Cal's left temple.

I dance with La for a bit. When she sees the hint of bruises my mum's grip have left behind, she leans her head onto my shoulder and squeezes me so tight I just stand there being rocked in her arms.

– This is for real, Lay Baby, you know that?

– Yeah, sorry, I got held up –

– It's not just a wedding, like Clit and Mag's. *This is real*. I haven't even touched the champagne your mum got us.

– Probably best. That bottle's older than me.

– Lay, I'm serious. Everything's going to change.

La pulls her head from my shoulder and faces me.

– Clit and Mag are moving out. The divorce, and all.

A grin spreads over La's face.

– Me and Cal will have the whole house. A home. A real home.

La rubs her stomach. I stop swaying, meeting La's eye. She has the expression she used to get, like she had a secret she wanted only me to know, it's the look of a junkie with a pocket full of gear.

– Shit, La. Does Cal –

She shakes her head and puts a finger to her lips, then mine.

– Nobody knows, Not yet. Except, me, you and little Laura Kay.

Little Laura Kay. I shiver, pulling away from La, imagining the birth of a miniature, purple Laura K. corpse, which, unlike Laura, would scream and spit and come back to life and have to do this thing all over again.

La's grip on my arms tightens, exactly where my

mum's fingers had been.

– Layla, we're sisters now.

La pulls me back into her. Swaying again with the music, she puts her cheek against my ear.

– Nobody's going to ruin this.

La squeezes me tighter.

– *Nobody*.

★

Miss's dad wanted Jasper and Miss at his in Oxford for his birthday barbeque. I ended up filling Jasper's seat in the car 'cause Jasper were a no show. And because Miss asked her dad if I could tag along while I was sat there with them.

Miss's dad promised he'd drive us into Camden on his way to work the following day, ahead of the party in the evening, but then work took him in another direction. So, next thing, we're booted out the car in Aylesbury.

I'd been pondering getting inked in Camden, as a souvenir, like. We couldn't find a tattooist in Aylesbury, just some guy on a market stall wearing a Native American headdress, and selling bongs and piercing jewellery. The Chief said he could pierce me any place I pleased, lifting up the tarpaulin behind him to show me a deckchair and a little fold-out camping tea tray with needles and a roll of kitchen towel...

– You could have AIDs now.

When I don't give a reaction, Miss tuts.

– I could have AIDs anyway.

– Why'd you do it?

– Why d'you always ask why?

– Why d'you always do it when you know I'll ask why?

– Why shouldn't I do sommet just 'cause you always ask why?

Miss fixes me with her best attempt at a scowl. I bare my bloody teeth at her before spitting the blood onto the cobbles, and digging for my phone, which has begun vibrating in my pocket.

– How do?

– Terry's taking us for a meal to celebrate Easter.

When I hear my mum's voice, I wonder why I didn't check who was calling before I answered.

– When did you find God?

– It matters to Terry. Caleb and Sarah will be there.

– If it really matters to Terry, shouldn't he be fasting for Lent?

– I want you here within the hour.

– Easter Sunday ain't for two days.

– I said one hour, Layla.

– I can't.

– I'm not arguing with you.

– Yes, you are.

– Layla –

– I'm in Aylesbury.

– Where?

– Oxford, I think.

– Oxford? What're you doing in Oxford? Why are you talking funny?

– A Native American in a tent just pierced my tongue.

– Oh for fuck's sake, Layla. What am I supposed to tell Terry?

– Remind him Good Friday is a fast day.

I hear my Mum huffing into the receiver before she hangs up.

Miss has pulled out a cinema timetable leaflet and is frowning into it.

– You didn't tell your mum you were coming with me to my Dad's then?

Miss is trying to sound casual.

– I didn't know I were coming to your Dad's.

– You could have belled her, when we were in the car. You probably should have asked her.

– What use would permission be, or lack of it when we were halfway along the M fucking 6?

Miss opens her mouth as if about to argue, but realising I ain't joking, only ends up laughing too...

★

Arriving back from Oxford at six this morning, Miss's Dad drops me off along Morecambe Road. I make it to college in time to rush a little dig in the visitor loos and still catch Peter-the-social-worker botch up parallel-parking his rusted Punto in one of the visitor bays in front of the reception area.

Peter is my allocated chaperone.

We're about seven feet from the main entrance while I finish a cigarette, when this typical tutor-looking bloke passes me flapping his arms about. I have the cigarette in my left hand, down by my side. The bloke coughs dramatically and says something about the cigarette smoke choking him.

Peter shoots me his best attempt at a 'don't do it' glare.

– He could be your interviewer.

Peter whispers in my ear, careful his lips don't brush my skin. I've to suppress an urge to cock my head like a gun so he kisses me, not to ruin Peter's career, but just to show him how some kid will try to, and that I ain't that kid. Next thing, this joker has stormed back out the doors. He stops inches from my face, closer to the cigarette than he ever got on his way in, only now he ain't choking.

– What was that? I want to know what that little remark was?

I take a final pull of the cigarette and stub it out, trying to walk round this maniac and into the college.

Peter follows, walking into me as I sidestep abruptly to avoid colliding with the guy who is trying to block off the door.

— Well? Not so fucking clever now are you?

Maybe my IQ has indeed dropped, because I don't get how some bloke having a tantrum and blocking off a doorway could in any way devastate my intellectual capabilities. But the thought of verbalising a sentence that length keeps my mouth shut.

— How dare you, how fucking dare you? Why should I have to breathe your smoke?

— I don't see no one begging you to keep breathing.

Peter reaches for my arm, but stops short as if trying to remember protocol on touching 'cases'.

I successfully sweep past the irate guy, Peter trying to hurry me away without having to actually touch me, or face the bloke.

— You should've risen above that, Layla.

Peter leans in the corner of the lift, his back to the mirrored rear wall, sweat patches appearing through his shirt. He looks like he is reassessing his whole life. But then, Peter always looks that way.

Inside the interview room, which is a vacant classroom on the third floor, he looks a little relieved to be greeted by a woman in a blue trouser suit. The woman, Kim Loveday, tells me to sit down and offers Peter a coffee, introducing herself as the head of the A Level Department.

Peter don't do caffeine; it gives him palpitations, so the coffee sits there, untouched.

— So, Layla, you want to study A levels?

Kim Loveday takes a minute to glance through some papers. School records and educational notes, which I guess Peter must've sent. Peter prods me, hesitantly, but still his message gets through: stop looking at the coffee and sliding down in the chair towards the carpet. The room is so well heated it's making me nod out.

— But you won't have the minimum requirement of five GCSEs?

When I still don't speak, Kim Loveday asks, more explicitly this time:

— Why is that?

— I got expelled from high school two years ago.

— Oh?

She tries to keep her voice neutral and sound surprised, despite the papers in her lap. The silence drags until she realises I really ain't pausing for dramatic effect before giving some repentance speech like I'm in an NA meeting or court.

— I could put in a recommendation for you to study for your GCSEs here?

— I came to do A levels.

— Yes, and you can, when you've achieved your GCSEs.

Kim Loveday sighs, and her voice softens.

— Have you studied literature before? I see you are

studying English language at GCSE.

– I'm literate. I have a library card.

I shrug.

– I'm not trying to be cruel, Layla, but A Levels are hard going...

– Hard going in comparison to what?

Kim Loveday studies me, my piercings, my greyed vest, arms bruised from lugging my rucksack around Oxford all week and my swollen mouth, my tongue within it almost engulfing the bar been forced through it days before. Glancing at Peter-the-social worker, she crosses her legs, and purses her lips.

– OK, so what have you been reading recently? Tell me what gets you going?

I give Kim Loveday some spiel. She catches on sommet I mention and asks about why I like Wordsworth. I reel off some shit about the Romantic aesthetic, but she stops nodding and instead makes this little hmm noise, the sort of noise an adult makes indulging a kid, before they patronise them.

I slouch back into the chair, sunk at the reality of trying to say a whole bunch of stuff, stuff you can't just recite, or edit, or pull from a textbook, or blame on a textbook.

Kim Loveday is looking at me harder now.

– I don't doubt you've read some theory, she says.

– But you did.

– I'd rather like to hear what *you* think, Layla.

She says 'rather' but she means 'now'.

We sit for a minute without speaking, until Peter makes as if to break the silence, and I cut him off at the thought of him speaking for me, or trying to. It's all part of the bullshit mechanics though; I cut him off at exactly the moment I know I'm supposed to.

– You know Coleridge used to go stay with the Wordsworths up at Dove Cottage? Like, he were a junkie by then and he used to wake screaming in the night, clucking real bad. Coleridge said in his journals even though the children's bedroom led from the room where he was seeing some demon pluck his eyeballs out, Wordsworth would bang through the walls, tell him to keep it down.

Kim Loveday frowns ever so slightly, not an expectant frown, but the sort of frown visitors to special school give when any of us start doing what the staff refer to as 'acting up'. Nervous, almost.

– I ain't saying Wordsworth weren't this great guy, or a great poet. Just, that he was just a guy. So were Coleridge. And people got to do what they got to do, right? No matter how great or clever or creative they are, right?

– Um, Layla, I think you misunderstood me, I –

– You want to know how I ended up fucked up. You want to know I ain't *just* fucked up.

I pause. A film has begun to develop on the coffee like a mist, swirling in the blackness. I still want it.

— No matter how Coleridge screamed, no one came, nothing came, least nothing but bad shit, shit that made everything, anything, impossible. School, least for me, it were like being Coleridge screaming in that windowless room; I couldn't do nothing there, *but* scream. But that don't mean I can't do nothing.

Peter shifts in his chair, his teeth clinging onto his fingernails like if he lets go he'll be washed off the earth or something. Kim Loveday ignores him. She clears her throat looking back down at the papers, shuffling them and placing them on the table, away from her. Then, she looks at me.

— And if I did allow you onto the course, would you be willing to take one GCSE alongside three A Levels?

I shrug.

— OK then. So, I'll put you down for A level Philosophy, Literature and History, yes? And, a GCSE, let's see, I'll put you down for —

— Spanish. It's in the prospectus, page twenty-three.

Kim Loveday blinks at me.

— I was thinking maybe a Maths resit. Your current, err, headmistress, has placed you in the lower band. At best, you'll achieve below a C this year. Yet, you were previously in the top set for Maths...

— Yeah, 'cause I can do Maths; I can't speak Spanish.

Peter even tries to sort of hug me when we get clear of the room and back outside into the reception area, patting my shoulders, smiling, then shrugging and settling back into his usual way of looking awkward about the whole thing, about everything.

★

Arriving at the house, my mum is washing up Cal's dirty breakfast plates, her gaze cast out the kitchen window as usual. I come up to lean beside her, flipping the kettle switch on and follow her eyes to where Sue from across the road is running out her house, her boy Chimp having just pulled his two-tone Subaru Impreza onto the drive. His fiancée gets out the passenger side with the baby.

She's sixteen, my mum tells me.

They all hug on the path before disappearing into the house.

– He's been back from Iraq for a while now. Sue's been bragging on the street for a month, and about becoming a grandma. Her Chimp earns over a grand a month.

– Would you really want Cal out there?

– He ain't out there. He's asleep on the fecking couch. So it ain't neither here nor there what I want. Anyway, were I even talking 'bout Caleb?

My mum pulls the towel from its hook and dries off the plates, making me wash my hands before passing me them to put in the cupboard and then leaves the room.

Returning with her handbag on her arm, she

tightens the cord about her pink dressing gown, hitching it up as she sits cross-legged at the table.

– Your welfare worker rang, that awkward bloke, Peter?

– He's not a welfare officer; he's a social worker.

– Don't split hairs, Layla.

I take the tea over and sit down opposite her.

– He told me you got on that college course, what is it again?

– A levels. I don't know yet if I want to –

My mum pulls the giro envelope from her purse and then takes a tenner out of her own purse slips into the envelope in front of me and before she pushes both over the table towards me.

– Get a taxi out tonight. Don't be walking round in the dark.

It's like I'm some battered-up ornament she's just found out is actually a valuable antique and warrants insuring.

– It's cool, Mum. Really. I'm walking into town first to meet Miss anyhow.

– Then get yourself some food or sommet, but if you want t'eat here then do. There ain't much, just paid off the last of the TV stamps, but if there is owt you fancy... there's a walnut pave. Want a slice with your tea?

– Ta, but –

– Have a slice, or even just a biscuit. I got some treat

bits in to celebrate. Here —

She gets up, bringing the biscuit tin to the table. Removing the lid, she pulls out a handful of custard creams.

— Your favourites. Remember? You used to try sneak them and think I wun't notice.

— Mum, really, ta, but I'm fine.

I don't tell her that custard creams were Dom's favourite, or that I used to steal them for him.

— I were going to bake a cake, but seemed a bit much, not that I ain't proud, just I didn't want to out-face you...

In the end, I pocket the giro and some biscuits and leave Cal sleeping. Rather than wait around to catch a staff taxi to The Hammer and Sink with him, I walk into town to kill some time and catch the free bus along with Miss at Dalton Square.

★

Meeting AJ on the stairs inside The Hammer and Sink where there's no cameras, I pass over the tenner and AJ spits the cellophane wrap of coke into the space between my tits, giving me an odd look as she does.

— Did a custard cream just fall out of your pocket?

I am teetering on picking up the biscuit, when both me and Jeanie pause, having to back up against the stairwell wall to watch the soldiers march past, crushing the biscuit as they make for the first set of doors leading into The Sink Bar.

The atmosphere round here changes when the soldiers come back. Following them through to The Hammer Bar, some are already flinging their post-traumatic stress like incendiary grenades at each other. Aiming fists at us dregs in the mosh pit, like they do on the street if they catch up with any of us between crawling the pubs in town; moshy banging, they call it.

The gangs generally keep the moshy banging to a minimum, only when a 'mosher' or dreg ventures into one of their clubs or onto their turf, say, but the soldiers actually come looking for it, invade our turf at The Sink. I guess, that's what soldiers do. Netty, the barmaid, says you'd think a tour of Afghanistan or Iraq would teach them it ain't clever to stand out, but they just seem to come back louder, madder, drunker, like they forget, or want to, that – unlike the rest of us – they signed up for whatever's happened to them. At The Sink you get no honour for being fucked up, for thinking you're the only one who knows what it's like to be armed, loaded with where you've been and what whatever politics have done to you. You want to get treated like a hero on account of being a squaddie? Easy: just don't come back.

– Him?

Miss, her face bloated and pink, nods, stifling a sob. The squaddie who had locked his teeth behind Miss's tongue bar and forced his hand through her tights, ripping them in the process is leaning on the back legs of his chair, and laughing. Five feet away, Miss is at the bar sobbing into a row of tequila slammers.

— You made her cry.

— I made her cum first.

At that, I slam my forearm into the soldier's throat and his fingers slip from the tabletop, causing his chair to topple backwards with him still on it. His soldier mates, all four of them, react instantly and then the bouncers join in, until half the club has dog-piled the squaddies, and me in the process.

I don't know who called the cops, seen as squaddies dread the army police getting called up much as us kids dread our parents getting called up, and The Hammer and Sink staff dread losing their licence. But I were already outside, waiting on a taxi; Netty, the barmaid had called to get us the hell out of there, and hoped maybe the staff wouldn't get too much shit.

As for Miss, the police can't do shit to or for her. Everyone knows it's really up to the Wyatts now — even the cops. That's why they won't tell Miss what they're going to do or when, but whether two weeks or two years later, broken legs are the standard. A shattered cheek or cracked ribs, that depends on whether the squaddie tries, like Miss did, to resist.

He's just lucky Miss is related to the Wyatts and not any of the Aldgate 212. If the 212 are dealing with a guy

who touches a lass up wrong, they send some of theirs
to have a dirty go, which is when someone bites off a
piece of you and swallows it so there ain't nothing to
reattach when you get to A&E.

★

My mum has to come pick me up from the police
station on account of me being under eighteen, even
though I ain't being charged or even cautioned. I
am trying to cool my head against the bus window,
convincing myself I am an orphan being driven to a rich
aunt while my mum, who didn't say owt in the police
station, is now telling me exactly what she thinks about
me. In the end, I pay one-fifty to orbit the police station
via Lancaster's one-way system, and I don't even make it
out of the town centre before my mum beside me causes
such a scene the driver throws *me* off the bus.

    Cal let me in the house this morning. I didn't bother
even trying to get let in last night, and I probably
should've left it longer before coming back; Mum is still
raging.

    — You saying you wouldn't have defended me if
some bloke bit my tongue and shoved his fist up my
dress?

    — So why didn't you call police when this bloke
supposedly assaulted Miss?

    — If I hadn't been arrested you wouldn't be asking
that.

– Do you know Layla, I don't know what to ask no more, where to begin. What I do, eh? What were it I did so bad to you? Do you really hate me that bad? And what if college finds out 'bout this? You ever think of that? They could take your place off of you, then what, eh? Then what, Layla? You think life is a game? A bit of fun, eh?

Mum keeps talking over me, asking the same questions I ain't been able to answer the first, second or third time.

– What makes a teenage girl punch a man, a soldier, in the throat, Layla?

Looking up and down the hall, from the plastic sunflowers spray-painted sunset-yellow to the knitted cat at the foot of the stairs, I wonder why I even came back.

★

Except the kettle – which Dave keeps on a constant boil – all the noise has stormed upstairs. I take my cup of tea through the patio doors into the yard, staring up at Miss's bedroom window.

– Oi, Rapunzel, wherefore art thou?

A metal bin full of paper, photographs and flames hits the crazy-paving. A burning photo album follows, showering the garden with smouldering baby pictures. Next, a slate ashtray almost hits me, with a brief rain of ash and butts. Before I can get back inside, I am forced to choose between protecting my head and saving the tea as more books are tossed from the window.

Heading back inside, slamming the empty cup on the kitchen counter, I make for the stairs, tea-soaked jeans sticking to my thighs as I go.

– Fight me if you want, but I'm coming in.

– I'm twice your size, you fucking idiot.

– So stop eating so fucking much then.

I kick the door open. Miss don't try to fight me. She is sat cross-legged on the floor. The carpet is burnt in a circle where the bin has been and the duvet is on the floor, partly singed. It takes me a moment to notice she's trashed the whole room as well – her usual debris is now even more broken. I laugh. Hell, I can't help it.

– Yeah, laugh at me. Make me a fucking joke, Lay.

– You are a joke. What, you expect sympathy?

– Your dad hates you, does he? Your dad thinks depression is a choice? Thinks you ask to be touched up in a fucking nightclub? He knows nowt about me, Layla, and he thinks because he gives me money that it's OK, that that'll solve everything.

– So take the fucking money and feel sorry for yourself with a full deck of smokes and sommet half decent to drown your sorrows in.

– Fuck you too, Layla. And fuck his bribes. You don't know what he's like. He hates you too.

– I nicked your Grandad's heart meds and ruined his

birthday barbeque. He'd be a dick not to hate me.

– That's just him. He judges everyone.

– He didn't chuck us out till I poured wine over your Nana and knocked that tray of cocktail onions into your lap. He was angry I'd hurt you, and he still offered us a lift all the way back to Lan–

– He just wanted you out of there. He was ashamed.

Miss resumes laggardly destroying the closest notebooks.

– So that's what you were burning?

– That's all my emotions are: fucking rubbish; that's what I am in his eyes.

– So why's he stick around?

– To torture me. Fucked if I know. Probably because of Jasper, his blue-eyed boy.

– Miss, let up. He could take Jasper and do one, anytime.

– I wish he would.

I bite my tongue. Literally. How you dream about it. And yet, when it happens, when you are left alone, how you wait to wake up from the reality of it like a bad dream. Because what else is there to do but wait, when everyone's upped and fucked off? To wake up one day and realise you've just become a part of the thrown-away stuff, the shit people have no use for. And, to have to try to explain to the social workers that the reason you couldn't just pick up the phone, couldn't just open the door, couldn't just leave wherever you were holed up, ain't because you *don't* know what is out there, but because you know *exactly* what is out there. I could tell Miss all about being abandoned by your father, about being the only kid your father left behind when he finally did as he always threatened and fucked off 'for good', but for what?

Miss will never be on the other side of that door, never hear the voices as they break it down, never know how it feels to have some gloved stranger peel you from your childhood like evidence from a crime scene, never understand that the only thing worse than being abandoned is being discovered having been abandoned. Just like Miss will never know the sound a plastic carrier bag makes beneath a ten year old's wet arse everytime they shift in the back of a social worker's alpine-fresh, grey plastic Mondeo to try avoid being eyeballed via the rear view mirror, or what it is like to while away the journey wondering whose place there is to go to from here and not being able to think of anyone, of anywhere.

Miss will never know the nothingness that is always there beneath the everything that, however shit, was *your shit*; *your* family, *your* life. Just like I've fuck all idea what it must be like to have your dad stick around, or what it must be like to dare to tell your dad you're suffocating beneath so much shit you slash gills into your arms when everyone's sleeping just to go on breathing, and just to get told by your own dad that your pain don't mean shit, that you're just an attention seeker, like wanting your parents' attention is a fucking crime and that makes you the bad guy, when you ain't even trying to argue you're a victim; you just want someone to tell you, I hear you.

Burning the cigarette on the inside of my arm while Miss tries to articulate what a dick her dad really is, I let both fizzle out.

— Fuck it, Miss. Y'right.

I toss a paperback to Miss, and she catches it.

— What?

I choose a hardback next, and skim it fast this time so Miss don't catch that one. It hits her square on the forehead.

— We're fucked. We're fucking fucked, I laugh.

Miss aims a wire-coiled photo album at me. I shatter a 'Best Daughter' mug above her head in retaliation and Miss charges me.

Hitting the wall, the shelf above my head gives way. Diaries, photo albums, journals, all pour over us as we exchange punches. Not because we don't care. Just because it feels good to hit something sometimes that you know won't just shatter upon contact.

★

— You're a bitch. You know that? You're fucking cold. I mean, what, if you smoke that cigarette here I'm going to propose to you or sommet'?

There's a bit in *Peter Pan* when Tink has drunk the poison meant for Peter. Unless the kids clap to show they believe in her, she'll die. That's what Trix fucks like since Polly died; the kids clapping: slow at first, unsure, embarrassed, then faster, harder.

But ultimately everything ends and kids grow up and people die. No matter how hard Trix fucks or how many people he gets to clap along with him, we will all die. That's life.

– You're fucking heartless, Layla.

I could've just pulled the hoodie over my head, or buttoned it up on the stairwell. I could've walked out topless, nobody would've cared or noticed in a house full of far bigger tits than mine, but I stay in the bedroom fiddling with each button while Trix shoots insults at me until he's emptied out like a shattered swear jar.

Downstairs, La's pupils, atypically large now she's on a script, yawn at me before she turns silently back to Cal. The music is loud, but no one is really listening, every person's brimming with coked-up philosophies, mantras destined to bounce off these four walls only. I slide down the corner of a wall and pick up a bottle of vodka. Rich, who's the kid of some middle-class couple who once fostered Trix, and has taken to appearing at the steps, and pattering about after me, slides down beside me, piggy eyes staring out at me from his doughy face. The sort of face, my father used to say, only a fist could love.

— Where you been?

— Elsewhere.

— Play nice, Lay Baby.

I gargle vodka, wiping my mouth on my sleeve, and take a joint from him.

— I ain't playing at all, Rich. What you want?

— You tell me.

Rich grins. He always meets my eyes, pretends like there's something between us. The thought, the memory, of Jim rises to the surface of my opiate-and-alcohol-flooded mind. Once upon a time, I'd have told Rich what I thought of him with the back of my hand. I press my headache against the radiator, closing my eyes.

— Come on. Push my buttons, Lay —

— Rich, you're one of them, not one of us. Give it up, already.

— That all you got?

— For you, yeah.

I make to pull myself up, but Rich takes my arm and pulls me back down.

— Come on, I know you —

I pull my arm free.

— No, you don't. You don't know nothing, Rich. And you don't want to. Thinking everyone else is shallow is too easy. You can try telling yourself it's your appearance that makes you unfuckable, that way.

And no one argues with you on that, 'cause they can't deny you're ugly, Rich, but if they told you so that'd just confirm to you that you were right; everyone else are the cunts. Don't you get it? I can't tell you owt you don't already know. No one can.

I think I'm about to cry, for some reason. When Rich don't answer, I look up from the joint I've been watching burn down in my fingers.

— When you've had enough of playing one of us you get to leave. You get to go home to your nice house, to your real parents. To your real nice parents. And that makes your shit bullshit. You want be one of 'us'? Want to be a fuck up? That's your fucking problem, Rich, and it makes you more fucked up than any of us; anyone here had that choice, there'd be no 'here' 'cause there'd be no fucking *us*. So, congratulations, Rich; you've got what you wanted; you're a real fuck up. In fact, you're so fucked up even the fuck ups won't even fuck you.

At that, Rich pins me against the radiator. Someone's turned the heating on and my back burns against the metal.

Only at Bull's place could a lass get strangled in a room full of people without anyone noticing. Rich's hands tighten as I try to turn my head, as if he thinks I'm trying to free myself. But I ain't trying to free myself. I'm being strangled facing the window beneath which I last woke being more-than-strangled, and just don't want that window to be the last thing I see.

Eyes burning, my words jam in my throat on the way up, until I have to half-shout them just to manage a whisper, or gasp.

— You ain't got a monkey on your back, Rich. You are the fucking monkey.

Rich lets go. The joint has burnt down and left a blister on my middle finger. Ignoring the swelling I can feel in my throat and pounding in my skull, I put the blister to my lips and suck at it till it pops. But that only makes it throb more. I swear I can feel my pulse in its rawness. Rich looks at what he thinks he's done to me like I am something that has happened to him and his voice breaks and cracks like he's the one just been throttled.

— I just wanted to talk to you...

Stubbing the joint out in the carpet, I climb up, turning my back on Rich.

— Next time you want to talk, fucking say sommet. Better yet, push your own fucking buttons. Ain't nobody's job, even 'mongst these people, to be your wank rag.

Miss glances up from the cocaine on the countertop only long enough to see it's me entering the kitchen.

— That hot bloke you know just left. He were crying.

It takes me a moment to realise Miss means Rich.

— You think Rich's hot?

Miss pinches her nose like a pro, sniffs hard and nods.

— What did you do to him?

— You think I fucked him.

— I think he looked fucked up.

— Miss, do me a favour...

— Depends what it is.

— Take your nose out of that shit and take a look around, and tell me, *tell me*, how I could possibly fuck these people up.

— Lay, *these people* are our friends.

I follow Miss's gaze through the open doorway into the lounge where it falls on Cal and La, sharing a blowback on the sofa.

— And this is supposed to be a party, so lighten the fuck up, will you, Lay.

— And how do you propose I go about doing that?

Miss takes another bump of coke and pushes the remaining crumbs over the Formica.

★

Write an essay about your hero, who they are and why you respect them.

Now I'm officially moving out, old enough to be on the list for a council flat and officially estranged from my mum, she's been hassling me to sort through all the boxes in the bedroom that were supposed to be mine. All the shit from my dad's place that beat me to my mum's, or followed me back here. All the shit my mum's been boxing up and tossing into that room since the divorce, almost a decade ago.

I opened one box the other night and found my old school draft book, swimming gala medals and a bundle of newspaper clippings from competitions I'd long since forgotten I'd won. The canvas tote bag my mum used to use to carry the books I chose home from the library. School calendars I'd won awards for designing. Basketball medals I'd won before I hit high school and were told girls weren't allowed on the team and I were made to play netball, wear gym knickers and only compete against other girls. The Christmas cards of baby Jesus I'd drawn when I still recited my Hail Marys and Our Fathers, out of fear of God and not just fear of *our* father.

I'd never before seen the newspaper stuff. Guess the last time I did, I were too young to even be able to read it.

The last newspaper clipping was dated 1996. And it were all yellow somehow, even though it's been in the dark all these years, like at some point it must've been on the wall or stuck to the fridge. It were one of the only photographs done in colour. In it, I am stood in front of the mural I'd designed for the Aldgate grocery shop, representing my community before the freshly-painted fruit.

February, 1996. A week before my brother, Dom, became a hero at our school for becoming the only kid, ever, to get expelled from Aldgate Primary. That newspaper clipping never made it into this box, course, even though it seems the only story that really mattered in the end.

Story goes, when our Dad said no to buying Dominic a new coat one winter, Dominic took one of Dad's petrol lighters to school. He told the teacher he were going to the toilet. Instead, he went to the cloakroom where four hundred polyester coats and four hundred P.E. kits hung. Dom sparked the Zippo and, dropping it into his coat pocket, he returned to class.

The whole cloakroom, the toilets and part of the junior wing were destroyed within an hour. They marched us out in lines onto the field at the back of the school as if only so we were in a better position to watch the place burn. And we did all watch. It's about the only time I remember the queues at school being orderly and quiet. None of us daring to look away, in case we noticed a gap in one of the queues of kids beside us where a kid sister or brother or cousin should be.

Nobody did die, though. Nobody even got hurt, at least not by the fire. And when they rebuilt, the teachers got a new staff room, and us kids got six foot, spit-green, barbed-wire fences to keep the 'baddies' out, they said, like some outside evil had penetrated and torched our school, not a nine-year-old boy with a petrol lighter. Before the fences, when a kid got pissed off, it were normal to see them breaking out onto Aldgate

Estate through the back of school, running through the field and into 'the long grass' through the hypodermic gauntlet. Even Mrs Armour did it once. She had her car out front, but when Daniel Barnes spat in her face, she took the long grass like the rest of us.

Nobody else seemed to notice the fences, though. Or care. From the day my brother burned his coat, all the kids were too preoccupied making Dom out to be some hero. I guess that's because they didn't go home that night to see Dom getting tanned with the buckle end of their dad's belt. Or hear him cry in the dark afterwards. And those kids didn't watch as, just after Dom were expelled, their parents sorted through all their shit, separating everything they'd ever known into two neat piles, all the time wondering which pile they would end up in.

What no Aldgate kid saw or spoke about after Dom got himself expelled were the inevitable collapse of my parents' relationship; my mum wordlessly packing all my belongings, counting my sweaters as she folded them and not stopping until the whole drawer were empty and there were nothing else to fold. And nothing else to pack, except me.

I relax my grip on the pen, watching it roll from my fingers, and the desk, imagining, for the first time, my mum having watched me being driven away, just the last of her ex's belongings. And, afterwards, my mum on her knees in the empty bedroom that had been mine, like she somehow knew there'd be no more trophies or certificates. The scream of masking tape winding layer over layer, sealing shut the baby-sized box she'd kept instead of me.

★

Some bloke has a handful of the other guy's hair and is smashing his face into his knee. I pull my hood up and keep walking, not looking, hearing horns blaring and cars breaking behind me as the riot spills out Algate Estate. The second guy flies past me. I hear the guy's bottom jaw smack the ground ahead, and the gritty sound of flesh mingled with shards of teeth grinding down into the concrete, shortly followed by the sound of his attacker running up behind me. He flings himself onto the kid again, with a grunt. The kid's face is such a mess I can barely make out where his nose and eyes go, but it is plain to see from his hoodie and trackies and to hear from his moaning that he is young. Around my age, probably.

The guy who's taken him down looks up at me, panting. It's Stevie. Too few teeth and too many tattoos to mistake. He nods, like being polite, then punches the kid's head back into the concrete. I acknowledge Stevie, pull my hood tighter round my head and keep right on walking.

★

The police have every road around Aldgate estate closed
off and have shut the bus lanes down. They'd already
begun redirecting all the traffic through the one-way
system when I'd set out from Pok. When I were walking
through the thick of the jam, I'd been met by people
stuck in the filter lanes on Greyhound Bridge who'd
started getting out their cars to try to quiz the cops and
listen in, lining up along the Quay to watch the fires
on the estate from across the River Lune like how they
do on Bonfire Night to watch the firework display over
Lancaster Castle.

I go round the back of the estate, not to avoid
the fighting, which is on the edge of the estate and
making its way slowly into town, but the folk who're
collecting on the peripherals like at a firework display. I
get to my mum's, but as soon as I arrive, feel like I can't
remember what it is I wanted to get, like when you
walk into a room and stand scratching your head. I can
only remember that whatever it was, it had seemed real
important only a moment ago. Right now, the only
thing that seems important to anyone is 'the riot on
Aldgate'.

The cops almost always ignore all that goes down
on Aldgate, ever since the nineties riots, as long as it
remains within the estate walls. And everything usually
dies down within a few hours. But this time, for the first

time since the riots back in the nineties, it hadn't died out but spilled out into town as the Dacrelands 414 and Gallows Hill 353 tried to retreat.

— I saw them dragging off anyone who ran out the estate. Got the whole place surrounded. Armed response units at every place the walls end.

My mum loses no time in telling Cal when he gets in around midnight. That's why she's been stood at the kitchen window all night; she'd been waiting for Caleb to walk through the door. Not because she were worried for him being out there; just, Cal is the only one who listens to her. Or so she thinks, on account of Cal being the one who *only* listens.

★

Next morning, Cal tells me Mum is out already. She's not gone to work, but over to Mon's 'cause Alastair's been in ICU up at the infirmary. The Dacrelands 414 and Gallows Hill 353 had all gone up onto Aldgate to get back for the notices they'd posted and Alastair had his jaw shattered.

The doctors managed to save his left eye – bone shrapnel from a shattered cheek had threatened to skewer his eyeball like a cocktail onion – but they had to crack his skull at the hospital to let his brain swell, Cal tells me. He died in an induced coma at 4.26 AM. They said there was nothing anyone could do. And that's true;

at least, it is now.

I remember seeing Alastair with a few of them last month, and then of Stevie yesterday afternoon, and the kid whose face Stevie had gone at. The kid with the pounded alien face. Thinking of that kid as Alastair, thinking of that kid as human, it is like trying to make opposing magnets join inside my mind.

★

I lift my head from the desk to find the room is empty, except for me and McQuaide. McQuaide is sat in front of me. The sweat runs like tears when I look up at her. Even then, she don't look surprised.

I wait for McQuaide to shout, but she just sighs.

– Don't you want your life to mean something?

She stares down at the blank paper like someone who's been called to identify a body, like it's already too late and she's asking like a coroner checks one final time for a pulse, not in case there is one, but just to tick the box to say they checked the right number of times.

– Don't you want to make a difference?

Slipping my hand back into my sleeve, I ball my fist and wipe the sweat from my forehead. It's an effort not to just kick the chair back, peel the hoodie off entirely, and then ask McQuaide if it looks like I give a shit. But even then, she'd probably just see my sweat, my scars, my ink as proof that I don't care.

People don't look at track scars or razor blade tallies and bother to count them, to count how many times someone has survived. They don't see someone trying to survive; people just see what's right in front of them; a kid, a junkie, a fuck up. I guess it's easier to say a person don't care than it is *to care*. So, a drunk drinks, a junkie shoots up, a bulimic throws up, a cutter cuts themselves up, a kid fucks up. And people with clipboards write it up; write people off.

– Everything we do makes a difference.

When I finally answer, and because she weren't expecting an answer, never mind that answer, McQuaide just stares at me, mouth slightly open, like a coroner who's been about to tick the box and then feels a pulse, like I've just risen from the dead, as if she believed she had been talking to a corpse this whole time.

– That's the problem.

★

When I hit the Steps, Bull tells me Stevie fucked some kid up real bad, he killed him, and now Stevie is being charged. Everyone at Pok's banging on about it. Bull says it's going to get like the nineties again, 'cause The Wyatts had sent the Dacrelands 414 up there.

– It'll have been going on for hours inside them walls before anyone even knew, La says, dropping down beside me and offering me a single-skin joint to ease the rattle.

— It's been going on years inside them walls.

Cal, reaching over me, takes the joint before I can.

— It never stopped.

Bull snorts in agreement.

— Aye, and the plod say they're confident it were a one-off.

Miss, who is bent forward so her hair draws like curtains over her face, stops digging dirt from between the steps with the butt of her lighter, and takes a hard, shuddering breath. Rich, sat beside her, shifts closer and puts his arm around her.

Jasper, Miss's twin and a member of Wyatt's, had been up there too, sent by the Gallows Hill 353 to back up the Dacrelands 414. Consequently, Jasper is in hospital too. He ain't going to die, but still, the only folk allowed by his bedside are two coppers. He'll probably just get a couple of years and he'll be out in less than one — he'd be out in less, if he didn't have priors. Sam pipes up, just when the conversation has burned so low it threatens to fizzle out completely.

— You think it's going to get worse, like last time?

I laugh mid-yawn.

— Worse? When'd it ever get better? Always behind them walls, innit?

Bull pulls my hood down so we can see each other, and winks at me.

— Aye, long as them walls stay up, ain't fuck all gonna change inside them.

I wipe my nose with my sleeve and accept the joint from Cal, surprised at how much he has left for me.

★

A sealed envelope has been placed on the desk at some point since I fell asleep. I try not to imagine how it got there while I was riding out the first full night of kip I've had since I last used, thanks in no small part to Mag and her own legally-acquired stash of Valium, which she shook into my pockets when I said I was heading to my mum's. Clit, who's back with Mag at the house along with Cal and La, suggested I leave it a few more days before making any 'big decisions', but he didn't hide my shoes this time.

I stare at the letter without blinking until it blurs and loses all definition, like a word when you say it over and over, before I finally go over to the desk and pick it up. It's a brown envelope with a small plastic window, in which my name and my mother's address have been typed. Turning the envelope over, I unpick the glue, pull the letter from the envelope and skim the paragraphs to find the address, my new address, home *Flat 24, Calder Court, Aldgate Estate, Lancaster.*

The words look vaguely familiar. Calder Court on the Aldgate Estate, the block I was born into. The block where my grandma died. The block where I spent the first year of my life sleeping in a fruit crate and being literally kicked from room to room. The last place my family all lived as a family. I replace the letter in the envelope and shove it into my bag, rather than leave it for my mum to find.

★

When I come downstairs, shouldering my bag, there is a cup of tea waiting in the kitchen. I sit down, sip the tea, and put it back down.

– That alright? Weren't sure it'd still be warm.

It ain't warm, and I don't take sugar, I've never taken sugar, but I finish it anyway just to avoid having to answer.

My mum busies herself, folding clothes she ain't yet ironed and wiping down the countertops though they ain't been used. She waters a spider plant on the windowsill, pouring the water so slowly it drips drop by drop from the jug. All the time, her eyes don't settle on anything, like even the weight of her gaze might leave a mark.

When she runs out of things to do, or pretend to do, she pulls out a chair. Sitting opposite me and nursing her own mug, she eyes the faded Moomins t-shirt I salvaged from the otherwise emptied bedroom. A smile forms along her lips like a cut that you don't feel until the blood begins to well.

– You know, when I were a kid my mum used to say to me, 'You'll get it when you're grown up'. All the time: 'You'll get it when you're grown up'. It were her answer for everything. I heard it so often, I actually wokened up on my sixteenth birthday expecting to know sommet I hadn't before. I thought I'd suddenly not just feel so...

She resumes blowing into her teacup.

– All I got were pregnant, 'course.

When she finally looks up, her eyes are bloodshot.

– And then I got old. Old and tired.

Everything I can think of saying, of doing, just seems to mean I don't say or do nothing, but try to keep my legs, which didn't feel restless till my mum sat opposite me, still beneath the table, so I don't end up just unintentionally booting her.

– I know we agreed once you turned sixteen, and once school were done with...

Again, my mum don't finish her sentence. Instead, she digs her hands into her dressing robe and pulls something from her pocket.

– But, well, now Caleb's upped and gone...

– Gone?

I half laugh.

– Mum, Cal ain't gone, he's just –

– Layla, please.

My mum interrupts, placing the key on the table

with more force than she seemed to intend. She takes a deep breath and lowers her voice again, but it's lost its soft edge.

– Who knows how long it'll take the Council to house you someplace? Without kids in tow you'll likely be waiting years. So, unless you've gone and got yourself knocked up...

My mum shakes her head like she's making a joke rather than asking a question. I don't return the gesture. And I don't mention the letter from the council or that the exams are over already.

The key lies on the table between us. Its tip is blackened with a permanent shadow where I recall Caleb tried use it to hot-knife a crumb of weed onetime when we'd run out of skins. It makes me think of the black spot in *Treasure Island*.

When I don't make a move, my mum does; she reaches across the table. I think she's reaching for the key, like she's about to force it into my hand or back into her robe pocket. Instead, she takes my hands from the cold cup and sort of squeezes them. I fight the impulse to pull myself from her, surprised at how foreign her fingers feel in mine.

I try to recall my mum's touch. If she felt this way when I were a kid. Realising I have no comparison, I just end up sitting there, dumbly, wondering how anyone can survive with such thin skin, until the taxi draws into the cul-de-sac.

The driver hits the horn. Flinching at the sound, my mum releases me. She gets up, glancing at the clock on the wall and moves to the window.

– Sure you've got everything?

Letting the net curtain drop back down, my mum looks over her shoulder. I nod, looking up to meet my mum's eyes, but my mum's not looking over her shoulder at me; she's looking at the key still on the table.

I clench my suddenly-empty fists, the scars from when I'd try to reach for the key and had the door slammed on my hand last year pulling at my knuckles, as I get up.

It's been raining. Moisture hangs in the air like static. Petrichor emanates from the sunbaked concrete, and worms litter the doorway. They look like petrified question marks, as if they tried to turn back not realising once they left the dirt behind it was always going to be too late.

Goosebumps raise along my bare arms as, behind me, I hear the door shut. It hits me like dèjá vu, the sound of the door *not* being slammed; the latch just tutting, like a gun firing on empty. So tenuous, it barely disturbs the dull mumur of traffic, far-off sirens and life out on the street.

ACKNOWLEDGEMENT

Thanks to you.